Praise for Paul McHugh

Deadlines — a journalism mu.   ...y

"Every reporter worth his or her notepad is a sleuth at heart. Paul McHugh brings this truth to life with crackling suspense and a true, ink-stained veteran's eye for the newsroom."
—Dan Rather, TV anchor and newsman

"The themes of Paul McHugh's companionable, rock-solid and soul-satisfying mystery *Deadlines* could not be more modern and relevant. But it is his wonderful character, the has-been alcoholic newspaper columnist Colm MacCay, who will stay with you, and who channels McHugh's considerable writing talent into a voice that surprises and delights. A superior story, not to be missed."
—John Lescroart, *New York Times* best-selling author

"With *Deadlines*, McHugh nails the desperation of new-millenium newsrooms and the quirky crusaders of the Bay Area. He also has a lot of fun with the unlikely culprits in this land-and-money murder mystery."
—Farai Chideya, author of *Kiss the Sky* and
The Color of Our Future

"*Deadlines* has everything a reader looks for in a mystery."
— Michael Krasny, host of KQED/NPR's
award-winning Forum

"People who love San Francisco and appreciate a good mystery will find Paul McHugh's *Deadlines* a page turner with unforgettable characters and a realistic view of crime."
—Sheriff Mike Hennessy,
the City and County of San Francisco

The Blind Pool — a political thriller

"A deftly crafted and riveting novel that's based on an all-too believable premise. *The Blind Pool* showcases McHugh's flair for narrative driven storytelling of the first order. The stuff from which blockbuster movies are made."
— *The Midwest Review of Books*

"This book is cinematic in its intensity, yet it's imbued with a sense of reality. Its violence has consequences and even its heroes are not immune to them."
—Jon Mays, *San Mateo County Journal*

"The narrative thread of his thriller, which features flawed heroes battling international criminal forces, could have been pulled directly from news reports. Some elements even look prescient."
—Clay Lambert, *Half Moon Bay Review*

"Paul McHugh is a writer who links vivid scenes with the thread of suspense. His new political thriller keeps up a steady beat of surprises."
—Jorge Imbaquingo, *El Comercia* (Quito, Ecuador)

"A taut thriller by a terrific storyteller. The political headlines of today make it timely as hell."
—Dan Rather, *News & Guts Media*

Came A Horseman

A Hard Ride in a Fierce World

Paul McHugh

Came a Horseman

Copyright © 2021 by Paul McHugh

Book production by Cypress House
Front cover illustration: Beth Garcia
Cover design by Kiersten Hanna
Author photo by Lari Shea

Print ISBN: 978-0-9987320-1-5
Ebook ISBN: 978-0-9987320-2-2

Library of Congress Control Number: 2020915555

Printed in the USA

9 8 7 6 5 4 3 2 1
First Edition

To Mom & Pop Garcia–
You've brought a great deal to life. Including my wife.

You can control your mind, but not outside events.
— *Marcus Aurelius*

Chapter 1

Rays of heat stabbed into his back, prodding Kyle out of his stupor. But his movement toward wakefulness was tardy. Bone-deep weariness had rendered him almost comatose. Only sounds he began to hear summoned him fully back into the world.

Some noises repeated—the thump of waves crashing on a steep beach, followed by a seething hiss as they withdrew over rough gravel.

Last night, as I came out of the ocean...did I crawl up far enough? Or am I still within the reach of high tide?

And he heard a nearby rustling. A creature that munched on something.

An animal? Scavengers? Raiding my gear bag? Can't say I blame 'em...I'm starving, too. And hella thirsty.

Kyle tried to swallow but he choked on the dry burn of salt. His lips were cracked and split, his tongue felt swollen to twice its normal size.

Coarse pebbles rasped against his fingers as they twitched.

It's a wild shore, far as I know, though it was dark when I came in. Could be more than one animal. A pack or a flock. Might start to bite or peck on me next. Be careful!

Kyle let his right eye slit open.

He saw a foot sheathed in a shabby boot, next a ragged pantleg.

He tilted his head slightly, widening the scope of his vision, and observed a thin youth, somewhere in his late teens, with his lank brown hair tied back with a strip of cloth.

Kyle's hazy brain tried to offer some helpful associations, memories of an illustrated book his grandmother had used to give him reading lessons. *If I'm like Rip Van Winkle just waking up from a sleep that went on God knows how long...he...well, that there is a young Ichabod Crane.*

This kid had certainly busied himself, rooting through Kyle's stuff. A pair of gnawed apple cores already lay at his feet, next to the spot where Kyle's sack of elk jerky had been torn open. The kid clawed nuggets of meat out of the sack with his right hand and crammed them into his mouth. Meanwhile, his left arm was plunged into Kyle's waterproof duffle—the only bag Kyle had managed to salvage from the wreck—pulling out more items. The lad gave them a glance, then tossed them on the beach.

Shit. If he gets to Roy's knife, he'll be armed. The survival rifle is way down at the bottom of my bag and it must be assembled before it'll work. So, knife's my big prob here. Must take him down before he grabs it. But have I the strength for a fight? Surprise will need to be everything.

Stealthily, Kyle pulled in a deep breath. A wisp of energy curled through his depleted body. He pushed one hand and his toes into the sand, did a mental countdown, then surged up to his knees. He focused on delivering the last of his momentum by slamming the heel of his right hand into the side of the guy's jaw.

The youth made a strangled yelp and fell onto his side, a red gob of half-chewed jerky dribbling out of his mouth.

Kyle saw a knobby branch of driftwood poking from a heap of seaweed and reached over to snatch it up. He hefted it as he lurched to his feet and turned back to the youth. The kid shrank away, eyeing him in terror, one elbow raised over his head to ward off any potential whack.

"No! Please!" he yelped. "No harm! I meant none! I was just—"

"Stealing?" Kyle snarled.

"You looked like you were dead!"

"Or so you *hoped*," Kyle said. "But if you bothered to check me for a pulse, you'd have found a man who could use some help."

Kyle poked one end of his branch into the sand, leaned his weight on its knobby tip. His head swam, all his muscles trembled from the sudden effort he'd just made. Yet he knew he still had to look strong and in control. Although both legs felt bruised and stiff, making him want to just lie down again. *Probably got hurt when I'd banged and scraped 'em on the cockpit as I exited.*

"Sorry! Thought I should check your stuff, find out who you were first. That's being smart these days, right?" The youth pled, brows raised, eyes wide and imploring. "I had to."

"You had to what? Eat my food? Pick the gear to take?"

Kyle used the stick to knock a spray of gravel at him. The youth scrabbled backward and raised his arm again. He had a pinched face that emphasized the ungainly beak of his nose. Big ears cupped the sides of his narrow head like dirty wings.

"I... I'm hungry," he muttered. "Your stuff tasted great. I couldn't stop. They don't let us eat much meat. The Elders, I mean."

Kyle pointed the stick's end at him.

"'Elders.' Mm. So, who the hell is that?"

The skinny youth shoved himself up into a sitting posture.

"Our bosses. People who run Elysian," he quavered. "Up there?" He pointed a finger inland. A broad slope spread away and upward from the beach. Its rolling landscape was bisected by the bright, wavering squiggle of a flowing creek. "Where we live."

Sunlight fanned out just above a forested ridgeline. Kyle squinted into the glare and began to discern swatches of dark, cultivated earth on slopes below the crest of the ridge. Long lines of green brush straggled downhill from this farmed area to braid together at the creek. The watercourse then spread out into a gleaming blue sheet that debouched into a marsh-ringed lagoon, at one end of the beach and just above it.

Kyle shaded his eyes with a palm to study that high hillside somewhat better. He made out threads of blue smoke that spiraled upward from a settlement, located a quarter of the way to the crest.

Wow. I crashed on the shore of a hidden valley that has inhabitants. What're the odds? Kyle mulled it over. *Many different paths got taken after the Fire-Flare. But few paid off. If they built a farm out in an unburnt stretch of wilderness, plus they beat back the marauders to keep it going, they're better off than most.* That appraisal sparked hope. *Perhaps they can resupply me, give me all I need to finish my trip and get on home to Luz Maria! Maybe even provide a horse. Because damn, man, that crash convinced me. I'm freakin' done with trying to paddle my butt all the way back. Anyhow, my boat now is likely only a loose clump of broken fiberglass bobbing around offshore. If it's not sunk. Or flung up onto the rocks somewhere.*

Kyle noticed that the youth had shifted, begun to gather his legs under himself.

"No, dude. Sit! Don't move till I say. Or I'll knock that gargoyle skull of yours into the middle of next week, okay?"

The kid grimaced. But he settled back down and wrapped arms around his bony knees.

While he'd lain face-down and groggy, a rising sun had started to bake Kyle in his wetsuit. Increase of its heat rays now didn't improve that situation. He jabbed the stick back into the sand so that it stood in easy reach. He swept a hand to the small of his back, grabbed the lanyard and tugged down the long zipper, then peeled off the black rubber suit.

The youth gaped at Kyle's lean V-shape of whipcord muscle and bone, seamed by a long pink scar than ran across his chest. Otherwise his skin was covered by fine reddish hairs that glimmered all over him like a light coat of fur.

"What're you lookin' at?" Kyle challenged.

The youth blushed, averted his face for a moment.

Kyle rooted around in his duffle, located a rugby shirt, his green canvas cargo shorts and a pair of river sandals and put them all on. He tugged out Roy's bone-handled Bowie knife, uncoiled its belt from the sheath, and strapped it onto his waist. He next pulled the stock of the semiautomatic survival rifle out from the bottom of the bag and popped its butt plate off to reveal the barrel, action and magazine nested within. He pulled these parts out and rapidly assembled them into a functional firearm.

The youth's eyes widened.

Kyle slid the bolt, racked a round into the chamber, clicked on the safety and grinned. His celebratory display of teeth was all dominance, nothing jolly about it.

A beat-up aluminum water bottle came out of the bag next. Kyle twisted off the cap, upended it and gulped. Fresh energy seemed to pour into him with each swallow. He rolled up the wetsuit, and stuffed it, the empty bottle and the jerky bag into the duffle. He snatched up clothes the kid had tossed out and put them all back.

He squeezed air out of the bag, folded over its top, then united the side-snaps to make a handle.

Meanwhile, the youth used fingernails to gather shreds of jerky off his cheeks and scrape them into his mouth. His eyes stayed riveted on Kyle.

"Uh-h, what's the plan..." he faltered.

"Tell me your name."

"Ephraim. I am Ephraim Coop-... I mean, James."

"Say what?"

"Ephraim! James!"

"All righty, Jimbo. We're taking a hike."

"Huh?"

"Up to your village."

"I don't think that's—"

Kyle made a curt gesture with the rifle barrel. "Up and at 'em, kid."

The youth went pale. He arose cautiously.

Kyle put an arm through the handle of the duffle, slung it over his shoulder. He beckoned to Ephraim, then ordered him to walk toward the village. He limped along close behind. *It's not the brightest idea to barge into a place before I've scouted it. But damn, I'm beat, so bad. And this kid would likely report me no matter what. So, I either go to the settlers right now or they'll find me later. Better the first way. Besides, if they're just a bunch of farmers, how bad could it be?*

After they'd gone a hundred yards, the youth halted, turned around. The look on his face was nervous yet resolute.

"This won't work," he said.

"Yeah? Why not?"

"March me into Elysian? A prisoner? You look like an enemy from Outside. It's how you'll be treated. People will be upset. A lot more people than you can ever shoot."

"Okay-y-y." Kyle scratched his chin. "Shooting people wasn't my goal. But what's a better way to go, Jimbo?"

"My name is Ephraim."

"Oho! Not James Ephraim."

"No. Ephraim James."

"Got it. Thanks, Jimbo."

"That's not my name."

"Easier to say. You'll always be Jimbo to me. So, what's your answer?"

Ephraim scowled. "First, don't be waving that gun around."

Kyle snorted. "What? I should pitch it in the creek?"

"No. Put it back in the bag."

Kyle guffawed. Then he paused, shrugged. He slid the bag off his shoulder, opened it, shook its contents to one side, then inserted the rifle so an inch or two of its stock hung out of the opening. He re-snapped the handles around it. "There," he said. "I'm happy with concealed carry if you folks are. Let's move."

The walk resumed, with Kyle gimping along as best he could.

"Hey Jimbo, did you ever see anybody who was, like, great at throwing knives?"

Kyle put this question to Ephraim's back.

"What?" Ephraim threw a puzzled glance over his shoulder. "Why?"

"Because I'm really good."

"I just helped you. And you threaten me?"

"Just don't take it into your head to try and run off."

"Why?"

"To reach your folks before I do. Offer a version of your behavior on the beach. But see, I plan to create my own first impressions. Get it?"

Ephraim didn't reply. His stride lagged for a moment, then he stepped ahead briskly.

As they went up a main path into the village, black dots of bent figures wandering among the row crops and orchards grew into vertical lines, then recognizable humans. They stood stock-still as they assessed the approach of Ephraim and Kyle, gaped, talked among themselves, then moved toward them.

Buildings became visible. Kyle saw tall walls made of slabs split out of redwood trunks, surmounted by slanting sod roofs. From these roofs sprouted a living, verdant thatch—grasses of a dark olive hue. A dozen big lodges had been erected this way, with a score or so of conventional, much smaller log cabins scattered between them. Nestled against the far hillside was the biggest structure, one with high domes of waving sod grass that crowned a row of three circular chambers.

As they headed toward it, they passed an amphitheater, carved into a hillside, where groups of children plopped on benches were being taught by adults who stood at plank tables. In the shade of some trees near the buildings, women were hand-weaving sheets of fabric on tall looms.

Workers from the fields had begun to parallel their course. But they kept off about thirty yards, staring hard at Kyle and Ephraim. Many of them carried tools—spades, rakes and hoes. Ephraim made gestures at the onlookers, pointed back at Kyle, awkwardly indicated his helplessness. The laborers began to mutter. But they were wary enough of a stranger that they attempted no closer approach.

Ephraim led Kyle straight through the village center up to that large domed structure tucked against the hillside. A fan of clay, pounded flat and smooth, led to its front entrance. Nearby, a long steel cylinder dangled from a tripod made of peeled poles. Kyle squinted at it, realized the cylinder was a welder's gas tank with its bottom cut off. It'd been transfigured into a kind of gong. *Probably to transmit signals out through the village....*

Between this ad hoc sonic device and the main lodge's entry stood a huge black man wearing a coarsely woven tunic. His body was a thick, wide column, with the round boulder of a head balanced atop it. Tight curls of hair lay flat against his balding skull. His broad nose showed many scars and dents, looking as if it had been broken more than once. He gripped an oaken staff, displaying it with an air of authority. Kyle guessed him to be in his mid-thirties.

Behind him, a bearded white man who looked a bit younger slouched against a wall. He was dressed in worn buckskins, had a shaggy mane of red dreadlocks that drooped past his shoulders, and held a spear with a gleaming steel tip in the crook of his arm.

"Ephraim," the black man barked, "why do you bring an intruder here? To our sanctuary? You *know* that's not how we deal with Outsiders!"

"Yes, of course. I know." The Adam's apple bobbed in Ephraim's thin neck. "But the Sayer also asks us to show mercy. I found this man passed out, down the beach. Seemed like he needed our aid."

Kyle snickered. Both men gave him a penetrating look. The black man's stare was particularly stern.

"Ha. What a load of crap," Kyle said. "Sure, I was down and out cold on your beach. And this charming lad thought I was dead, or at the very least, dead to the world! So, he raided my gear bag. Ripped me off."

"Nope," Ephraim denied. "Just inspecting it. Which is how I found out this guy is carrying weapons."

"Weapons?" The red-haired man shoved himself away from the wall to take up a more poised and athletic stance. He pointed his spear at the sheath knife on Kyle's hip. "Y'mean, besides that blade?"

"There's a gun in his duffle. And he put bullets into it."

"A gun, huh?"

The black man took a step to one side and two more forward. He placed both thick hands, side by side, fingers down, on the center of his staff. Kyle found himself flanked by a pair of men who looked more like warriors than they had five seconds ago—keyed up, ready to take action.

"Do you?"

"Yes. But I can explain."

"Take your bag off," the black man rumbled. "Do it slow. Put it down on the ground. Then step away."

"Hey. I'm not trying to threaten anyone."

The man's grim gaze altered not a jot. Kyle turned to that red-head with the spear. He smiled. Yet he also held his spear level, with its keen tip pointed right at Kyle's belly.

"Prob'ly should, bro!" the redhead said. "Samuel's a regular terror with that staff. Saw him kill a bull with it, one time. So, don't want to make him mad. Do as he says and he'll like you better. Me too."

Kyle glanced at the massive black man, then swept his gaze around at the field hands who'd closed ranks to surround him. Most held farm tools that could do major damage, especially if they all got swung at the same time. He considered his options. Just one made any sense. He plucked the duffle from his shoulder, set it down and took a step backward.

Samuel hooked the bag's handle with his staff and dragged it closer to him. Both men peered at the black plastic of the gun butt that poked out of the opening.

"Just an old military survival rifle," Kyle said. "Semiauto, called an AR-7. Shoots .22 longs."

"Nice!" the redhead said. "Yeah, we can sure use one a' them. Hope you've got lots of ammo, too."

Kyle felt a tug on his attention, a tiny, invisible hook that'd snagged on a hidden lobe of his brain. He involuntarily turned his head to see Ephraim slink back into the crowd of villagers. And he noted the smirk on his face, a sly and satisfied gleam in his eye. *Kid played me. Pretty damn well, too,* he realized. *Must be savvier than he looks.*

Chapter 2

Samuel thumped an end of his staff against the dangling steel tank and it released a deep, resonant *b-o-ng-g*. Wasn't clear to Kyle if the guy hoped to signal somebody or was just making noise for the hell of it.

The red-headed man leaned his spear against the wall, seized Kyle's duffle and yanked it open to dump its contents out. He kicked through all of Kyle's gear with a moccasin-clad foot, then plucked the survival gun up with both hands to inspect it. He hauled back the bolt just enough to see the gleam of a brass round in the chamber.

"What did you plan to do with this?" he asked.

"Hunt. Or use it to defend myself," Kyle said. "If I had to."

"So, how's that workin' out?" He snickered.

Kyle shrugged.

A thick canvas cover that hung down to form a door flapped back and a short, wizened man stood in the dark entry. His scrunched skin, dark beady eyes and an aureole of white hair and wisps of beard made him look like an apple doll that had been attacked by a fungus. He gave Samuel an irritated look.

"And why do you disturb the Council?"

"Beg your pardon, Elder." Samuel pointed his staff at Kyle. "But we caught an Outsider," he said.

"Uh, no sir. More like, a so-called 'Outsider' walked right up here of his own free will," Kyle clarified.

The Elder squinted at Kyle. It didn't seem that his vision was all that keen.

"Yeah, but he was toting this." The redhead brandished the gun.

The apple-faced elf rummaged around in a fabric purse that hung from his sash, took out a set of wire-rimmed spectacles and perched them on his snub nose.

"Well!" He peered at the gun, then at Kyle, and pondered for a second. "Then it may be a blessing for us that our Council is already in session. We can discuss whether this might be the Outsider we've hunted for."

The red-haired man cocked his head. "Ri-i-i-ght," he said. "Or may know about him. Since marauders rarely travel alone."

"Check the man over with care. Then bring him in."

"Yes, Elder Ez. As you wish."

"You people on the lookout for someone?" Kyle asked.

Nobody answered. But a murmur in the crowd behind him grew more agitated and menacing.

"Shed that knife you got strapped on, dude," the red-haired man said. "Then Sam here needs to feel you up some. My advice? Just relax 'n' enjoy it."

Kyle raised both hands, palms out. "Hey," he said. "I'm no danger to any of you folks. I'm here looking for help. You got none to give, let me have my stuff back, I'll take off. Won't bother you again."

"Sorry brother," the red-haired man said firmly. "You're already on a 'nother path. Got to walk it."

"What's your name?" Kyle asked.

"Call me Red."

"Makes sense."

"Yep. Don't it?"

"Where you from?"

"Ol' Rocky Branch, Kentucky. Brought my trimmin' scissors out to work the Triangle 'bout twelve years ago, liked it well and never left."

"So, Red—"

"Nah. Shit-can the chit-chat now. Got stuff to do." Red clicked the safety off on the rifle and aimed it at Kyle's chest. "Drop that knife, like I told you. Step over 'n' visit Sam for a friskin'. I'll take care of that pig-sticker. Promise, you can have it back when you leave."

"But I—"

The end of Samuel's staff made a blur in Kyle's peripheral vision just before it whacked his solar plexus. Kyle's breath whooshed out and his body folded in half as he flopped over backwards. His vision swam as he struggled for breath. Eventually he realized the biggest reason he couldn't breathe was that Samuel had a knee on his chest and was shoving his full weight down on it while he stripped Kyle of his knife. Next he ran those big hands below his shirt, and next all over Kyle's torso and thighs.

"Clean," he pronounced, and stood.

Sam gave Red the knife, who grinned as he buckled its belt around the waist of his leather shirt.

Kyle gasped, managed to coax a wisp of air into his lungs. One more. But before he could win a third, Samuel flipped him over, picked him up by the waistband of his shorts, dragged his limp body through the lodge entry, then hurled him down onto a dank floor of pounded earth.

He lay there as odors of musty clay, wood ash, and an aroma of fresh cedar floated up into his nostrils. Finally, he recovered enough to push himself up to his hands and knees. He leaned back, haunches on his heels, and tried to take in his surrounding while his vision adjusted to dim light.

Before him lay circular firepit formed of river rocks. Whorls of smoke spiraled up from it to exit from a hole in the top of the dome roof. To either side of the heap of dying embers stood a long plank bench mounted on stumps, and on each bench sat a row of five men. Those on the left, including the Elder called Ez, wore tunics of fabric so rough it appeared to be woven out of jute. Those sitting on the right were clad in loose, soot-smeared, patched-up buckskins.

The men all studied Kyle as though he was some type of varmint snared in a trap, and they wanted to assess how dangerous or bothersome he might be.

Ez cleared his throat. "This is the Outsider. Don't fear him. He's been disarmed."

"True," Kyle wheezed. His diaphragm still felt half-paralyzed. "But I'm not here with any ill intent. And I wasn't so armed as all that, actually."

Samuel's staff poked him in the back. "Shut up now, you," he rumbled. "Answer their questions. That's all."

"Oh, so this is a court? But I must keep my lip zipped? Well where's the kangaroos? Don't see any."

One of the buckskin men in the center of that bench chuckled. But Samuel wasn't amused. His staff prodded Kyle again, harder, and right on a kidney.

Oof. Now's not the right time to offer these guys any sass, Kyle thought. *No matter how much I'd like to.*

"Where did you come from?" Ez demanded.

"Your shore. Down on the cove. I crashed a sea kayak there last night."

"Last night? And where were you before that?" This question came from the buckskin man who'd laughed—the oldest of the leather-clad men. He had an aquiline face with high cheekbones and hooded eyes, and a mane of grey hair swept behind his ears and held back by a folded white bandanna.

"At sea, mainly. Stopped only at night to make my camps. I started out from San Francisco last week, paddling north to get home to Arcata. But my voyage got cut short by a big-ass wave."

"Crazy. Why risk your tail on such a long, rough journey?"

"Well, originally it was even longer. First part was getting from Arcata south to Frisco. I drove that inland on what's left of I-5, with an ol' gas-burning car. A Mustang. But that was literal hell on wheels. I thought paddling back would make for a much safer way home."

"Which didn't turn out to be quite so safe as you'd hoped, then."

"Right."

"And how many companions had you?" An Elder who sat next to Ez spoke up.

"What you see is the whole shebang. Been a solo trip from the get-go."

"Hah!" The Elder scoffed and spat into the firepit.

The buckskin man stroked his chin. "Don't buy it," he said. "Why'd a guy attempt such a tremendous trip by his lonesome? Not just your paddle back up, but that long drive down t'other way."

"Loyalty."

Buckskin man's smile was thin. "Whoa. To who? To what?"

"My friend, Roy. Well, he's my father-in-law. We heard that he and his wife and neighbors had all gotten in a ton of trouble. The Bay Area's begun to look like Chernobyl. We hoped to rescue Roy and his wife Felicia, and maybe someone else. Take them back up to Arcata to live with us."

"We?"

"My wife and I. Well, me mostly, I guess. Luz Maria hollered for while that she didn't want me to go. However, I knew that she truly did. And in the end, she admitted it."

Buckskin man chortled. "Ha. Women! 'M I right?"

"Yeah. So, what's your name?" Kyle instantly felt sorry he'd asked, since the business end of Sam's staff bonked his other kidney. The guy seemed to be a stickler for rules. His own rules, at any rate.

"I'm Carlos. You okay there? Take a deep breath. All right. Now tell us yours."

"Kyle. Kyle Skander."

"What's goin' on up in Arcata these days, Kyle?"

He swung his gaze around the room. "Same thing that's going on here, I'd say. People doing whatever they can to live. There's bouts of tough fighting, sometimes."

"How so?"

"Arcata's sort of rural. However, three highways run straight on into our town. After the Flare, we got hit awful damned hard by marauders. Ever hear of the War at HSU?"

"Nope."

"Can tell you all about it, if you want."

"Later, maybe. What sort of stuff were you up to in Arcata?"

"You mean, my gig? Before the Flare?" Kyle half-smiled. "I was a new professor. Taught logic, rhetoric, and philosophy. But that was only after I met Roy. Way before, well, then I was an indoor pot farmer."

The Elder Ez scowled. "All right, let's us then get back on track here." He lifted a fuzzy eyebrow. "Let's imagine for a moment the possibility that you did truly go on down then to the Frisco area to rescue these other people. All right, so now, where are they? Where's any of them?"

Kyle exhaled, glanced at the floor. "I reached Woodside too late. Know where that is? A town south of San Fran. Way-y-y too late," he said. "My fault. So now they're gone. Not with us. Dead." He looked up, eyes glistening.

"Convenient," one of the buckskin men said.

"A story," Ez commented, after a pause. "All its parts fit. You tell it convincingly. But let's see if there's a different angle, one that still accounts for all our available facts. Carlos?"

"Thanks, Ezra," the buckskin man Carlos said. He stared at Kyle. "Was it truly last night that you crashed here? Where were you six days ago?"

"Woodside. As I just said." Kyle's face puckered in thought. "What's so special about a week ago?" He flinched, anticipating a poke from Samuel. But that impact didn't arrive.

Punishment is more effective if it's sporadic.... So, he'll pick a reason to swat me again.

The men around the firepit all exchanged looks. No one wanted to speak next. Then Ez cleared his throat. Apparently he was the big pooh-bah among the five Elysian Elders.

"We had a killing," Ezra said. His voice was thick with emotion. Sounded as if this victim was someone he'd cared about. Perhaps a person they'd all cared for.

"Okay. And?"

"Know something about it?"

"How could I?"

"See now, that's what we intend to find out! Can you prove to us that you weren't here when the killing happened?"

"What?! Prove a negative? Give me a break."

Samuel got back on task by awarding Kyle's collar bone a brisk rap.

"Jesus!" Kyle swiveled his head. "Knock that shit off! You want that stick rammed straight up that bent nose of yours? Jerk."

When he looked back at the assembled council, he realized his show of temper had been a tactical error. Everyone now looked at him as if he might indeed be a man of violence.

"Sorry," he pled. "But can you please get that guy to quit whacking me? It's maddening. I'm already being as straight with you as I can be."

Ez lifted a hand, waggled an index finger at Samuel. Kyle heard him shuffle backward a step or two.

"Hey, help us out, here. Make it easy on yourself," Carlos coaxed. "Toss us some hard info we can work with. Any part of a defense."

Kyle thought.

"Okay. You send someone to scout your shore, and they find a wrecked sea kayak in a spot where nobody saw one before, ought to prove something, right? Far as any other clues go, well, I just left tracks on your beach last night. Up to the high tideline." He pointed at his sandals. "This morning, I put these on for the first time. Only shoes I've got. Since some of you folk go barefoot, and it looks like all the rest wear moccasins, my tracks would be unusual on any trail or patch of dirt. And I'm saying, you won't be able to find those tracks in any other place. Just between the beach and here."

"Unless you'd traveled along our paths either barefoot, or in moccasins yourself." That was Ez. "Which would be clever."

"Come on." Kyle locked eyes with him. "Why would a bloody-handed killer, who'd slain a person from your village, next be dumb enough to march straight on into it?"

Ezra stayed silent and poker-faced.

"Oh well now, he might," Carlos drawled. "If our killer happened to be bold. Or crazy. Or hoped to use a display of innocence to deflect blame. Get accepted in Elysian. Then, once we were off guard, he might try his hand at another crime." He swung his gaze around the council chamber. "Maybe we should try to pound a more detailed confession out of this sucker. Just yacking with him won't cut it. He's too glib."

"You people," Kyle said, shaking his head. "Are friggin' nuts."

As Carlos spoke, a short, chunky boy who wore a monk's robe with a raised cowl that hid his face moved into the council chamber from a hallway. The child whispered something to Ezra, then left.

Elder Ezra held up a palm. "Our time for argument is over," he said. "I declare the council adjourned. We have a suspect in hand. He shall be detained till his guilt can be proved. A righteous vengeance may soon be undertaken. Then our community can perhaps move on, with justice done, in satisfaction and in healing."

"Or not," Kyle said. "Can't I get just a scrap of presumption-of-innocence, here? You're *starting* with a verdict? That's some real Lewis Carroll, through the looking-glass shit right there."

He was ignored.

"Should our Tribe take him into custody?" Carlos asked. "We can beat a tad more truth out. I say, drag the guy. Or something. We've got methods to apply. That's why intruders haven't posed much of a problem."

Ez shook his head. His wispy fringe of white hairs waved around as they trailed a half-beat behind his face.

"We built a cell in the rear of this lodge. Tiny, not much used. But it's stout, and it shall work perfectly well to hold a miserable fiend like this one."

"That's it?" Kyle looked aghast. "My hearing? The whole thing? How in the hell is this fair?"

"Samuel, put this creature in his cage."

Thick fingers twisted into Kyle's hair, began to haul him to his feet. He jumped up in order to keep his scalp from being torn out by the roots.

"You just want a scapegoat! Maybe the killer's one of you. But hey, let an Outsider take the fall... UGHH!"

Samuel had snatched one of Kyle's arms and cranked it so high up behind his back that it felt like his shoulder joint would pop. A knee then hit him in the lumbar region. Sam held Kyle up so that his feet barely scraped the floor.

Kyle took the deepest breath he could and yelled, "You're a bunch of raging assholes!"

Those words echoed around the dank chamber as Sam shoved him out of it, frog-marching him into a deeper part of the building.

Chapter 3

Samuel half-carried, half-shoved Kyle out of the Council chamber, moving him past a heavy oaken door, through a second chamber that boasted an oculus in its roof—an octagonal, open-air skylight—and dim walls that had arched hallways radiating out from the chamber on three sides. Sam delivered him into a final space, cool and shadowy, with a pit the size of a bear's den at its far end. This jail cell was a hole spaded deep into a hillside, then lined with crude bricks. Its door was an oblong grid of iron straps, spot-welded at the cross-points.

Samuel flung Kyle in, secured the door with a brass padlock, spun around and left without uttering another word.

Kyle arose to explore his dim surroundings. Didn't take long. The cramped space measured only ten feet long by eight wide. And about seven feet high at the center of a curved ceiling. A low sleeping platform along one wall was merely a shelf of more uneven brick. It bore a pair of scrofulous sheep fleeces laid end to end as a mattress, plus a musty quilt for a blanket. A pail served as commode. A dinged metal canteen leaned against the wall next to it. He grabbed the canteen and shook it. *Half full!* He drained it immediately.

Kyle plopped his butt on the shelf and sat with his elbows propped on his knees, his head in his hands, and struggled to sort out his thoughts. He'd already felt weary and beaten up back when he woke up on that beach. And now just a few hours later he'd been battered still more, by the very people he'd imagined might help. The settlement didn't appear as if it aimed to provide succor of any kind.

I'm just a pest they aim to paint as a villain. Then stomp flat. Y'know, if a man really let himself go, he might get depressed by a situation like this. But it's like Roy used to say. If a problem crops up and you let yourself get all stressed over it, then you've got two problems. Kyle's smile was both wry and sad. *Nothing I can do except refuse to freak out. Oh yeah, maybe also take a nap. As it just so happens, feels like I could use about a month of sleep....*

He leaned back, swung his legs up onto the shelf, and tugged the moldy quilt up to his chin, his nose wrinkling as he did. *Phew! Oh well.* Almost instantly he felt himself drop off, as if falling back into a well of shadows. His last conscious thought was an epigram from one of the philosophy classes he used to teach. *'Patience is bitter, but it can bear sweet fruit.' Plato, I think. No, no, it was Aristotle.... Yep, Ari. Roy's fave. I mean, right after his Stoics, of course.*

———

Sounds again became a stimulus that prompted him back to consciousness. But since he'd been dreaming about Luz Maria, he fought to grab a few more fabulous seconds of imagining that he could see her, feel near her, before he let himself fully awaken.

There's Luz in our garden acre where she so much loves to hang out, skirt hiked up so she can squat down easily and pull carrots and radishes, brushing the dirt off, dropping them into that wicker basket she wove from willow shoots. Now she feels me watching her, turns and smiles, God that great smile, so wide and joyous and all those bright white teeth and that way her brown eyes seem to glow when she gazes at me, in a way no other woman ever has, and she's standing up, so I score a glimpse of both those swee-ee-eet copper thighs that flex so deliciously before the hem of her skirt drops and she pirouettes toward me, I can tell she wants a kiss, but...now she's looking over my shoulder, frowning... and I hear someone else come up and I turn....

The cell door clanked, as if someone had bumped against it.

He opened his eyes to see a golden glow flicker above his bed, dancing on the arched ceiling. He turned his head. A tall figure moved in the shadows bearing a lit candlestick, accompanied by another figure half as big that dragged a wooden stool over in front of the door and then backed away. The tall person sat on the stool, set a fat beeswax taper in an iron holder on the clay floor. It was a blond woman with an odd aspect to her face—a black blot where her left eye should've been.

Kyle flopped the quilt back, put his feet on the floor, and swung around so he could score a better look. She wore a shapeless grey garment somewhat like a monk's robe, belted at the waist with a cincture braided from multicolored yarns. She threw the robe's hood back. He realized then that her odd appearance was due to a black eyepatch, suspended from a string that ran over her hair on one side and under it on the other. The eye without a patch appeared to be large, blue and luminous, although its focus wandered vaguely. That eye did not seem to be ever aimed at him, or indeed, at anything, which puzzled him.

He just sat there, taking her in.

Then she said, "May I touch your face?"

"Huh?" He was startled. "Why?"

"I want to see you. But I'm blind. I need to use my fingers."

"Why bring a candle in here, then?"

"So that you can see me."

"Oh."

Kyle didn't want to cooperate with anyone in Elysian. Yet thanks to his brief dream of Luz, he'd awakened less angry and depressed than he'd been when falling asleep. This midnight visit felt odd, but the blind woman only seemed weird, not threatening. He slid to the end of his sleeping shelf and put his face up to the cell door.

"All right. Give me your hands, then."

Pale hands with long, slim fingers came in through the gaps between bars. Kyle took them by the wrists and placed them on his face. The hands paused, then the fingertips trembled and fluttered against his skin as gently as the wings of moths.

Despite himself, Kyle found her touch erotic to a startling degree. It had been a long while since anyone had touched him that way. Indeed, he thought, perhaps no one ever had.

The hands withdrew.

"Once you sought to be a man of peace," she said. "Not so any longer. True?"

What the hell kind of question is that?

"These days?" He hedged. "Might say that 'bout a lot of people."
She raised one hand in front of the door. He watched those fingers wave and shudder like long grass in a stiff breeze as they poked about in the air some two feet in front of him. Somehow it felt as if those hands had remained contact with his skin.

"But now, you've become a genuine killer."

"Oh, great," Kyle said. "This is Bogus Trial Part Two? You're what, Miss Detective Lady of Elysian? Wait, no, you sound more like a judge. Blind justice for real, huh? Ready to find me guilty of something I know absolutely zip about."

"I am not your judge. I am merely an interested party."

"Well, I'm *not* interested. Okay?"

"I do not pick up any particular sense of your guilt or blame in this crime. The deed that so many here suspect you of. The one that dismays and saddens us all. Yet, perhaps that's because you excel at concealment. And you have killed otherwise and elsewhere. True? Because the shadows of many deaths have darkened you."

Kyle felt his impatience accelerate. All he really wanted to do right now was go back to sleep, not suffer another specious interview. "Yeah, sure. I live in the woods up north. Where I hunt and fish. So, a lot of blood on my hands."

"I see, animals. But what about people?" she persisted. "Other humans?"

Kyle's mouth worked. Suddenly, he wanted to put a gob of spit in the center of that pale face, with that strange pair of eyes that weren't truly eyes. He remembered, way back before the Flare, a friend of his who'd been in Army special forces told him the one question he hated getting from a civilian the most was, "Hey, did you ever kill anybody?" Now he understood why. No matter what you told them, they'd never get it.

"Can't see that's any of your business," he said coldly.

"Ah, but it truly is."

How do I rid myself of this nosy bitch? She bothers the tar out of me. So cocksure about her bullshit.

"Look. I told those old council boys of yours about times of heavy fighting up in Arcata. I was right there on that scene. Which is the only way I could ever tell them about it. Enough said, all right? Go away. Let me get back to sleep."

"I know what you said to the Council. Tell me more about Arcata."

He uttered a groan of frustration. "What on earth does that have to do with anything now?"

"You had been a teacher there?"

Kyle's forehead wrinkled. This lady not only bounced fast between topics, she veered all over the map. He began to wonder about her mental competence. *Jesus. Maybe if I just answer some of it, she'll go away.*

"Yes. But a professor, of philosophy. At HSU, the college. I taught logic, rhetoric and coached debates, too," he summarized. "Geometry as an elective, for our adult classes. Ran a mystery and thriller book club for everybody. All of that well before the Fire-Flare hit, of course. And so, irrelevant now."

"Ah, the Reckoning," she said. "That's our name for the Flare, down here in Elysian."

"Reckoning? You mean, some kind of Hand-of-God crap? No, lady, it was only a giant solar flare. What scientists used to call a coronal mass ejection, I mean, back when we had scientists. Biggest such event in recorded history. Fried just about every microchip on earth, blew up transformers, burned down power stations. Really thumped our civilization reset button. Yanked us backward more than a century. Maybe two."

"Yes, it was from the sun," she said calmly. "Our sun, which is the face of the Creator. Behind its purifying light stands the All-Father."

"Uh-huh. Well, if you want to interpret a star-fart as a message from God, I guess it's your call."

He thought for a moment. *Okay. If this gal keeps insisting on staying so chatty and chummy, maybe I can steer her toward a useful topic. Learn about my captors. Even if I must force myself to stay awake to do it.* He sighed. "So, then. Tell me something. I mean, take a turn on getting a question. I get the impression you're a religious community here. What type?"

She nodded. "We are Readers of the Holy Writ. Or RHW or the Writ Readers, for short. And this," she said, as she waved one of those graceful hands in a circle, "is the land that was promised to us. A new Canaan. Our reward for keeping among the true faithful." She cocked her head. "But you, don't you have a spiritual belief?"

"Sure. You bet," Kyle said. "I believe religious talk is a crock of total hooey. An old, old con that we should call The Invisible Friend Industry. And when I say, 'we,' I meant me and my pal Roy. That was his line. He just had to cite it to me one time, and at that moment a lot of guff about so-called 'matters of faith' became crystal clear."

"Ah." She seemed unperturbed by his blanket criticism. Her fingers waggled in the air for a second. "So-o-o, I gather that you had been very close to this man."

"Very. Yes, sure. I taught plenty of others, but Roy was *my* teacher. Not just the school stuff. He taught me a ton about hunting and fishing. And other things, too. He's the father of my wife, Luz."

"Yes. A lovely one who enjoys gardens."

Kyle stared at her. *How on earth did she get that information? Everything else, she could have been told by those guys in the council room. But not that.*

"Who are you, then?" he asked. "And what's your role? You a type of leader here, like the Elders?"

She smiled. "I serve the Writ Readers. It's my honor to be anointed as their Sayer."

"Wow, sounds important." He eyed her. "And might an infidel Outsider ask your name?"

"Ruth. I'm the Sayer Ruth James."

He thought about that for a second. "Any relation to a teenage creep here in Elysian, called Ephraim James?"

"Yes. He's a cousin unto me. Not by blood, but by baptism."

"How's that work?"

"Elysian was founded by several extended families. Where there's not a blood bond, others may take that family name and join them by a mutual adoption. It's how we of the Writ bring new members into our circle of the blessed. So, Ephraim's my cousin, and our Elder Ezra is my uncle."

"What about actual blood relations? Got any?"

The glow of her pale face seemed to dim and her mouth sagged down at the corners.

"Well, I did have, once," Ruth said softly. "Yet, no more." Her chest heaved. "She's traveled on to Paradise and her reward. Six days past, now."

"What? Who're we talking about?" His eyebrows rose. "The one killed?"

Her posture stiffened. She seemed to struggle with the right way to answer. Her wandering blue eye abruptly ceased its drift. Instead, it appeared to settle and glare at him. Kyle had a hunch that he wouldn't like what she said next.

"Yes. She was my sister," she said. "Our beloved younger Sayer. Her name was Rebecca."

A single tear broke loose from the lower edge of the eye patch. It skated down her cheek to trace a glistening, wavering snail track. The other eye—that now seemed to watch him—followed soon, dropping a tear of its own.

Kyle was stunned. He felt tongue-tied. For a long minute, he and Ruth sat face-to-face without speaking a word.

What the hell, she won't believe me. But I might as well say it. Put it on record with her from the get-go.

"Listen," he said slowly. "I had zero to do with her death. Rebecca's. Never met the lady. And I don't know any person who had anything to do with it."

She simply sat there with her chest rising and falling in slow and measured breaths.

"I…" he started, but then stopped as he realized he couldn't put it any simpler or make it any clearer.

"Sayer Ruth?" A suave, tenor voice rippled out from the shadows of the chamber. "Does all go well with you?"

"Almost, Michael, almost. For now," she said. "But I am done. We can leave."

She stood up and turned away.

What the hell was she trying to get, from me, then?

That short figure Kyle had earlier seen accompanying Ruth as she'd first arrived at his cell door now reentered the ring of candlelight with his own hood thrown back. He realized it was the same person he'd seen whisper to Ezra in the council meeting. Given a moment to study him, Kyle realized he was no child, but a short, stocky young man with a big head, fringe of beard and a wild mop of brown hair.

Legs of the wooden stool scraped on the floor as he pushed it off to one side. He stooped over to pick up the iron candlestick then reached up to place it gingerly in the hand that Ruth held outstretched and cupped to receive it.

Kyle gaped. *Hey, this dude isn't just short, he's way-short! A real half-pint. Veritable midget. No-o-o, an actual dwarf.*
The guy gave Kyle back a hard, *"Yeah, I'm a small person, so what?"* glance. And Kyle could guess at the rest of his thinking. *"Perhaps I also help decide how long you stay in that cell."* The dwarf's glare was insolent, bold, a gauntlet flung down—if not swung across Kyle's face.

The woman glided toward the exit tunnel. Although blind, she had a dancer's poise and balance. Maybe her lack of vision had awakened a certain unusual skill in movement, as a compensation. Like those long fingers of hers, that could wig-wag so hypnotically, as if using semaphore to signal to ghosts.

The pair began to walk away, the dwarf moving with his own special gait to keep up with her, a blend of waddle and strut. Kyle almost shouted after them, "Hey, when can I get out of this rathole?" Yet he found himself unable to do it. He was still too befuddled by his encounter with Ruth. All parts of it, but particularly the final minute. *This Sayer gal acts like both an interrogator and a judge. And it's her sister who was killed. Damn. Does that ever give her an ax to grind—right into my neck. And that could be the first item on her agenda at sunrise.*

Well, let's try to not have any more depressing thoughts. Then you need a distraction.... And holy smokes, think about that dwarf with her. I'd say he's no lackey. Far from it. A power behind a throne. Or a stool. Her éminence grise. Half of a Cardinal Richelieu, or maybe the entirety, but coiled up and compressed into one untidy lil' package.

Chapter 4

A thin sheet of light slipped beneath the black iron-strap door of Kyle's cell like a tiny note from the sun. The grey glow had dribbled in from the skylight in the next domed chamber, then seeped along the dark corridor to slide into his place of confinement.

This faint square slowly broadened, became a trapezoid that slid up his cell walls.

Kyle awakened, stretched, yawned.

A jumbled thumping of many mingled footsteps could be heard. The marchers sounded as if they might be approaching his cell. He rolled over, flung off the decaying quilt, stood up. Saw the yellow flare of a torch rounding a bend in a tunnel. Its smoky glare overwhelmed the vapid gleam of sunlight.

Shit. Here they come. Do I try to fight 'em in here, or should I wait till they drag me out into the chamber? Well, how many of them are there?

Big Samuel led a crew of three others. Sam clutched the torch in one of his giant paws, but curiously, did not hold his oaken staff with the other. Kyle wondered what its absence meant. At least, maybe that gave him a slightly better chance to fight his way out.

Four against one—hey, I've seen worse odds. Okay, truth be told, well no, I haven't.

Samuel went down to a knee in front of the cell door. His eyes were liquid, beseeching. His wide mouth twitched in an attempt at a smile but he gave up on it. He heaved out a breath.

"Kyle Skander," he said. "I've wronged you. I dove into a black pool of rage and lost my way in that darkness." He took another deep breath. "I should not have let myself grow so upset. The demon of anger is the heart-destroyer. I did so because I was truly mad at myself. Because I failed to protect Rebecca's life, and let myself blame you for it. The Sayer and I have spoken, and she has revealed to me that I treated you more harshly than was just. And I apologize. I ask for your forgiveness."

Kyle gaped at him, astonished. The man didn't appear to be joking. *What's changed?*

Samuel arose. He opened the padlock, swung wide the cell's creaky door.

"Please come with us." Samuel was trying to sound pleasant. Well, his voice held more formal and friendlier content than before, but it still amounted to not much more than a bass growl. "It is our Elder Ezra who summons you. He wishes to make you an offer."

An offer? One I can refuse, or no? Hey, Outsider, if you just throw yourself off a cliff, we might not need to hang you from an oak limb.

———

Kyle was brought into the domed chamber with the oculus. A cribwork of small logs framed the octagonal skylight hole. He looked through it up into blue sky, with clouds still tinged rose by sunrise. Ravens were calling to each other in the distance. A dark shape flitted low across the opening with a rustle of feathers.

He looked down to see a rough table and a pair of stools had been set up in the center of the room. Off to one side and against a wall was a more ornate sort of chair, almost a throne, carved out of hunk of redwood log that had been set on end. Around its base and arms was strung an elaborate network, bas-relief carvings of symbols and glyphs that he couldn't quite make out.

"Sit," Samuel invited. "Your breakfast is being brought."

Kyle fought an impulse to go leap onto the throne. However, he suspected that no one but him would find it amusing. He opted for a stool.

Samuel went over to a wall where his staff leaned, awaiting him. The big man stood there, thick legs spread apart and thick arms folded, formidable-looking as ever. The other men exited.

A girl in a tunic entered, holding a wooden bowl that emitted curlicues of fragrant steam. Kyle had eaten nothing for more than a day, and saliva jetted onto his tongue. She set the bowl full of a kind of lentil and veggie stew down on the table. He wasted not a second. He sat, grabbed the handle of a spoon that projected from the stew and fell to.

He was wiping his lips with the sleeve of his shirt when Ezra strolled in. He nodded at Samuel, then placed himself on the other side of the table.

"How do you like our food?" Ezra asked. He pointed at the empty bowl. "You seem to have paid it a compliment."

Kyle eyed him. *Oh, he plans to go all friendly on me now, too? Yet another switcheroo. Must be good-cop day in Elysian. To be chased how soon by a fresh batch of their bad-cop approach?*

"Oh. passable for a starter course," Kyle told him. "But if it's all that's on tap, how about seconds?"

Ezra looked at Samuel, who whistled into the next chamber. The girl reappeared and took the bowl. "She'll bring you more," Ezra assured him.

"Let me ask you a question," Kyle said. "What the hell is up with you? The way you treat me now is the total opposite of yesterday."

"Well." The Elder Ez folded his hands over his small pot belly and offered Kyle a faint, polite smile. "We no longer put you in quite the same category as we did then."

"What's different?"

"Several things. The Tribe pulled their scouts in off the Pale to review their reports of all entries to Elysian. At no trail, at any time in the past week, had anyone left footprints like yours. So, that was a good point you made yesterday, in your own defense."

"What about *your* point? That I could've hiked in barefoot?"

Ezra shook his head, and his white fringe of hair nodded and bobbed. "Their trackers are skilled enough to read an individual by weight and stride. Each imprint is unique, as I understand it. Going barefoot wouldn't have made much difference to them. Carlos and Red described you, and the trackers said no one had passed through who resembled you."

"Great. And were any parts of my sea kayak found along your shore?"

"No." He smiled again. "But the picket who helped you yesterday did get questioned more closely."

"Jimbo. Oh sure, he was a big help. You bet."

"Ephraim."

"Whatever. And?"

"He said nothing that contradicted your story."

"Nice. And what about him attempting to rip me off?"

"He maintains he performed a proper inspection. He never planned to keep any items for himself."

"Including all my jerky he ate? How exactly does he plan to give *that* back? If it's in the usual way, not sure I want it."

Ezra shifted on his stool. "You don't understand Ephraim's job as a picket. He walks our perimeter, day after day, up to the Pale and back. To report what he sees. Especially things that vary from the usual."

"Such as me."

"Indeed. You vary considerably, Kyle Skander. And our Sayer agrees heartily with that assessment."

"Right. Your Miss Ruthie. After our chat last night, I thought she had me sized up and written off as the evil killer of her sister, Rebecca."

Ez shook his wispy white aureole. "No, quite the opposite. She's now sure of your innocence. And has sought to convince many of us, as well."

"Well, I hate to act as my own devil's advocate. But how on earth *could* she be convinced?"

"She's a Sayer. She has a gift. She has the sight."

"How special. Ruth's never wrong then?"

"Rarely. Yet sometimes! The prophetic gift in and of itself is holy and perfect. Yet we are inferior vehicles of any higher power, even the most blest among us. As the Writ has it, we all peer at the truth through a glass darkly. Yet she tells me you are an unbeliever, so I won't try to convince you. However, the upshot is, both her expert testimony and the evidence we have at present seem to support your story."

"It did that yesterday, too. So, why have your goon pound me and then toss me in that shithole cell?"

A grumble came from the wall. "Clean up that language, please," Samuel said. "Show more respect for our Elder."

Ez waved a hand at him. "It's all right, Sam," he said. "No Outsider can be healed in a day." He leaned toward Kyle. "We had to put on that kind of show to keep you out of the hands of the Tribe. To stop them from taking you away with them. You see, Rebecca was greatly beloved by the Tribe, as well. They're as angry about her killing as we are. And their means of interrogation are—shall we say—harsh. Even cruel. They're far more interested in fast results than in any social nicety. Had we not confined you in our cell, they might've dragged your body down a trail behind a horse yesterday. Until you babbled out all that they thought they wished to know."

"I see. So, this Tribe, Carlos and Red and the rest of 'em, they're the local tough guys. And they're a different group from you. Yet what, some type of ally or partner for you as well?"

"Yes. We farm here and create this sacred refuge that is Elysian. The Tribe hunts the forest and guards the Pale, which is the outer border of our joined territories."

"Okay. I'm getting a picture. But I'd like to make a tiny part of this big picture much clearer. Can I be done with the entire lot of you now, root and branch? Can I get my tail the hell out of Dodge?"

"By no means." Ezra gave his white-fringed head an emphatic wag. "You must finish absolving yourself of suspicion. Remove all doubt."

"Hey, wait! Aren't *you* the guy who just said that my alibi held water?"

"Sorry, no. I only meant to observe that your status had improved. Somewhat. Presently, you bear no more potential blame than any other suspect. And the Sayer Ruth has suggested a way that can help you win yourself through to a *full* exoneration." He beamed.

"Which is?"

"We ask you to investigate, both down here and up on the Pale. As an Outsider, you have no vested interest, you should not favor one side or the other, neither we Elysians nor the Tribe members. As a teacher, especially of logic, you have been trained to look at facts objectively. So, we hope you shall help us find and catch the real killer who might be concealed amongst us."

"Unless it's me."

"Right. In which case you'll of course fail to find him. And if that's what happens, then next, I'm afraid, you'll need to confess."

Kyle half-shut his eyes and nodded slowly while he processed the Elder's bizarre pitch.

Y'know, Elysian isn't quite the right name for this lil' burg. Crazyville would be much more fitting. But if I seem to play along with them, intriguing options other than this gonzo game may present themselves to me. At some point. Such as a chance to escape. And I should consider that, 'Any day spent out of jail must only be a fine day.' One of Roy's puns.

"Absolutely," Kyle said. "'Cos by then, my guilt should be obvious, even to me. Right?"

Chapter 5

Kyle hunkered down on his haunches. Stretching his thigh muscles in that manner felt pretty good, since swelling of bruises he'd suffered while escaping from his boat wreck had begun to diminish.

He'd concealed himself among thick tufts of bunch grass in order to watch dozens of the denizens of Elysian file past him on a slope far below. His observation post was a grass patch on the end of a bald spur ridge that jutted up between a pair of emerald valleys crammed with tall redwood trees. Those groves swayed gracefully in an onshore wind. The bunch grass around him did its scrawny best to echo that dance.

The Elysians had returned his duffle of gear. Whereupon he found his whole jerky sack emptied to the point of even being turned inside out. That hadn't surprised him. He'd just been delighted to see how much of his other gear remained. It meant that he could deploy a lightweight, waterproof, 10× monocular to scan the slope below.

Through that scope's circle, he saw people go by in small clumps of five or six, heading for a cabin down in a fern-furred and moss-upholstered gulch. The cabin had been built on a row of logs felled over the creek where it flowed through a notch in the hills. After emerging from this shaded canyon, the creek coursed on down to fill the lagoon that shimmered near the beach.

Elysians dubbed that cabin the Cold House. In it, they usually stored milk, cheese, butter and fresh greens, to help such food items keep a tad longer. But at this moment, the place hosted a vigil to bid farewell to the late Rebecca James.

Her wake was due to end shortly, Ezra had informed Kyle. Her mortal remains would soon be surrendered to the clay even as her soul was commended to Paradise.

Way-y past high time to stick that lady in the ground. A corpse must've turned darned whiffy by now, whether kept within the Cold House or not. Still, could be good that she's not been buried already. Just need to figure out how to turn that happenstance into luck. What discovery can I make about her now that'd feed a proper investigation? Sad to say, I'm not trained to investigate, or I'd know! That whole summer I spent repossessing cars from deadbeat HSU students all those years back...somehow, I don't think it qualifies as detective work. So instead.... Let's just use what's always on hand—pure logic. Puzzle this thing out. Think of all that you've been told here, all you've seen thus far. What might be the most promising thread I can tug on?

It's like Roy says. Always strive for your deepest possible situational awareness—since that's the only power that ever lets anyone turn mere chance into luck. Dig and think, man.

Kyle put his full attention back on the slope below him and the long trail that led from Cold House over to the rest of Elysian. He studied the knots of people moving back and forth along the pathway. He realized this also might be a chance to backfill his knowledge of the community. How many men, women, kids? What age ranges for each? How many healthy or weak? What inklings could he pick up on the village's general mood and ambiance?

He wondered if he'd be so fortunate as to win a "tell" in body language—a signal that drew his attention to a certain individual. Someone who acted scared, or awkward, or ashamed as he or she moved toward Rebecca's wake. *Just one of those real, real, slim possibilities.*

He raised his scope to take in the layout of the entire settlement. From this perspective, it looked well-ordered, once you grasped the notion that these structures, the pathways, roads and fields all had been laid out according to natural contours of the slopes, to ensure good drainage and to forestall erosion.

That coot Ezra sure yacked my ear off about it. Said he'd taught geometry himself in junior high for years before the Flare. His design for Elysian combines geometrics, hydrology and soil engineering. Pleased as the dickens with how well his plan worked. Good thing that man is guided by logic at least some of the time. A place where we overlap, where we can communicate. Since he's logical, he's able to see some benefit in me being an unbeliever; I can't be swayed by sympathy for any Elysian while I investigate. Of course, I won't cut those Tribe folks much slack either. They owe me a thing or two. Such as: my gun and my knife!

Kyle's lips twitched in a wry smile.

Still, they've both allowed me space in which to work. Or to save my own butt, to put it another way. The Elders of Elysian and the leaders of the Tribe have made a pact. I can ask anyone in Elysian anything. Even go up to the Pale and grill members of the Tribe. But one thing I am forbidden to do is scoot off across the Pale by myself. Got to travel always with a guide, who'll really be my minder. And if I try to escape and they catch me at it, straight back into that tight little brick cell I go. And I'll also fall under deep suspicion once again. So, I must appear entirely accommodating. At least for a while.

Hysterically funny though, in a way, these weenies see me as a man of no beliefs. Hell yes, I have beliefs. Well, I have one. The simplest and oldest of all philosophical ideas: pure reason lies at the heart of the universe. Thus, the more poised and the more rational a person can be, the closer you draw to an imperishable Logos. Roy taught me that. One of the last of the great Stoics, was he. Well, since I now stumble along in Roy's footsteps, maybe I'll be the last. That is, until or unless I bring Luz Maria around. She thinks emotion trumps reason, as Spinoza did. She's got a point, but only sometimes.

Kyle noted a tall figure with a gliding gait now passing by below. She was a woman, with the cowl up on a grey robe that she wore. The fingers of her right hand rested on a child's shoulder as they moved along side-by-side. *Hey that's no kid, that's the dwarf. What did Sayer Ruth call him? Michael. Hmmm. If she and Mike are heading into the Cool House together, it's the right time for me to be inside too. The mourners will look more at them*

and less at me. She's the big cheese around here, the one who sets
the tone...and he's...well, I need to discover more about who he is.
More there than meets the eye, though.

—

Elysians emerging from that cabin in the shadows flicked damp-
eyed glances at Kyle as he himself neared its doorway. Many had
clearly been weeping—red and puffy eyelids appeared on most
faces that he saw. He himself scored looks of fear, doubt and suspicion, not much else. Some visibly shrank away from him as he
approached.

Hey, how 'bout a little respect, folks? Don't you know I'm your
brand-new detective-in-chief? Well, the only detective that's been
assigned. That should make me chief.

He could hear a chant as he approached, the invocation-and-
response of a litany.

"O Lord of All..."

"Forgive us our sins."

"O Heavenly Father..."

"Help us keep faith."

"Most blessed Sayers...

"Show us our path."

"Dearly departed..."

"Be a light unto us."

"Elders and Brothers and Sisters..."

"Defend our unity."

Many voices braided together in the community song, male and
female, young and old. It was broad and spontaneous harmony
woven of discrete elements, such as the bark of a grandpa, the
trill of a maiden and the lisp of a child. To Kyle the blend seemed
charming, even inviting, but the song became muted then went
silent as he entered the door.

Inside, the Cold House walls were festooned with fir boughs
and wildflower bouquets—mainly pink-to-red boughs of fresh
rhododendrons. Corsages of herbs and fern fronds also dangled
from pinned-up ribbons.

On the cabin's rough puncheon floor, rows of benches arranged like pews held seated mourners who had lingered to pray and sing. Among these, he spotted the Sayer Ruth and Michael sitting up front. Wisps of cedar smoke twisted up from braziers at each end of a bier that supported an open coffin. A line of people was slowly forming to approach this bier. The first man took a long moment to gaze down at the face of Rebecca, murmur some words of grief or blessing or farewell, then turn, face agonized, head down, and plodded back to his place on a bench.

Kyle put himself at the tail of the line. The closer to the corpse he drew, the better he grasped the use of those cedar-incense braziers at each end of the bier. Potent as the fumes were, they only managed to fight the sweet-sour reek of death to a draw.

Wrapped round the deceased woman's head and bunched around her neck, a white shroud revealed only her face. Kyle saw that Rebecca had been beautiful. Wisps of champagne-blonde hair peeked out from the shroud to frame a pale oval visage with long-lashed eyes, a delicate chin and full lips. Her mouth had been rouged with a substance like red berry juice. Apart from that single lurid touch, dead Rebecca appeared sadly young, innocent and virginal.

Kyle guessed her age as around sixteen. *Virginal.* That impression made him recall questioning Ezra about motive. He'd asked the Elder if Rebecca owned a boyfriend, suitors, or had any major emotional involvements. No, Ez told him, not at all. Sayers were elevated as virgins and then charged with keeping celibate. That way they could become pure conduits of spirit and focus their attention solely upon care of the flock. And should they ever desire to launch into intimate relations with a mere mortal, well, they were required to surrender their high office first.

Sure, right. But a girl so gorgeous? Kyle shook his head. *There'd be more than a few people leaning on her to renounce her vows.*

Kyle felt his knee bump into something solid and looked down. It was Michael, who'd inserted himself in Kyle's path, planted his feet, and now stared up at him. Fury lit his eyes.

"How dare you?!" His whisper was low and harsh.

"Uh, double-check with your Elders, pal. I can go 'most anywhere."

"Not here. Not now. A sacred place, in a special moment. You are *not* wanted. Leave!"

Kyle glanced over his shoulder and around the room. Several

heads were raised, and on those upturned faces he read anger and accusation, and full agreement with what they'd just overheard. Next he felt a sudden and keen pain on his right shin. Michael had kicked him.

"All-ll righty, dude, I'll go," Kyle said. He gave the dwarf's hostile stare straight back to him. "But only if you exit with me. If not, well, let's find out who can kick the other guy the hardest. Won't do any wonders for your holy and peaceful ceremony, but hey, so what?"

As their glaring match endured, Kyle shifted his stance and drew back a leg. Michael nodded imperceptibly. "No. Not before the Sayer," he muttered. "Or all these others."

Kyle turned, sauntered from the building. And Michael followed him out.

—

They found a place to sit on a clump of mossy rocks, beneath spreading branches of a coast live oak, far enough away from the Cool House that no one inside could overhear them.

"The Council and I do *not* agree," Michael brusquely informed him, seeking to regain balance and reclaim turf. "Not an iota. We should have kept you in that cell, or let the Tribe have their way with you."

"Hey, pleased to meet you too, guy," Kyle said. "And you're what, a cute altar boy for the Sayer? She's your boss? And Ruthie has said I'm probably okay, right? So, what's your opinion of *her* opinion?"

Michael scowled. He had a square head, prominent brows and jaw. His facial expressions all came across as dramatically enhanced. "The next time you dare to call me 'boy,' or say anything dismissive to me, or about me, all you'll score is an enemy for life," he said. "Just so we're clear."

Kyle thought that over. *Let him win this tiff. Then maybe I'll start out a point ahead on our next one.*

"All right," he replied. "Fair enough. I won't..." He realized he needed to speak carefully. *Belittle,* he thought, *might be the worst possible choice of verbs at this moment.* "I won't insult you again. Here's my hand on it."

Michael eyed Kyle's outstretched arm, then looked him in the face for a long moment.

"You watch that stuff," he warned.

"I promise that I shall."

After they shook hands, a degree of rigidity seemed to drain out of Michael. He crossed his stubby legs and leaned back against a taller rock, behind the one he sat on.

"Well, I have to admit that you *are* right about one thing," Michael said. "If our Council of Elders rules, we all must go along, like it or lump it." He raised his hands, dropped them. "I'm forced to comply. Yet, know that I do so under protest."

"Acknowledged. Do you get my own reasons for taking on this job? First, I've got to prove my own innocence, beyond a flicker of a doubt. Then I can move on to number two, which is getting the hell out of this place so I can go back home to my wife. What I'm trying to say here is, I'm motivated. Hugely."

Michael tilted his head. He paused. Nodded.

"If you truly can't stand the sight of me, Michael, your solution is easy. Work with me some, and you can be rid of me that much faster."

Michael couldn't help himself—he had to grin. "That has a certain appeal," he admitted.

"Great. So, here's something I need to know. How much has the body of Rebecca been examined? Is it obvious how she died?"

"Strong blow to the back of the head. Blunt object." Michael tapped himself on the rear of his own blocky skull. "Fracture. And there were bruises on her neck also, as if she'd been strangled. Not sure if that was before or after."

"Where was her body found"

"Up on the creek. Well, truthfully, she was *in* the creek. Held down under a pile of rocks. We found her there four days ago."

"Ezra said she'd been dead for six? Or it would be seven, now?"

"That's how long ago she disappeared. Failed to return to Elysian. As far as the exact date of her death itself, we're unsure."

"Where had she been?"

"Up on the Pale, preaching to the Tribe."

"I see. Are the Tribe guys a conversion project then, for you Elysian folks? Bring 'em into your fold, as it were?"

"Yes. But it's not easy. You see, the Tribe has strayed even beyond unbelief. Some of its members are actual pagans. We're able to take one or two from the Tribe into our circle of the Blessed, only by dint of unrelenting effort. I myself went...well, that's not relevant or important."

Kyle tugged on his chin whiskers. "I've just thought up something we need to know, before Rebecca goes in the ground," he said. "Because finding stuff like this out afterward could be impossible." He gave Michael a half-smile of apology. "So, was a close exam ever performed by anybody on Rebecca's female parts?"

Michael jolted upright as if stung by a hornet. "Such a thing would be an outrage. Sacrilege!"

"Would it, now? Why?"

"Sayers are virgins. Everybody knows that."

"They are? Or are they just supposed to be?"

Under his heavy brows, Michael's eyes bugged somewhat. His lips pursed and his throat worked convulsively.

"Give me a second here, Michael," Kyle said quickly. "Look. A killing is a huge deal. Mighty emotions are invoked. Like it or not, we need to study where those feelings come from. And if you don't think sex is the wellspring of a whole lot of 'em, well, go back and study your Holy Writ. Got the Old Testament on a shelf, don't you? Well, does that sordid affair between Solomon and Bathsheba ring any bells?"

"You mean, David and Bathsheba?"

"Sure, okay. Come on, I was close."

Michael eyed him while rubbing his bearded jawline and chin.

"How can you, an unbeliever, know enough Writ to even make such a mistake?"

"Well, back in the day, I made it a point to try to study a little bit of everything. I thought getting my arms around western culture was my basic assignment."

"So, you've read the Bible."

"Some of it, not all."

Michael gazed down in thought, then looked up again.

"I'm not sure I wish to hear it. But precisely what measure are you asking us to take?" His voice was low and quiet.

"Elysian's got a few midwives, right? I mean, you must, since there's so many lively kids bouncing around. Well ask a midwife or two to check Rebecca over closely, down there. Fore and aft. Is she a virgin still, yes or no? Are there any signs of injury or violence to her lower frontside or backside? If we know that..." Kyle's voice trailed off for a moment. "We'll know something important," he finished. "And—of course—this absolutely needs to happen before she's buried."

Michael's face clouded. "All right." He sighed. "I shall do it. I'll ask." He swallowed, averted his gaze. "But I *can't* report to you what they find out. Words like that shall not leave my lips. The midwives will need to tell you the results, themselves. Not me. Definitely!"

Chapter 6

Kyle stared at Ephraim. "You?" he said. "My guide is *you?*"

Ephraim nodded. "Yuh. Elders told me to."

Kyle sighed, shook his head, looked away, back. The lanky youth stood slouched, diffident, near the same location where Kyle had last seen him—on the beige fan of pounded clay that sprawled out just before the entry to the Council Lodge.

"Why?"

He lifted and dropped a thin shoulder. "Know the trails, I guess."

"Guess? I can do that by myself. Don't need you."

"Um, no. We both must do as they say."

Kyle had spent a lot of time scanning Elysians. Now he could pick out key differences. Ephraim, from a crooked part in his long and tangled hair all the way down to the hem of his burlap tunic, looked typical. Yet below that line, he differed. He also wore a pair of brown jeans ripped out at the knees, and leather boots that had once been cowboy-style—before the heels were knocked off and both soles reshod with a flat patch of tread from auto tires.

Most Elysian men wore neither pants nor boots. *So, how come Ephraim rates 'em? Find out. But not from him. Remember, he chooses to play dumb.*

"You sure you want to come with me, Jimbo? 'Cos, I'm all out of jerky. Of course, maybe you already knew that."

Ephraim's mouth worked below his narrow balcony of a nose.

"I have to travel with you," he said sullenly. "And to try to answer your questions. It's a chore. Assigned."

"Okay, here's a question. Why do you act like such a freakin' geek?"

Kyle watched Ephraim stiffen, his head tilt back, something flash in his eyes. *There. Glint of a buried force that I'd glimpsed... What? Resentment? Hatred? It's way older than any interaction with me. Okay. Now, lighten up, bring him back. No need for another poke right now.*

Kyle smiled at him. "Sorry, Ephraim" he said. "Not a nice thing to say, is it. Don't know what got into me. Y'know, we didn't get off to such a great start. Maybe I still carry a charge from that. Well, let's just drop it, right? Looks like we've got to spend time together. Ought to make an effort to get along. What do you think?"

Ephraim stood frozen, wary.

"Tell you what. You're *not* a geek, all right? That was stupid. And I'll stop calling you Jimbo, too. Shake on it, okay?"

Kyle used two hands. He took Ephraim by the right forearm with his left hand, gripped Ephraim's hand with his own right, squeezed and shook with a show of enthusiasm. He got back thin, cool fingers wrapping slowly around his own in a limp, damp coil. Felt like pushing a hand into a bait bucket.

Hey wow, I've dropped way-y back into a Tolkien storybook land, Kyle thought. *Now I know what it feels like to shake hands with Gollum.*

"C'mon, Ephraim," he said companionably. "Let's hike up the hill. What do you say?"

⎯

They walked a broad trail onto a spur ridge, above the spot where Kyle had lurked in the tall grass, using that compact telescope to study mourners as they filed by below. Forests to either side of this spur went from bishop pine and Monterey cypress to redwoods, then up higher turned into a broad and rippling belt of Douglas fir and spruce.

Kyle stopped on a switchback to take a breather. He turned to see Ephraim plodding on uphill, considerably in Kyle's wake. Ephraim's gait was pigeon toed and his loose boots made a clomp with every step he took. The effect was comical, but it wouldn't do to snicker at him. *Not right now.* Kyle looked out over Ephraim and down-hill. He saw a line of people walk toward the Elysian graveyard. In their hands they carried dots and dabs of color that were prob-ably bouquets from the walls of the Cold House. The light brown splinter borne aloft in the center of the crowd was Rebecca's coffin.

Ephraim reached his side and turned, panting, to glance down-hill too. Out of the side of his eye, Kyle looked at him, trying to pick up and read a reaction. But Ephraim stayed impassive.

"Did you care about her at all?" Kyle asked. His question, so blunt and abrupt, was a tactic.

"Wha- what?"

"Good thing you didn't say, 'who-who.' Could've made you sound like an owl. Rebecca. Did you care for her?"

"Everybody here loves our Sayers," Ephraim replied steadily.

Kyle could almost hear a silent postscript that added, *See, be-cause we're supposed to.*

"Sure. But I meant, you personally."

"'Everybody' includes me. Doesn't it?"

"Thank God. Nice for a guy to feel like he belongs."

Ephraim frowned slightly, nodded indifferently.

They continued onward and reached a bare rock knoll on the spine of the ridge. Up here, the vegetation mosaic switched over from conifer forest to oak savannah, brindled with swaths of gold-en dry grass and drab clumps of coyote bush that emitted a minty aroma. Kyle took a moment to step up onto a long and flat boul-der that footed the knoll. He poked his toe at a deep, symmetrical depression in the boulder's surface.

"Well looky there," he said. "Old mortar. Kind the Indian wom-en once used to grind acorns. If we look around, maybe we can find the *metate,* the grinding stone."

"No," Ephraim said, "you won't."

"Why not?"

"The Tribe women went around, gathered them all up. To use on rocks nearer their settlement."

"Wow. They actually do acorn mush up there, like the old-timers?"

Ephraim nodded. "Sure. Mush. Plus everything else."

"What's that mean?"

"You'll find out."

From their high perspective, Kyle could see that the spur ridge they were on dropped off into a saddle before it rose again to connect to the tall and long, north-to-south crest he had seen from the beach. Looking into the broad main valley that dropped all the way back to Elysian, he caught the glint and sparkle of running water.

"Hey. Way over there. That the same stream that runs past Elysian?"

"Uh-huh. Balm of Gilead Creek."

"Where Rebecca's body was submerged?"

"Yes."

"Pretty damn wild."

"Why?"

"Well. Putting her in there could be like a big 'screw-you' to the community. See, you people then are forced to take your drinking water from a creek with her dead body soaking in it. And do so for days and days, hm?"

Ephraim went pale. "N-no," he said. "Our water comes from another branch, the south fork. Through a flume. You're looking at the mainstem, over there. And Rebecca was found way over in the north fork. At Bethesda Pool."

"What's that?"

"Big round pool about halfway down. It's real cold and deep. We go there to swim in the summer when it's hot."

"Aha." Kyle nodded. He tapped his chin. "I wonder if any Outsider would know about it."

"Outsiders don't know much about Elysian."

"Meaning maybe yes, maybe no, huh?"

Ephraim frowned, shrugged, and looked at his feet.

"Tell me. How did Rebecca get found?" Kyle asked.

"Oh, we had search parties."

"Did you help?"

"Of course. But... Samuel, well, he was the one who found her."

"That so?"

"We spent hours and hours looking. Everywhere. Samuel took a rest by the shore of the pool. Glanced down, saw some of her hair floating out. Said later that the Spirit must've moved him to look there."

"I see. Which prompts a follow-up query."

"What?"

"Samuel and that young Sayer Rebecca. How did those two get along?"

"Oh. Well. Samuel is very strong in belief. Of course, he honors our Sayers too."

"I hear a 'but' in your voice."

"Samuel has a hard job. A hard man must do it. That's what he is."

"Talk loudly and carry a huge stick, huh? The big guy is what, part enforcer, part town constable?"

Ephraim nodded. "He serves the will of the Council to keep order in Elysian. But it's not like he does it by hurting people." He glanced at Kyle. "Except, just sometimes."

"Seems to me like a guy who both hurts and has been hurt."

"He fought a lot in his past. Samuel had been a football player, for a famous team. Called the Raid, I think."

"I remember it, the Raiders. Moved all over the place."

"Next he was in big martial arts cage matches like they used to have. But he gave that up when Elder Ezra converted him."

"Okay, so his violence is more channeled now. But does he drop that tough-guy *shtick* and his big stick, ever? Did he make friends in Elysian? And was Rebecca his friend or no?"

Ephraim lifted and dropped his shoulders. "Can't say. Didn't see them together, not often. Maybe she avoided him? Could've scared her. Still does scare some people. Why he doesn't lash out so much now. But really, who knows?"

———

Kyle caught the smell of horses before he could see them. Redolence of old hay and manure and of sweaty leather mingled together and floated to him as he and Ephraim hiked toward a clearing at the flat center of the dip in the ridge. Then he saw corrals, a crude barn. He heard snorts and whinnies. A large horsefly buzzed passed his ear.

"What's this?"

"It's called the Cuadra. I don't know why. Horses are bred and trained here. Then some are brought down to work the fields in Elysian. Most go to the Tribe. They say they need horses to patrol the Pale and trade with the Outside. But really, they just like to ride all over and act like bigshots."

"Tribe people aren't your favorites, huh?"

Ephraim leveled a look at Kyle. His eyes were close-set, and their perch atop the blade of his nose awarded him a bird-like aspect when his face turned straight at an observer.

"I know why you asked about Samuel back there," he said. "You're right. There's a chance he could've been the one."

"The one, what?"

"Who killed Rebecca. Then he tried to shift blame away from himself by pretending to find her. Maybe he did that. But most likely, it's somebody from the Tribe."

"All right. Among those rasty Tribe folks, who might you suspect?"

He smirked. "Hey, that's your job. You need to investigate. Maybe you're smart enough to find out and get yourself off the hook. I'm only here to answer questions."

"Answer that one."

"I can't. Yet I can say, Samuel at least struggles to keep himself under control. Those guys in the Tribe don't, not much at all. Could be any of 'em. They're wild. They're ready, willing and able to do really bad stuff to people they don't like."

"Makes me look forward to meeting them again."

"Come on, then."

Ephraim led the way past the crude board fences and paddocks of the Cuadra. Kyle gazed at the animals, trim mares and geldings with thick necks, bay coats and glossy black manes. Most were Morgans, he guessed. Maybe with some Quarter-Horse tossed in. He inhaled the horsey aromas, grateful for this brief reminder of his untamed boyhood, when he'd grown up on Bald Hills Ranch, to the north of Redwood Creek. That was long before his college years, before Roy, and certainly before the Flare. He often felt nostalgic for that time and place. *A world forever lost to me. A case might be made that our post-Flare world is becoming wilder and more natural than the countryside we enjoyed back when. But our overall situation is so-o-o much less tranquil nowadays. No matter where you go, you've got to watch yourself, keep on your guard.*

The Cuadra's final corral had the beefiest fences, and they confined a solitary horse, a muscular grey stallion with a skull that looked as broad and thick as an anvil. Kyle stepped up to the fence and held out a hand, wondering if the horse would respond to this invitation. But the stud did not approach, merely slanted his ears back, rolled his eyes and stamped a hoof.

"Hmph. Another tough customer," Kyle said.

"That's Buck," Ephraim told him. "The stud they mate to all the mares. But not for much longer."

"How come?"

"Carlos plans to geld him."

"Why, if he can sire such pretty colts and fillies?"

"Oh, he's an ornery one. No one can ride him. Can hardly even touch him with a rope. Just plain mean, bites and kicks at anyone who gets close. Won't do a thing you want."

"Stallion? Can sometimes turn that way. Doesn't make him completely useless. Maybe Carlos ought to get gelded himself, see how he likes it."

"Yes!"

Kyle's head swiveled toward Ephraim. A *cri de coeur* had burst loose, quite unlike the half-hearted mumbling that constituted most of Ephraim's speech. Kyle eyed him, then realized the instant of revelation had vanished as quickly as it appeared.

Ephraim slouched back to form. He swung around to plod along in his pigeon-toed gait on the trail that led out of the Cuadra.

As he followed, Kyle heard a *whoosh.* He looked over his shoulder and saw a stocky, black-haired man who wielded a wooden pitchfork fling a fat clump of hay down into the corrals from an open window at the top of the barn.

—

They left the flat ground where the Cuadra was located and descended into the drainage of Gilead Creek, approaching what Kyle reckoned as the upper south fork. Two large fir trunks had been felled over the tumbling, sparkling freshet. These logs had then been barked and peavied next to each other and secured in place by deep-driven hardwood stakes. Sawn sections of puncheon plank were spiked crossways over the logs to form an ad hoc footbridge, one wide and sturdy enough to even carry a horse. *If your mount doesn't get too skittish, that is. One spook, and over into those rocks and that water you go. Ought to put some rails on the blamed thing.*

They crossed over the brook and started to ascend again, moving toward the crest of the main ridge. As they left the drainage, Kyle picked up the vanilla scent of flowering buckeye, then the lavender fragrance of ceanothus. Atop the ridge, they paused to take in the view, a green expanse of the Elysian valley to the west, and the somewhat browner foothills that rolled off toward a hazy eastern horizon.

Kyle felt impressed to find himself standing on a road. Not much of one, a dusty, rutted track, but still a wider and more robust thoroughfare than any trail he'd seen so far.

"What's this?"

"The Haul Road. It runs along the ridge, then down by the north fork, and around to reach Elysian through the fields."

"For trade?"

"Goods back and forth, yes. A wagon circulates once a week. Tribe handicrafts and Outside goods go down, produce from Elysian comes back up."

"Outside goods? So, there must be a link."

"Yes. Over at Treetown One, a route heads inland as far as the Portal gate."

"Treetown?"

"Where the Tribe groups dwell. Huts built up in trees. They have four Treetowns."

"Cute name."

"I think it's stupid."

"Where do Red and Carlos live?"

"In One. The biggest."

"Take me there."

Chapter 7

A faint clop of a hoof against a distant rock provided an alert. Someone was riding up behind them, perhaps trailing them.

Kyle glanced back, but a bend in the Haul Road kept him from seeing anybody. He looked ahead.

The top of the ridge leveled out then dropped away to the east in a more gradual and gentler slope than any they'd seen from the crest so far. At the head of the nearest valley, a dense grove of blue and black oaks arose, a huge hillock of vegetation. A light brown haze drifted toward him from it, and he realized he was looking at dust. He shaded his eyes and squinted in that direction. Now he could spot a knot of horse riders galloping furiously around each other in an open field next to the grove.

He looked back again. A rider had emerged into view on the Haul Road, then halted to study them. He held a long lance upright, its butt caught in a kind of holster on the side of a stirrup. Honed edges of his spearhead winked in the sunlight. Another rider appeared, coming from the opposite direction. He too paused. This one had an animal horn suspended from one shoulder on a baldric. He raised it to his lips and blew out a short and sharp blast.

Kyle saw Ephraim's head settle between his thin raised shoulders like a turtle's head pulling back into its shell. *Yep, they're really not Jimbo's favorite guys. No question.*

Then he heard a thunder of many hooves. The horsemen who'd been playing down by the oak grove were all galloping straight uphill towards them.

—

They wound up being marched toward the oak grove amid a laughing, jeering gang of Tribe light cavalry. As they neared the grove, shapes of walls and windows incongruously appeared among the giant tree limbs. Kyle realized he was looking at an enclave of shingled cabins built around the upper trunks of many of the trees. Some structures were lofted thirty feet or more above the ground, and these had spiral staircases winding around the trunks to provide access.

On a landing of one of these staircases, a man with long red hair, clad in fringed buckskins, observed their approach.

"Hey! Heard that you-all had planned to drop by," Red said. "Howdy-do. Come on up."

—

When they reached the landing, Kyle pointed to Roy's bone-handled Bowie knife, which Red wore strapped to his side. "That's mine," he said.

"Said I'd give it back when you left." Red grinned. "But see, you ain't left yet."

"If I'm gone, how could I ever get it?"

"Might could be a prob," Red conceded.

"Guess we should discuss it."

"Love me a good debate. Happy to oblige, at some point. But go on up now, Carlos is waiting."

Kyle climbed the stairs, but as Ephraim attempted to follow, Red planted a hand on his chest and shoved him. "Not you, scarecrow. Scoot on back. Hang out 'n' wait."

"But I—"

"Worried you might get bored? Idle hands, right? Well heck, maybe our boys will let you play some Kav Kaz with 'em, then. Ephy, bet you can't ride for shit, but we'll let you sub for the carcass. Tie that sheepskin 'round your skinny butt. Should work out just peachy."

Kyle had paused and turned around on the steps. He looked at Red and Ephraim, then out at the churned-up pasture, where a white lump with four legs poking up rested in the dust at the spot the riders had dropped it. Apparently, the Tribe's young horsemen liked to play a gory form of Asian polo, one that involved dragging or carrying a dead animal to various goals.

"Leave that kid alone, Red," he said firmly. "Just let him be."

Ephraim shot Kyle a look that mingled both gratitude and suspicion.

"Ah, didn't mean no harm," Red said. "Only just get bored myself, kinda."

"I see. Picking on people entertains you? Want to try it on somebody your own size?"

Red grinned. "Now, there's a thought," he said. "Any suggestions as to who?"

Kyle leveled a gaze at Red, by way of answer. Red met it for a moment then shrugged the challenge off with a grin.

Ephraim rotated, glumly stomped a few steps downward, sat down in a huddled heap, wrapped arms about bony knees and looked off into the distance. His face was blank, but he was obviously wishing himself someplace else.

Kyle ascended the rest of the steps up to the treehouse deck and its front door, Red at his back.

"Just head on in there," Red said. "Seeing as we're all set for your visit."

He popped the wooden latch. Leather hinges creaked as the door swung inwards. A wave of odors washed out to him from the dim interior—cured hides, spicy food, funky bedding, unwashed bodies, reek of old smoke, and a light hint of the floral perfume of hashish. As Kyle's eyes adjusted to the shadows, he saw a raised bed under a shuttered window where a woman with long grey hair knelt on a fur coverlet. She was braiding cornrows into the hair of a younger, dark-skinned woman. Carlos sat in a rocking chair nearby, sipping smoke from a brass pipe.

"Ahoy," Carlos said. "The sea-farer! Our castaway. Or so he says."

"Hi Carlos. Right. But how good are you at remembering the old movies? Am I Tom Hanks, or Wilson? And who are you guys... the Lost Boys up here, at play in your tree forts?"

Carlos laughed. "Sure. But hey, if your game is to play keep-away from all the field mice and woodrats and ticks, living up in a kid's tree fort works out just fine."

Kyle looked around the space, saw longbows and quivers of arrows that hung from wall pegs, a wooden barrel with a dozen or so spears and lances jutting up from it, a woven basket that held river rocks with hardwood handles attached to them by rawhide lashing.

"Care for a puff of local product?" Carlos held up the pipe.

"No thanks."

"Teetotaler, huh?"

"Nah. Used to grow, myself. But that was before I grew up. Anyhow, I can't partake, since I'm here on a serious matter."

Red chortled. "Yeah, we heard 'bout that. Your butt be stuck on the hotseat, pal. Can only stand up and walk off if you finger somebody to take your place."

"In a nutshell? That's a hundred percent correct." He looked at Carlos. "So, Ezra and the Elders say I've got a pair of broad permissions. I can travel around within the Pale, and I can ask anybody anything. They said my deal has got full buy-in from the Tribe. So far, so good?"

Carlos nodded. He scraped a match alight, touched it to his pipe, inhaled, and fanned the match out with a wave. He held his breath, then released a cloud of fragrant vapor.

"Yep, those are the basics," he acknowledged. "But 'fore we dive on into the matter at hand, let's finish introductions. Red, you know. Over there on the bed is Sally, our wife." The grey-haired woman smiled and waved. "And Jade, our fiancée." The dark-skinned woman tickled the air with her fingertips.

"Our?" Kyle echoed.

"Don't do things up in our Treetowns same way folks do 'em down in Elysian," Carlos explained.

"Guess not."

"Ladies, this here is the Kyle we've told you about. Straight off the bat or out of the boat, he was considered a bad guy. Now some think he's maybe an okay guy. Still on probation, far as I'm concerned. But we can show the man some hospitality. Since you're not into *humo*, Kyle, can we fetch you something else? Coffee, maybe?"

"You've got *coffee?!*"

"Sure. Not every day, but right now. Awesome, what our boys can snooker out of the trade routes inland at times. Jade, you want to go fix this man some?"

"I'll do it," Sally said, and jumped off the bed. "Jade, you keep still until I'm done with you."

"Great, thanks." Carlos fixed his grey eyes on Kyle. "Here's my opening statement, mister investigator. Far as we're concerned, the Elysians are late adopters, true come-latelies. We cut a deal to let them stay down in their valley, a deal that works out okay for the most part. Now, we're not exactly best buds with every single Elysian. But we do own up to having a few favorites 'mongst 'em, and Rebecca was way-y up at the top of our list. Everyone liked and admired that gal. She was spunky and funny and sweet and sharp as a blackberry thorn. To sum up, I'm here to say that nobody in the Tribe, no one up here on the Pale, would ever harm a hair on Becky's head. Not in any way, shape or form. So, roam about, do your chore, then we'll hear whatever you've got to say. We want to find her slayer bad as you do, likely more. But you can start off your hunt easy by cutting it in half from the git-go. It weren't none of us in the Tribe. And that's a lock."

"Whoa, damn!" Red exclaimed. "Preach it, brother."

"Okay, then," Kyle said. 'I should just turn around and go back down the hill. Every minute I spend up here is time wasted. That right?"

Carlos' lips twitched in a smile, and he gave a slight shrug.

"Rebecca apparently hiked up to the Pale a number of times, in her role as a Sayer. To make converts to her Writ Readers faith. Her trying to do that didn't bother you any?"

"Why should it?"

"If she had success, you'd lose members."

"Not many. And if some idiots prefer the muddy farming life, or all that spiritual jabber, way I see it, they're better off trotting on down and staying there. Godspeed and good riddance to 'em."

"How many people have you lost? Say, over the past few years."

"Oh, just two or three. The last one was Michael."

"Michael? The dwarf?!"

Red, Jade and Carlos flicked amused looks at each other.

"Sure, why not? He could do far better in Elysian. Wretched as Michael was as a horseman, he was much worse as a hiker. So, not well-suited to life up here."

"Yet he's no idiot."

"Nope," Carlos said. "That for sure Mike is not."

Sally returned from a back room of the cabin holding a mug atop a saucer. Kyle accepted it from her with a nod of thanks. Aromas wafting from the top of the cup almost made him faint with delight.

"Don't suppose you've got any milk?"

"Mare's milk, sure. Fresh today."

"Um, no."

He sipped, cocked his head and closed his eyes for a moment of bliss, then sipped again. He cleared his throat and looked at Carlos.

"Erhem! Thanks for this rare gift. A true taste from before the Flare. Now, let me ask, does that conversion process ever go the opposite way? I mean, do any bored Elysians come up here and try to sign on with your circus?"

"Hah! Yep!" Red slapped his knee. "Always got us a trapeze for a 'nother monkey. Can take *you* in, if you want. Just need to give you a lil' test, first."

Kyle ignored him. "I mean, all those strict morals and rules in Elysian must feel like a straitjacket, to some people."

"Oh, we've adopted runaways," Carlos said. "For the reason you mention, plus others. Numbers vary. But our books kind of balance over the long haul."

"How about Rebecca?"

"What do you mean?"

"I mean, what about her lover? When did she come up and take a lover among you folks?"

Eyes of the other four people in the room widened as they turned to him simultaneously.

"That's ridiculous!" Carlos spluttered. "Sayers are virgins, everybody knows that."

"Heard the same thing down in Elysian. Except that rule doesn't seem exactly ironclad, does it? Because I asked the midwives to check Rebecca before she went in the ground. They said they saw zero evidence she was a virgin. On the contrary, seemed likely to them she'd had a fair amount of sex. At every available port of entry."

"Aw, them ol' hags can't know what they even be talking 'bout," Red objected. "When did they last push their cobwebs aside 'n' get their own damn selves laid?"

"Doesn't make any sense, they'd try to ruin the rep of a poor girl that way," Carlos added sadly.

"You mean, Elysian midwives deliberately set out to harm the reputation of a saintly Rebecca?" Kyle shook his head. "Not hardly. Strong tendency would be to go the opposite way, I'd think. That's one thing that makes their diagnosis believable. The other is, Rebecca looked to them to be about two months pregnant or so on the day that she was killed."

This time a silence lasted unbroken while glances got flung around the room. Kyle waited it out.

"First we've heard of that," Carlos said flatly.

"I know," Kyle said. "Now, I'm sure you've got good sources of info down there. Otherwise, you wouldn't have heard I was heading up to the Pale to visit. That decision was just made this morning. But this info about Rebecca, or Becky as you call her, was too tightly held for you to be warned. Told straight from the midwives to me. And now, you're the only other people to hear about it. So, let me repeat my question. Who was Becky's lover?"

"Total bullshit," said Red. "Just shut your mouth. Damned if we know."

"Red, you yourself shall likely get damned about six different ways from Sunday," Carlos drawled. "Hush, now. Don't harass our guest."

"Okay, Chief."

Carlos eyed Kyle. "Guess the Writ Readers do take stock in at least one virgin birth. But I very much doubt they'd want to buy into another. Let's say Becky got pregnant the usual way. Decided to toss her vow and take a stroll on the wild side." He shrugged. "Could've had any man she wanted, a gal that pretty. A farmer out in a field. Some guy she met on the trail. Maybe even a stray Outsider she ran into."

"Is your Pale that leaky, then? Outsiders can sneak in?"

"It's happened," Carlos conceded. "Not often. We catch somebody, we drag him on the Haul Road a tad, then make him clean our latrines. After we let 'em go, they don't seem all that eager to come back. But since Becky got killed, our rangers have been on high alert. Guaran-damn-tee you there haven't been any crossovers lately."

"Thought experiment," Kyle said. "What if an Outsider got in, camped solo and covertly. Kind of guy that possessed some mad woodsman skills. Could someone like that hide for a while?"

"Possible." Carlos rubbed his jaw. "But again, real unlikely."

"However, say he did pull it off. With your rangers tightening the border, someone like that could then be trapped within the Pale."

"You mean, like you are?" Carlos' smile was slight and sardonic.

"Yeah," Kyle deadpanned.

"Oh, I can ask around. Get some more checks for recent sign on trails. But that chance is remote."

"You're the big dog 'round here, Carlos? You say jump and everybody else asks, how high?"

"Not like that," Red interjected. "The Tribe runs on pirate rules. In full!"

"What he means is, we're a baseline democracy. You know how buccaneer ships used to organize? Captain is elected by the whole crew. If he blows it, he gets unelected, and pronto. Got to take care of everyone, or he's out. There're more rules, about shares of earnings, taking fights outside, care of gear and so forth. Not too many. Quite simple, actually. Only rule of ours that ought to concern you is, don't piss off the redhead."

"Can you get someone to contact all your people, and ask about the points I've raised?"

This time, Kyle was not able to read the looks that shot around the cabin. *There's something that all these people know and which I'm missing.*

"What, do your work for you?" Carlos chuckled. "Why, you lazy bum! All right, sure. Take a load off Fanny. We can do that. And what are your plans? What's next?"

"Keep on walking around, keep on asking."

"With that lame-o Ephraim for a guide?"

"Hey, that's how the Elders set up my gig. What's your problem with him? Or his big problem with you, for that matter?"

"You know that list of our favorite Elysians? Well, your boy just ain't on it. Too light-fingered. Bits of our stuff have a kind of strange way of disappearing whenever he comes around."

"Could say I'm shocked. But I'm not. Why did the Elders make him a picket, then? Seems like a sweet assignment, especially if you put it next to having to go out and hoe-hoe-hoe those fields all day."

"'Cos he's a lazy-ass little punk, too," Red said. "Can't make the kid work, might as well have him mosey about, try to get something out of that. Leastways, he's not in your hair. And not setting a shitty example for everyone else."

"Tell you what," Carlos said. "Let that scarecrow go. Dismiss his scrawny ass. Our Tribe will take you on. Keep you in check but take you wherever else you want to go. Help you talk to folks. Can you ride?"

"I was raised on a ranch."

"Cool."

"The Elders might not like you being my guide."

"Oh, screw that. Let 'em lump it, then!"

Chapter 8

Kyle peeled back the cover of a sleeping sack made of bear fur and raised his head. Out from the rim of the cabin door drifted a cacophony of snores. The noise of inebriated slumber was what he'd expected—and hoped for.

After a supper of venison stew, the cabin's denizens had floundered on through a flight of *digestifs* that consisted of cups of potent moonshine, crumbly hunks of hashish, and even a few drops of opium sap—heated on a knife blade over a candle, with the spiraling lavender fumes then sucked up the nostrils of everyone in turn.

But Kyle didn't even pretend to partake. He sat quietly and observed. After a while, people simply stopped offering. Even so, the cabin's air was so thick with drug vapors that he couldn't avoid taking a few wisps into his lungs. The net result was that he'd been rendered a bit giddy, yet not catatonic.

He raised his head a little more. A few hundred yards away, one lonely spark of light bobbed as it glided along in the black distance. Probably, a lantern held by a horseman trotting along the Haul Road. The spark vanished, moving in the same direction Ephraim had taken before sunset, right after Carlos and Red had 86'd him out of Treetown.

Ephraim had waved his arms around and complained that if they forced him to drop his guiding assignment, it would cause major trouble for him with the Elysian Elders. Yet his protests lacked sincerity or enthusiasm. He was clearly delighted to find himself shed in a single go of Kyle, the Tribe and the Pale—likely an unholy trinity in his eyes.

Kyle craned his neck to peer out over the edge of the landing. A sentry posted at the foot of the staircase sat limply flopped on the last step. From the slow rise and fall of this man's back, he looked to be deep in slumber as well.

Kyle slipped out of the loaner bag, shoved his sandals onto his feet and cinched their straps.

He'd exited the cabin hours earlier, after telling its occupants he'd only be able to sleep outside in fresh air. It had an advantage of being true; the cabin's stale atmosphere had begun to nauseate him. And he had other motives. Before he went out, he'd paused over that woven basket of what seemed to be rocks with handles. He pretended to puzzle over these implements as he examined them. At the last moment, he'd slipped the head of one into the cargo pocket of his shorts and taken it out onto the landing.

Now, as he stood up, he slipped its wooden shaft down through his belt. He'd noted at his very first glimpse that these things were neither toys nor tools, but formidable weapons.

To make one, a river rock had been stuck in the partially debarked fork of a green and growing hardwood limb, then these branches had been lashed tightly around it and allowed to graft back together. Once that was accomplished, the limb had been harvested, fire-cured, and the stone head further secured by bands of wet rawhide and allowed to dry. The result was a sturdy war hammer—the backwoods equivalent of a medieval mace.

Kyle pondered how best to sneak past the sleeping sentry, then devised a plan.

He slid off the landing until he hung by his hands, and then swung, hand by hand, dropping down the risers by gripping the back of each step. When he was just about seven feet up, he felt his toes touch. He let go to land flat-footed. The impact was nearly soundless. And the dozing guard never moved a muscle.

He walked around and found that most of the horses had been taken away to a corral or barn further off. Yet a few were tied up on a picket line at the next tree.

Well worth a try!

Kyle moved cautiously toward the herd. All asleep. But a small mare awakened at the soft crunch of his footfall. He paused. She gazed at him for a while with her ears up. He blew his breath out in a gentle snort, as if he were a horse himself. She nickered a soft reply. He went to her, held out his cupped hand and she lowered her muzzle and sniffed it. He sniffed her too, right above the muzzle. Then he spent a minute scratching her lightly under the jaw and behind her ears. She sighed and half-closed her eyes.

This mare had been moored to the picket line with a soft rope halter. He untied her, and she followed willingly as he led her off.

"Like heading out for a night jaunt, don't you, hon'?" he whispered. "Guess the rangers got you used to it."

He unclipped the lead line, threw it over her neck and tied both ends to the chinpiece, turning the halter into a crude hackamore. Then he gripped a handful of her mane and hopped up and swung a leg over, landing just behind her withers. She shied a tad but settled quickly. He found that her spine was lower than the ridges of muscle that ran alongside it, so she'd be comfy to ride bareback. He touched his impromptu rein to the mare's neck and his heels to her ribs. She acted in a well-mannered and responsive way. He trotted her up toward the Haul Road.

A shrill whinny came from the picket line. Another horse had woken up. Kyle paused the mare, to see if any Treetown dwellers would respond. None did, and his own mount chose not to whinny back. *All good.* He turned her north on the road. The light from stars and a fingernail of moon were enough for him to discern the road edges. He would've bet the ranch—if he still had one—that the little mare knew this route well, anyhow. He brought her up to a canter and thudded off into the night. She had a silky gait, and it was a splendid sensation to feel a horse's back rocking rhythmically beneath him once more. This dark morning was cold enough that he appreciated the warmth of the mare's body seeping into him through his thighs.

He reached the proverbial fork in the road at first light. Birds had begun to twitter and flit around in the underbrush. The eastern horizon held a broad band of dark blue light, with the yellow flare of a rising sun just starting to paint the underside of clouds.

The broad track of the Haul Road bent left here to descend

into the Elysian valley, while a path split away to the north like
a narrow twig forking from a thick branch. In that direction lay
Luz Maria, Arcata, and home. But he saw to his instant dismay
that northbound trail took a precipitous drop over rocky ground
to enter a canyon jammed with tangles of manzanita brush. A bit
further along, the route wavered on across slopes that had been
plundered by clear-cut logging and were now clotted with thick-
ets of young firs. Be tough to lead a horse through there, even on
foot. Each mile traversed would be slow and hard-won.

He leaned forward, swung a leg over the mare's croup and slid
down off her flank. The crotch and inner legs of his canvas shorts
were damp with horse sweat. He didn't mind, in fact he enjoyed
its acrid aroma. Then the mare spread her hind legs, leaned forward, raised her tail, and pissed.

*Thanks girl, now I've got the full bouquet of horsiness! And I've
got some major decision-making to do.*

As he looked over his scanty options, Kyle's sense of dismay began to tilt toward despair.

*Damned soon after sunrise, the Tribe will discover that I've run off
and their rangers shall give chase. Their trackers will have no doubt
about which way I went. They know this country far better than I do
and they'll all be on their fastest mounts. My one hope was racking
up the miles and getting to country that I do know before they could
catch me. Now that looks like a non-starter. I've only succeeded at
making my situation worse. They're going to be irate. Whatever trust
or freedom I've won thus far will be snatched right back. I could get
dragged on the road or I could get thrown back into that tiny cell in
Elysian. Perhaps first one, then the other! That'd be fun....*

He sucked in a deep breath. What would Roy do? Well, he'd drop
back to basic principles, just as he always did. Since that's what
philosophers do. Kyle mulled that over. He remembered a time he
and Roy had been camped near Prairie Creek while out bow-hunt-
ing for elk. They sat around the fire, sipping wine from Sierra cups,
as a frosty night descended. Roy tossed a few hunks of rotten log
on the blaze, and it leapt up, flinging spirals of sparks into the sky.

*Ayn Rand claimed that emotions weren't tools of cognition, Roy
told him. Another thing that bonehead was wrong about. Emotions
are fine tools of cognition, simply our most primitive ones. And that's*

how a man of logic and wisdom should utilize them. Basically, see emotion as a raw energy source.

Kyle's face was being toasted and his clothes getting starchy from the heat of the blaze, so he scooted back a foot or two.

Exactly, Roy said. That's what I'm talking about! When you feel the power of an emotion, allow it to engulf you. After you know everything about its heat and potency, back away from it while keeping it in view. Go willingly into its grip, and then slip yourself right out of it. Analyze it rigorously and objectively. Compare and contrast it with all other inputs. See what parts of the feeling are true and advantageous. And on the other hand, which parts might be illusions or impediments that can only cloud your vision. Accurate emotion can powerfully fuel an action. Whereas imprecise emotion is a mere distraction and a disruption. After you see that difference, you can move on into the essential business of living. You will be able to plan coldly, then act boldly.

Well, there was no question about what Kyle felt—immense regret and gloomy sadness, since his bid to rush home to Luz Maria now appeared to be pointing toward abject failure. And he also had to dread that his status on the Pale and in Elysian would take a quick fall that could only end in a hard landing.

How should I analyze this? How can I change it for the best? No matter which way I go, the rangers enjoy high odds of catching me. Even ditching this sweet mare and trying to bushwhack on foot likely won't work. I must admit, then, Arcata is just plain the fuck out of my reach. And if I solely focus on that, if I keep feeling sick about it, I'll only end up disheartened and paralyzed.

What could possibly be my Plan B? Well. Guess I need to allow those rangers to catch me, since it's inevitable. And when they do, I ought to make it clear to them that I've been investigating, not fleeing. Y'see, I was only feeling so eager to start my detection work early. Of course, they'll be wicked mad I set out on my own. But my ride can't look like an escape attempt, or it'll be taken as a huge sign of guilt. There's nobody all these people would like to blame more for Rebecca's murder than me.

He faced north and closed his eyes. *Luz,* he thought, *this isn't hope destroyed. It is only hope deferred.* He opened them.

So, I guess Kyle's Investigations, Ltd., now must spring back into action.

He went to the mare's head, blew gently into her nostrils, and she blew gently back.

"Hey. What's your name, sweetheart?" he asked. Now that the light was better, he could give her lines a better look. He judged her to be at least half Arabian. And she had a bright chestnut coat that gleamed with health. She rubbed her head against him, hard, even shoving him a bit backwards. She wanted her jaw scratched again. He smiled. "Guess that *is* it! Sweetheart that you are." The mare eyed him, patiently waiting to see what he wished to do next.

He remounted, neck-reined the newly re-named Sweetheart to the left, put his heels to her sides, then galloped away through the dissipating shadows of night on the road that led down to the north fork of Gilead Creek. That should take him to Bethesda Pool, the site of Sayer Rebecca's death. Or, he reminded himself, at least the place where her body happened to be found. Since the slaying might've easily occurred elsewhere.

It won't do to jump to any quick conclusions. No matter how much I want to rush things and be totally friggin' finished with this crazy place!

Chapter 9

The Haul Road dropped through switchbacks and went by a bluff where mossy stones bulged through a green tapestry of ferns. Water drooled out of this vegetation from a hidden spring to collect in a rivulet that wrinkled and bubbled as it slid downhill. This trickle was bolstered by other threads of water garnered from folds in the landscape. Within a quarter mile, the rivulet had swollen into a creek that tumbled over small but steep rapids.

From a glimpse of the distant seashore provided by a brief gap in the trees, Kyle calculated that he'd traveled about halfway down the drainage to Elysian. He rounded a bend, then used his improvised hackamore to haul Sweetheart down to a walk. There lay the pool, a shimmering sapphire oval. This gem was set between steep, rocky banks. Above them, the firs and spruce of higher elevations were shifting over to the redwood groves of lower slopes. A waterfall about ten yards high tumbled into the pool's upper end to fill it, while a rocky rapid choked with boulders at the lower end permitted the pool's waters to then churn away downstream.

"Could be the place," Kyle muttered to himself. The mare snorted what sounded like her agreement. But it was merely an effort to blow a few strings of dusty snot out after her morning gallop.

Kyle halted, dismounted, and used the lead-line to secure the mare to a slim tanoak at the side of the road. Here, she could nibble on vegetation if she wanted.

He walked up to the shore and gazed down. A soft and level spot by the water's edge displayed signs of a lot of activity—the place was a veritable chaos of overlapping footprints, crushed plants, and long drag marks. *A body recovery might easily have churned the ground up this way.*

Kyle studied the calm oval pool itself, about ten yards across and twenty yards long. He guessed it had a depth of twelve feet or so. At the pool's center, where blue shades darkened to indigo, he could just make out a ring of small boulders on the bottom.

Ephraim could be right. If Rebecca's body had been sunk completely to the bottom, seeing a flash of light from her hair might require more than luck. It'd be easier for Samuel to discover Rebecca if he already knew she was here.

He tugged the stone hammer out of his belt and undressed. He waded into the pool, took a breath, and dove to the bottom. The water seemed chilly a few feet down and impressively cold at its deepest point. *Must be what kept Rebecca as preserved as she was.*

Kyle returned to the surface, took in breaths, then dove again to swim the length of the pool, a few feet off the bottom. This time he spotted a dark ribbon that waved at him as he swam over it. He had to roll one of the boulders over to free the thing, then swam with it back up to the surface. He held it up in the air and saw it was a long strap of the same coarse fabric he had observed girdling the tunics worn by the men of Elysian.

Huh. The killer tied her to one of the rocks to sink her, he guessed. *Then piled all those other rocks on top of her to keep her down.*

He swam to shore and his clothes and dressed again, shivering as he did so. He rolled up the strap and shoved it in a pocket.

A pair of ravens cawed hoarsely off in the distance. Kyle saw them land on the high branches of a fir, twigs that nodded beneath their weight. The black birds launched into a litany of odd gurgles and croaks that make up a raven conversation. And as he gazed at them, he saw something else. A huge, mature tanoak on a knoll nearby held something in its branches. He recognized it as a hut of some kind, a tinier version of a Treetown cabin. But this structure had been decorated in camo. It was painted with light and dark patches, and branches that bore clumps of live mistletoe had been draped over its roof.

Seems intriguing. It's something else to check out.

He hiked up to the knoll, looked up to the underside of the hut, then stood there baffled. The tanoak's lowest branch was more than ten yards up its trunk. No damn way to climb the thing. Then he spotted a rope that drooped from an upper limb and went across open space to the fir where the ravens roosted. Now, that fir had plenty of low branches. He clambered up into them, ascending till he could grasp onto the rope. The fat knot on its end looked like a foothold.

Stand on the knot, grasp the rope, then swing. Pretty straightforward. But if you don't stick the landing on the oak, you'll eventually pendulum to a halt in mid-air. And brother, it's a long way down.

He made his calculations, hopped upward, and swung. After a thrilling swoop between the trees, his feet slid off the knot and thumped down on a one-plank landing just outside the hut. He nearly let go of the rope, then realized he had to keep it in order to swing back, and so gripped it desperately with one hand while flailing around for some branch, any branch, with the other hand. He was able to wrap his fingers around one and stabilize himself. *Phew!*

A hook on the wall of the treehouse looked as if was meant to retain the rope. He hung the end knot on it. Then he pushed aside a deerskin that draped over the entry.

The hut looked to be a cramped space with minimal furnishing. Its main features were four broad view slits that ran the width of each wall up near the low ceiling. There was a sleeping shelf with bedding, a pottery jug with a saucer on top that likely held drinking water, a chamber pot also made out of clay that sported a hunk of board for a cover, and a clotted sheep fleece used for a rug on the floor. A half-melted candle stood in a square lantern with glass sides.

Kyle peered out of each of the view slits in turn. Two of them provided surprisingly good views: the eastern one looked all the way up to the head of the drainage to the point where the Haul Road turned off the ridge; the one facing west afforded a view of the coast and the distant fields of Elysian. So, this elevated hut was a watchtower of some sort. But cobwebs over the ends of the slit windows told Kyle it likely hadn't seen a lot of recent use.

All right, O Master Detective. Why don't you see if you can manage to detect anything?

He sank to his knees and began to poke and probe about in the wool of the fleece rug. When he got to its far end, a fingertip touched a hard, round pebble. He spread the fibers apart and found a simple earring made of a red glass bead and a length of copper wire. He'd seen earrings on some of the men of the Tribe, but those were all thick metal hoops, a good match for their joint pirate fantasy. This seemed more like a female item. But he didn't remember what the Tribe women wore and couldn't recall if he'd seen earrings on any Elysian women or not. The latter did seem to shun decoration. *Other than Sayer Ruth's eyepatch, of course. A fashion accessory that would work great in the Tribe, too.*

Kyle looked around for more stuff. The water jug indeed turned out to be just a jug and the candle lantern was only that. His inspection of the chamber pot yielded merely a slight worsening of the hut's atmosphere. He turned his attention to the bed. It offered a redolence of old body odor, but not much more. A blanket had been rolled up to use as a pillow. Kyle found this blanket's corners, spread it out and took it to the slit window.

He found a long hair on it and plucked it off. He wound it around his little finger, so the coil of adjacent strands could reveal its true color. It looked grey. He continued his search and found another, even longer hair. This one was reddish and showed kinks in its windings. He sorted through more fibers until he found another that looked different. *Aha. Let's see, now.* And it was…champagne blond.

Sounds drifted in through the windows. A man's shout, plus a hollow rumble of multiple unshod hooves.

Kyle exited the hut. From its landing plank, he could see a mob of Tribe rangers making a swift descent on the Haul Road. He grabbed the rope, swung back over to the fir, then clambered down. The rangers spotted him as he hiked off the knoll. They lined up in a semicircle with the tips of their lances lowered and aimed at the point where they saw Kyle would arrive.

"Good day, gentlemen!" he greeted them. "Really nice and cool out this morning, huh? Perfect time for a ride."

"What in hell you up to, you damn fool?" Red responded.

"Oh, my job," Kyle said. "And I'm pleased to announce that I've made an inch or two of progress."

"So what?" Carlos said. He leaned against the pommel of his saddle. "Mister K, you've been a bad boy. Have to go some, chump, to make up for the grief you just caused us."

"May I approach?" Kyle asked.

Carlos nodded curtly. Kyle walked up to his left stirrup.

"There was a way-old movie," Kyle said, "old even before the Flare. Called, 'Three Coins in the Fountain.' Ever hear of it or see it?"

Carlos shook his head and looked annoyed.

"My granny collected old movie DVDs, so I did see it. It's all about good and bad luck in love. I now have a similar story, one I'd like to call, 'Three Hairs on a Pillow.' Care to hear more?"

Carlos narrowed his eyes. Kyle noticed for the first time that the irises of the man's eyes were nearly as silvery as his hair.

"Might be best if I just showed you." Kyle held up his little finger. "This hair is grey," he announced. He held up his fourth finger. "And now, a red," he said. Then he brandished a finger that happened to be his middle one. "An-n-n-d to finish up, blond. How 'bout that? Pretty interesting, huh?"

Chapter 10

Carlos straightened up in his saddle so he could level a stony glare at Kyle.

"Bull!" he said. He waved a hand. "Means nothing. All sorts of guys use that watchnest."

"And it's guys-only? No ladies?"

Kyle looked at the other rangers. All of them, including Red, avidly swung their own gazes back and forth between Kyle and Carlos. *Hmmm. Outcome here appears to be much more than a bit loaded. Am I closing in on something they all know or suspect?*

Carlos aimed his forefinger at Kyle as if it were a pistol barrel. "You don't look so great to us this morning, pal. You stole a horse, and you stole a tallywhacker. You ran off from Treetown with no permission to leave. Trying to escape? You answer for all that, right now!"

"Sure, why not change the subject." Kyle nodded. "So, I'm trying to escape? Wow, obviously. Must be why I tied up my horse and waited here for you." Kyle gestured at the tethered mare. "Excellent ride, by the way. Who really owns this horse?"

"She's mine!" one of the rangers said. "And you best not've done my girl no harm."

"Nope. Didn't press her hard, and we got along great. Really knows her stuff. I began calling her Sweetheart."

"Penny. That's her real name."

"Okay. Like to swap you something for her."

"Yeah?" the ranger scoffed. "As if you got anything I want."

"Shut up!" Carlos roared. It was the first time Kyle had seen him lose composure.

"How about this?" Kyle pulled the stone hammer out from his belt. "What you call a tallywhacker, huh? I'll swap you this. Seems like a nice one."

"Belongs to us already," Carlos grated. "And there's a rune carved into the handle that tells us 'zackly which of us can claim it."

"Okay. Speaking of real owners..." Kyle pointed at the Bowie knife that hung in its sheath on Red's side. "That blade is mine. Didn't keep this asshole from trying to steal it, though, did it? Besides being a cool tool, it's got a ton of sentimental value for me. Want it back. Now would be a good time."

"Red?" Carlos said. He leaned back against the cantle, hooked a knee around the horn, and let the braided reins he used to control his bay gelding go slack. "How about you hop off your mount there and see if you can teach our uppity Outsider a few manners?"

"Happy to!" Red handed off his lance to another rider, then vaulted from his own bay to land lightly on both moccasin-shod feet. He swiped his hands to shove his dreadlocks behind his neck, then pulled a stone hammer from his own belt. "You like that 'whacker?" he said. "Show me how well you use it!"

He danced forward and made a swing at Kyle's head, then spun in a circle to continue the momentum of the first swing and as he came around, bent forward and reached to take his next swing at Kyle's ribs.

Kyle arched away and the blow missed by a hair, nearly scraping against the front of his shirt. *Uh-oh, this guy's got skill. He's practiced at this, and I'm not. Only thing I can think of is to handle it like a knife fight. Focus on hindering Red's weapon hand while you wait for him to make a mistake.*

Red tried for an uppercut, swinging from his knees. Kyle backed up as he turned sideways, leaned in, and swung his own hammer on an arc that tracked right behind Red's. It smacked into the bottom of Red's 'whacker handle and nearly made him drop it. Red's eyes widened. He spun and swung the hammer one way, then another. Kyle kept on backing up. Now he was at the rim of the pool, with no more room to retreat or maneuver. *Maybe I'm running out of luck too,* he thought. *But does Red know how to swim? Maybe, maybe not. So, my next move will be a total gamble.*

Kyle fell forward, landing on his free hand and a knee while sweeping his hammer around in a manner that caught its stone head behind Red's left knee. He yanked hard. Red whirled around and staggered toward the water. Kyle jumped up and tackled Red around the waist, driving him into Bethesda Pool. Both men then submerged in a gout of splashes and a tangle of thrashing limbs. With one key difference: Kyle had drawn a deep breath before going below the surface, but Red hadn't.

Kyle felt the stone hammer thump him on a shoulder blade. It hurt. He also felt panic surge through Red's body as he clutched at his torso. Red wanted to get back up to the surface badly, yet Kyle wasn't about to let him go. Red's leg kicks became more enfeebled. *He's running out of air. And water's soaking into those buckskins, making 'em heavy, hard to move in.* Red's body twitched and spasmed. *All right, time to bring the dude up.* Kyle let go, frog-kicked up past Red, then gripped him by the collar of his shirt as he went by. He tugged him up to the surface, then towed him over and dragged him out onto the soft part of the bank.

Red was gurgling and choking as he fought to draw breath. Kyle helped him roll over and get up onto his hands and knees. He thumped Red on the back with the palm of his hand and he vomited a gout of water onto the sand. He wheezed in a puff of air. Kyle dropped his hammer, reached around Red's waist to unbuckled Roy's belt and his sheath knife.

Kyle stood up with the knife in his hands. He'd expected to be crowded by rangers ready to leap on him simultaneously. Instead, they all still sat up on horseback, rocking back and forth as they slapped their thighs and shook with laughter.

Except for Carlos. He swung down off his bay and strode toward Kyle with his grey eyebrows jammed together in a scowl. He plucked a stone hammer from the left side of his belt as he walked. Kyle looked over to the spot where his own purloined 'whacker lay on the sand. He saw it would take about a half-second too long for him to bend over and grab it. So instead, he yanked the Bowie knife out and brandished its gleaming blade.

All laughter abruptly ceased. Carlos skidded to a halt and eyed him.

"Uppin' the ante for round two?" Carlos said. "Fine. Fine. I'm in! Match and raise you."

He dropped his right hand to the handle of a long knife that hung over his right thigh in a fringed and beaded sheath. That sheath looked slim, suggesting it held something like a long fillet knife.

"HAGH!!" Red sounded like a cat trying to bring up a hairball, or perhaps a seagull coughing out a rotten herring. He came all the way up onto his knees to aim a shaky forefinger at Kyle. "You dickhead," he accused. "How the devil did you know I can't swim worth a goldern fuck?" He spat out a series of soggy chuckles punctuated by hacking coughs.

The rangers began to chuckle right along with him. Against giant odds, and despite himself, Red had managed to reset the tone... and just in the nick of time for Kyle.

"Always tried to figure me just what a drownded rat might look like," opined the ranger who was Penny's owner. "Now, I got me a lil' clue."

"Yuh," another one said. "Y'know, his name might be Red, but he sure 'nuff wasn't *ready*. Not for that move!"

The laughter rose by a decibel or two.

The group energy had begun to blow in a favorable direction. It was the right time for Kyle to pat that breeze on its gossamer butt and keep it going the same way. He rammed the Bowie blade back into its sheath hard enough to make a noise. Everyone took note. He then looked over at Carlos with raised eyebrows. *Isn't this better?* Kyle glanced down as he buckled the belt and sheath around his waist. When he looked up once more, Carlos had tucked the haft of his 'whacker back into his own belt. And yet, Kyle noted, the man's right hand still rested upon the hilt of his blade.

Red got up to his feet and clapped Kyle on the shoulder. "Y'know, y'ain't nearly so much of a wuss as you look," he said.

"Thanks," Kyle replied. "Nope, nor you neither." And that scored him some of his own chuckles.

"You kicked my tail fair'n'square," Red said. "Frogman cunt that you are!" He flung an arm across Kyle's shoulders and pulled him to face him while thrusting out a hand. "Let me shake your hand."

"Sure. And luck always owns a stake in any win," Kyle said, as he locked fists with the ranger. Unsurprisingly, shaking hands with Red proved a renewed test of their respective strength.

"Red, I told you to teach this guy some manners," Carlos said.

"And it seems like now, you have."

Aha, Kyle thought. *Must be hard to pretend to command a mob of pirates like this. Or "freebooters" might be a better term for 'em, since there's no ship. I'd guess such rambunctious scalawags can be ordered around just once in a while. Even then you've got to pick your shots. Rest of the time, you need to keep a weather eye on where they're already heading, then scurry around to get in front of them before you yell out, 'Follow me!' Wonder if Blackbeard and Morgan and Kidd had that problem. They most likely did.*

Kyle leaned over to pick up his tallywhacker, then saw Red's club lying over in the shallows. He walked over and picked that one up too, then held up and waved both. "Well then, how 'bout I swap you a pair of 'whackers for Penny?"

"Hey! That one's mine," Red protested.

"Nuh-uh, man," a ranger said. "A guy loses a duel, he loses his tool. Them's our rules."

"Penny's worth more'n even two 'whackers," her owner groused. "A big bunch more."

"How 'bout a rental, then?"

Her owner ruefully smiled while shaking his head.

"Don't know as to how we want to see you on a horse," Carlos said. "Makes it kind of hard to keep a string on you. Y'know, I just don't buy this idea that you had no plan to run off."

"Yeah, well, sorry. But this is the only way I could think of to get some of my work done without one of you bums clamping a hand on my shoulder. For example, if you were out with me, would you have let me dive into the pool or climb up into your whatchamacallit, the watchnest?"

No one replied, which made the answer obvious.

"I must stay as objective and independent as I can be. Otherwise, my work here won't be worth spit. If I've got a horse to ride, I'll get a lot more done, and much faster. That's in everyone's best interest, right?"

"We're *not* going to let you keep a horse." Carlos sought to make his statement sound both firm and final.

If I buck his authority now, he'll be my enemy. If I give in and treat him like a chief here and now, right in front of these men, could make him more of a friend.

"Okay," Kyle said. "You're the boss." He shrugged. "But can we at least discuss letting me ride down to Elysian today? I planned that as my next stop."

"We've got a ton more than that to discuss," Carlos said.

"Well then, let's you 'n' me go somewhere to have ourselves a chat."

Red was stripping off his buckskin shirt so he could wring water out of it. He exposed a pale, lean, freckled upper body decorated by ink-black tats with themes that ran a gamut from macabre to romantic. Kyle dropped both 'whackers onto the ground in front of him. He gestured to Carlos, suggesting that they should stroll by themselves over by the waterfall end of the pool. Carlos gave him a thumbs up.

—

They stood there in the wash of sound and a spray of fine mist from the tumbling whitewater—which meant they could not be overheard. The rest of the rangers paid no heed, anyhow. They were still preoccupied with giving Red a ration of shit about losing his tussle with Kyle.

"You run off? That's bad for me," Carlos said. "When and if it happens again, I'd make sure it's really bad for you."

"Understood."

They stood still and silent for a moment, taking each other's measure.

"So, what else have you found out?"

"You mean, besides the hairs?"

"And which hairs are those?"

Kyle looked at his hand. His fight with Red in the pool meant that the tell-tale hairs wound about his fingers were long gone.

"Gee," he said. "Missing evidence! But hey, no biggie. I had plenty of witnesses when I waved 'em around that first time. And how many rangers already suspected that Rebecca did sleep-overs with somebody up there? Or maybe, with somebodies."

Carlos' stare, blank and steady, gave nothing away.

"What else do you imagine you discovered?" he insisted.

"Enough to put more questions to Ruth, and then to Michael and Samuel."

"Care to drop a hint? I can help you think this stuff through."

"Bet you'd like to. Didn't you watch *any* movies, or read detective novels before the Flare? Poirot, Columbo, Holmes and Bosch and Hardy need to build their case first, next get all the suspects in the same room."

"Screw that!" Carlos shook his head. "Pre-Flare crapola is your playbook? That's old hat. Obsolete. What a piece of work you are."

"Everybody alive right now is a piece of work."

"Red's right. You're a major dick. But I'll give you a leg up anyhow." Carlos sucked a breath in deeply then released it slowly. His grey eyes bored steadily into Kyle's. "One of the things that you're thinking is true. But the other thing you might be thinking—I mean, as a consequence of that first thing—isn't true. I told you earlier that we all loved Becky up here. Two of us who loved her the most were Red and I. Because she asked us to. She invited us to love her, and rather damned often at that. And by that very same token, we are the least likely, by far, to ever have done her the slightest harm. Get it?"

"I do," Kyle said calmly. "But *you* need to understand that I must figure out if jealousy is a motive in her killing. Since it appears to be the most obvious one. And if it does apply, then how, and to whom, and why, and to what degree. Do you get that?"

Carlos had stiffened during this last recitation, yet he still nodded in reluctant agreement. "Sure," he said. "But don't grab for any easy conclusions." He shook a finger in Kyle's face. "I'm always ready to discuss findings or help clear up some of the muddle. And not just by talking to you, pal. 'Cos when it comes to named suspects, don't forget, you're still in the mix! We both know what that means, right? You've got every goddam reason there is to blame somebody else and blow us a bunch of smoke."

Chapter 11

Ocean scents grew stronger as two horses cantered around the final bend into Elysian. Kyle could see a broad expanse of deeply furrowed sea dotted by whitecaps, and dense flocks of birds that swirled and fluttered above fresh lines of seaweed and wrack the parading swells had heaped up all along the coast.

As he made the final turn, Kyle swapped his view of open water for the green fields of the settlement. Between Penny's upright ears he saw workers bent over the rows of plants straighten up to observe the arrival of the horsemen.

"Yeeeee-haw!" shouted Red.

On the straightaway into the village he pounded past Kyle while lashing his mount into a full-tilt gallop with the ends of his reins. Kyle put his heels to Penny and gave immediate chase. Eight hooves kicked up dust, raising a floating beige cloud that the onshore wind shoved at the farmworkers, making the people nearest to it cough and avert their faces.

Red's bay was a bigger, stronger horse. Kyle noted that keeping up was hopeless. He reined his mount back to a trot. Penny objected with a head shake yet complied.

Hey, why not let Red the Wildman win this round, he thought. *Keep that guy happy. Plus, I can also show everyone down here that there's a difference. Got to deal with Elysians now. So, I'll act more like an Elysian. Sedate and disciplined.... Do draw a line at reverential, though.*

Red awaited him on the excited, dancing bay at the clearing in front of the Council Lodge. A grumpy Samuel—his staff gripped in his fist—stalked up to them.

"What's the meaning of this?" Samuel demanded. "We never let horses run here. It puts our children at risk!"

"Don't look at me," Kyle said. "I was only trotting."

"That's near enough to a run. And you, you broke your word to us. You ditched our assigned guide."

"Okay. Must plead guilty, there. But only a little. Was a group decision, y'see. Undoing your Elders' mistake. Should've set me up with a person who gets along better with the Tribe."

"Elders will pick a suitable punishment," he groused.

"Buddy, count your blessings. I'm back among you now."

"It's no blessing."

"Sam, what's turned you so touchy?" Kyle asked. "Get up on the wrong side of your bed-o'-nails this morning?"

The big man chose not to dignify that with a response.

"Looks to me like our welcome here already done got wore to a frazzle," Red observed. "So, guess I'll blow and head for the Pale. Want to hand me that lead for Miz Penny?"

"Nope," Kyle said. "But I guess I have to." He slid off the mare, untied the lead rope, clipped it to the tie ring again, then handed it over. He stroked the soft top of the mare's nose. "See you again, Sweetheart. Real soon, I hope." The mare eyed him and blinked.

Red swung a hand from his forehead, giving both men a salute so languid it was nearly contemptuous, then trotted both of the horses away, his dreadlocks swinging around the collar of his jacket.

"And slow down!" Samuel bellowed after him.

Red promptly kicked his horses up to a canter, vanished around a bend on the trail that led to the Cuadra.

⸺

"I need to talk with Sayer Ruth," Kyle informed Samuel. Samuel grunted.

"Huh? One more time, please. Didn't quite get that."

"Why?" Samuel growled. He fingered his staff. "What about?"

"Need to go over some of my newest findings." Kyle smiled at him. "And after that, I'd like to talk to you too, Sam. About Rebecca. I hear, you're the one who found her. Got to congratulate you. Did not sound like an easy search for anyone."

"Wasn't," Samuel said.

He regarded Kyle impassively for a long moment.

"Wait. I'll see if Sayer Ruth wishes to make time for you." He knocked aside the entry flap with one end of his pole and vanished inside.

Kyle seized the time to adjust the way he wore Roy's knife. During his ride, he'd pushed the sheath to the back of his hip and draped his shirt over the hilt. Now he had a better idea. He whipped off his shirt, unbuckled the belt, re-fastened it and hung the belt over one shoulder like a bandolier. He positioned the knife at the small of his back and pulled his shirt back on over it. *Sam doesn't know I've gotten my blade back. That's an edge. For now, my only one.*

The flap opened and Samuel beckoned. He brought Kyle inside the council space, with its plank benches and open hearth.

"Sit."

"Thanks so much." Kyle picked a berth that would keep any suspicious wrinkles or bulges on his back angled away from Samuel's eyes, then plopped down.

From the hall leading back to the oculus chamber, the dwarf Michael emerged, followed by Sayer Ruth, with her hands folded into the joined sleeves of her robe.

"My greetings, Sayer," Kyle said. "You too, Michael,"

"We are told that your day spent apart from us has borne fruit," Ruth said.

"Yes," Kyle said. "And now, I suggest that we should peel that fruit. Make us a snack."

Ruth glided to halt and stood, a tall and spectral presence in the dim light. The hood of her robe was up, and its shadows heightened the somewhat spooky effect of her black eyepatch.

"What have you learned?" she asked.

"We should confer privately. By which I mean, you and I only."

Samuel snorted at this, while Michael exclaimed, "Ridiculous!"

"Nope," Kyle said. "Here's why. Everyone's story must be compared to everyone else's story. That's the only way I can spot interesting differences. If everybody knows everything, all their stories will end up the same."

"And who put you in charge of that?" Michael sneered.

"Well. You guys did."

"To investigate," the small man fumed. "Not to attempt to act as a judge and jury over us, not to order us around. Especially not our Sayer. How dare you?"

"Michael, peace. He's quite right." Ruth's voice had suddenly turned silky, calm, persuasive.

"But dear Sayer, we must keep you safe from him," Samuel rumbled. "He's an Outsider. Not to be trusted."

"I ask that you wait out past the entry. Both of you. I'll call out should I need anything. But, please, do not worry. I shall be fine." Her tone now had an authoritative edge, one that brooked no defiance.

Ruth can sure talk, I'll grant her that. Understands the use of voice. Well. She's like one of the Bene Gesserit women in that old sci-fi book Roy liked so much. By that newspaper guy. 'Dune,' I think it was.

Samuel gave an uneasy, one-shouldered shrug that made clear he did not agree, turned and left. Michael flung Kyle a sour look before he followed him out the lodge door.

The Sayer Ruth moved forward till she felt her robe touch a bench. She turned and sat, then patted the plank beside her. Kyle got up, went over to sit next to her. He noticed that she had a pleasing smell, something that combined the keen tang of pine and the sweetness of lavender.

"Welcome back to Elysian," she said. "But I must ask. Why did you not try to flee us, while you had the chance?"

She's guessing, Kyle thought. *Leading this witness. That, or somehow the story of my crack-of-dawn ride has already come to her. But how?*

"Well, the chance I had to run off wasn't really so great," he told her. "Besides, this job has begun to intrigue me."

"Oh." Her lips quirked, as if she didn't quite buy this. "So then tell me, what did you find out?"

"Your lads up on the hill seem to be quite the wild bunch."

She chuckled. "Such a finding does not require any probe."

"No," he said. "But I did also find a curious item. Sayer, I note that you wear a special kind of belt, or sash on your robe. I'd like you to compare it to something." He pulled the cloth strap out of his pocket. "May I have your hand, please?"

She extended it and he put the coiled strap on her palm. She pulled the coil open and stroked the fabric.

"This is hempen cloth. Fibers like this come out of the Tribe's harvest. They and we both use it to make items, from twine to rope to clothing. When they make a sash of it, they weave in designs, bumps and patterns. But this is plain, so it must be Elysian."

"Thank you. Would Rebecca wear something like this, then?"

"No. She'd wear a braided cincture, like mine. Where did you find this? What do you think it means?"

"I can't really say."

"Can't, or won't?"

"Well, both, actually. It's not really the right time to do that yet. Can I have it back? Thanks. Now, here's something else."

He removed the red glass earring from his pocket and placed it in her hand. She weighed it, poked at it with the forefinger of her other hand. Raised it to the lobe of one ear after she recognized what the object was, as if she sought to assess its merits.

"To your knowledge, did Rebecca own any jewelry like this?"

She lowered her hand and wrapped her fingers around it. "Not to my knowing," she said, "but perhaps."

"If so, how would she get it?"

"Someone must've given it to her. Such vanities and adornments can only come from the Outside. We're not supposed to make or have them ourselves."

"Do you think Rebecca planned to stay on and keep her role as a Sayer?"

"Moments come for us all when we must wonder how we're best able to serve the Spirit."

"Doesn't answer my question."

"Not every question can be answered. Not in a clear or definite way."

"Yet, some can be. Did you learn Rebecca was no longer a virgin?"

"Yes," Ruth admitted, after a second of hesitation.

Sounds reluctant, a bit mournful, yet not in the least bit shocked.

Perhaps she's known for quite a while that Rebecca was sexually active. Really, how could a sister living right beside Rebecca not know? Being blind doesn't mean you fail to pick up on signs that aren't visual. In fact, you're probably great at that.

"How did you learn? From midwives who looked at her, or did Michael happen to tell you?"

"Why's that matter?"

"Trust me, it does."

"What a funny man. You say you wish to tell me things, but next all you do is probe me for more information."

"Actually, I'm doing both."

"Are you? Well, anyway, Michael told me."

Aha, then Mike's nowhere near as squeamish about Rebecca's condition as he pretended to be. That little weasel.

"Did he mention the pregnancy too?"

"Yes."

"Who was her lover?" Kyle blurted out the inquiry, making it loud, sudden and blunt.

The lid of Ruth's unveiled eye fluttered. "Well, who do *you* think?"

"Answering a question with a question. Another classic evasion."

She sighed. "I have no idea."

"How about your best guess?" he persisted.

She shook her head.

"Let's try a different tack. Did Rebecca have any enemies? People say, who envied her, or had some other reason to hate the girl?"

"None that I can think of."

"Really? You mean, not even you?"

Ruth's spine straightened with a jerk as a blush flooded her pale cheeks.

"Take care, Outsider," she warned. "What you suggest is highly offensive. Rebecca was my beloved sister. And of course, as a Sayer, she held a lofty post. All here did Rebecca due reverence, and I include myself in that number. Sayers are sacred to us."

"Uh-huh. I heard Rebecca was quite popular with the folks up on the Pale. And was she just as loved here in Elysian?"

"Yes."

"Even more so than Sayer Ruth? To such a degree that she might displace you, in terms of position or authority?"

The lid of her unveiled eye trembled as she turned her face toward him, but her voice was calm. "I know what you're after," she said. "You attempt to provoke, to see what may be lured out into the open. Yet you're also being fantastic and absurd. How could I, sightless as I am, do any being any harm? Even should I wish to? Which I certainly don't."

"Yes, you're sightless. But quite far from unseeing. Also, I must assume there are many here who'd do just about anything that you request."

Ruth sniffed disdainfully. His suggestion wasn't worth a response.

"Can I get that earring back, please?"

"I'd prefer not. Wish it for a keepsake. A reminder of my sister."

"But we don't really know it's hers, do we? And there might well be others I need to show it to."

"Where was it found?"

Changing the topic again. She's good!

"Small cabin, up in a tree near Bethesda Pool. You know of it?"

"No."

He observed no signs of agitation. But then she gathered the folds of her robe between her knees and stood up.

"Sufficient to each day is the trouble thereof," she said. "Thus, sayeth the Word. And you've given me more than enough trouble for this day. I declare our discussion ended. And so, be off with you."

"Sorry," Kyle said. "Let me just say, you're correct on two counts. I did mean to provoke, and you and I have spoken enough. Now, let me have that earring back. Please."

She tossed it vaguely in his direction and it bounced on the dirt floor.

She turned away from him and walked with her hand outstretched so she could touch the wall of the corridor as she got close. When she reached it, she paused, turned her head. "You walk inside our Pale freely now because of me, Mister Kyle. Because I used the Sight and vouched for you. Otherwise, you might still be held in our cell. Or an even worse place. And this is how you repay me, with doubt and accusation? Leave," She ordered. "Go outside. And tell Samuel to come in. But you, away with you now!"

Then she glided off into shadow.

Chapter 12

Samuel flung Kyle's waterproof duffle onto the ground in front of his feet.

"There," he said. "Now let's get going."

"Thanks," Kyle said. "Appreciate you keeping an eye on it for me."

Samuel replied with his implacable gaze.

"Anybody refill my jerky bag?"

"Don't make me laugh," Samuel growled.

"No worries. Don't see a way to squeeze even so much as a chuckle out of you. But hey, the day is young." Kyle waved a hand that swept in the whole arc of Elysian. "Just for the record, if I were allowed to stay down here, where would I have been lodged?"

"We'd put you in the Bachelors' Cabin. Sleeping with the other young men."

"Whoo. Exciting. Another thing. Am I getting this heave-ho by order of the Elders? Or is it just on Sayer Ruth's say-so?"

"Hers. And mine."

"Well then—if you don't mind—I'd like to chat at least with Elder Ez about all this before I go."

"I *do* mind." Samuel aimed the end of his pole at Kyle's nose, then swung it around to point up the south fork trail. "Cut the jive, Outsider. Just march. Go!"

———

They reached a switchback and viewpoint where Kyle had paused with Ephraim. Samuel growled for him to stop.

"What's that you've got there, under your shirt?"

"Oh, that? My knife."

"Pull your shirt off of your back right now."

Kyle smiled and complied.

"You had that blade on you when you went in to talk with the Sayer?!"

"Yep. But I pulled the shirt down over it, so that good lady would not get frightened if she saw it. I mean, if she happened to bump into it."

"Horseshit."

"Sam, your language!"

"Pull that belt off your shoulder. Hand it over."

"No."

Samuel's boulder of a head tilted on the wedge of muscle that constituted his broad neck. He showed his teeth. "Then you force me to take it away from you."

"Maybe you can. Or, maybe not," Kyle said. "Either way, it'll be a mess."

"Seem really sure of yourself."

"Not that. It's more, like, I'm really tired of being dicked with."

"Welp? Get yo' narrow white-boy ass oiled up fo' one mo' dick-in'," Samuel told him. Suddenly, he sounded a lot like an ex-con from Compton.

"There now, see? You talk more like you."

"The hell you sayin'?" Samuel took one stride toward Kyle then banged the end of his staff on the ground.

"You a player. Won MMA brawls, right? And before that, you were some kind of Raider dogface. Silver and Black, Pride and Poise. All true?"

Samuel's frown shifted from angry to puzzled.

"Where you be hearin' all that shit?"

"Ephraim."

"Oh. That swishy twat." Samuel glanced at the ground, then looked up. "Part you be missing is that I was a pro bouncer, too. And you don't hand me that knife, I'm fixing to bounce your tail back into the sea."

"No."

"Think I can't do it?"

Kyle rolled his eyes. "We've been over this! Yeah, you got a shot. Still, it's no lock. So really, why bother? Got to admit, could go south for you. Luck's an element. And I've got way better things to do with *my* time. I prefer to gamble on surer things. Y'mean, you don't?"

Samuel rolled his head to the other side. "You be one wacko piece a' work," he said.

"Yeah-yeah, people always sayin'. Should be right up there to the top of my C.V."

"Ah, you what?"

"Never mind. That stuff is so-o-o gone now. Listen, Samuel, you were told to take me up to lodge at the Cuadra, and you've got me walking straight there, no? Once I'm up at the Cuadra, I'll be out of your hair. What's left of it. So. Why act so cranky now?"

"Don't need to," Samuel said. "Hand over your knife, we all be cool."

"Forget about it."

"How'd you even make the Tribe give it back to you?"

"You mean, how'd I get it off Red? Took it from him. And yes, we had to negotiate a little bit first."

Samuel eyed him with a fresh level of respect. He decided that laying his hands on the Bowie indeed might cause more trouble than it was worth. Really, with Kyle forced into exile from the Elysian settlement, why bother? He raised the tip of his staff and poked Kyle with it. "Go on now," he said. "Get up the trail. Don't waste my time! Got 'portant things to tend to, 'sides herding a narrow ass all over this place."

———

The paddocks and barn of the Cuadra came into view, and an errant swirl of breeze awarded them a hint of its equine aromas at the same moment.

Kyle saw a thick madrone log lying in the shade by the side of the trail. He glanced at Samuel, then went over and sat on it.

"What you up to?" Samuel asked suspiciously

"Oh, taking a break. And something I want to talk to you about, Sam. With nobody else around. And before you need to go back down to Elysian."

"Yeah?" Samuel did not sit, but he held his staff in both hands and leaned on it.

"Tell me about finding Rebecca."

"Why?"

"Because that shall be more interesting for both of us than you not telling me."

"Man, you might be too much of a wiseass for your own good."

"Or too dumb to live. Guess I'll figure that out someday."

"Straight up."

"So, what was finding her like?"

Samuel heaved out a breath. He looked down at the ground and shook his head.

"You got to get, we'd pounded all trails on the Pale, way too hard. For days. With plenty of messy bushwhacking thrown in. Any place we saw buzzards circle, we'd go there, with our hearts in our mouths. And I was gassed. That pool, Bethesda, is the place we all go to soak our butts when it's hot. So, it just felt natural for me to sit on a rock there with my feet in that water and chill, just thinkin' 'bout what things was like before it got so whack. I mean we've had years of peace out here in Elysian without anything like a Sayer vanishing on us...and then Rebecca did."

"You were resting on a rock by the pool, and you looked down and saw her hair?"

"Yeah. Like this tiny flash, off in the corner of my eye. Like the glint of a lightning bug under the edge of a bush. Know what I mean?"

Kyle nodded. "And so then, you dove down and pushed off the rocks and untied her—"

"Oh, good Lord no! I can't swim a lick. And deep water scares the holy crap out of me."

"Who brought her up?"

"I don't know."

"Why?"

"Well..." Samuel rolled his eyes, appeared chagrined. "I passed out. Fainted. Just barely managed to point down into the pool as a ranger walked up. And by the time I finally came to, guys already had her out and on the shore. Then I cried my damn eyes out. Well, all of us did."

A rotund man with a mane of black hair—the same one Kyle had spotted pitching hay at the Cuadra's loft the day before—noticed their approach and stood waiting for them as they walked up.

"Samuel."

"Abraham."

"And who's this?"

"Kyle Skander. Young man who swam up on our beach few days back. Done nothing but cause trouble ever since."

"Come on, Sam. Hardly fair. You know I was tasked to look into Rebecca's death. What I've been trying to do."

"No small chore," Abraham observed.

"No."

"Well, it won't get easier," Samuel said. "Guy's pissed off Sayer Ruth, and she tossed him out of Elysian. Hard to say what his status is now, exactly. The Elders got to chew that over. Meantime, all I could think of was to come up and see if you'll keep him at the Cuadra with you."

"Oho!" Kyle lifted an eyebrow. "So, moving me out of Elysian was actually your idea?"

Samuel rolled his shoulders. "Best out of a bunch of bad choices."

"How long?" Abraham asked.

"Don't know. Few days."

"Can always use help 'round here. You know anything about horses?"

"Some. I grew up on a ranch in Humboldt."

Abraham studied Kyle, who studied him right back. The man was almost as tall as Samuel, but thicker, rounder, softer. His hazel eyes held a quiet steadiness. *This man's more'n a bit like a horse himself,* Kyle thought. *But a big one, a draft, strong puller, a Clydesdale. Percheron!*

"All right," Abraham said. "You can stay. On these conditions—number one, you listen to me, and do things the way I say. Two, you do nothing to hurt or scare my horses. Three, you keep your word to me. No rambling off. If Samuel asks me where you are, I want to be able to tell him."

Kyle thought it over. "Agreed," he said and extended his hand.

Abraham's paw was massive and thickly callused, yet it closed around Kyle's hand as tenderly as a grandmother's hug. One quick shake, and their deal was struck.

———

Kyle's first chore was helping Abraham to trim hooves.

Yet initially, Abraham would only let him pick clots of mud, pebbles and manure out from around the frog of a hoof.

But after he performed more than a few credible cleanings, Abraham let him move on to helping manicure. To level the sole and stratum of a hoof with a curved knife, trim it with pincers and then finish the job with a rasp. Which Kyle had done many times before, so Abe was satisfied with his performance. Then, they both began to work the string of waiting horses. They fell into a rhythm, working steadily side-by-side until all animals waiting in a special corral had had their feet groomed.

"That'll do 'er, for now," Abraham said.

"No shoeing though?"

"Nope. Trimming and shaping's all we got. Works okay 'less some idiot tries to gallop 'em for a long stretch over rocks. You hungry?"

"Could eat."

"Come on."

The upper floor of the barn held a hay loft, a space for spare tack and equipment repair, plus a small apartment for Abraham. His kitchen space wasn't much to brag on, a sheet metal wood stove with a cast iron pot on it, and a sink that drained through a hole in the wall. Abraham heated up what was in the pot—a bean and vegetable stew—then served it in a pair of wooden bowls so cracked they could barely hold it.

"Not bad," Kyle said, as he took a second helping.

"Like they say, hunger's our best sauce."

"You live up here full time?"

"Do now. Wife and I couldn't get along. Elysian doesn't allow divorces. It's a separation we figured out. Relate just fine nowadays, since we don't see each other so much. Not anymore at all, hardly."

Kyle pondered what sort of woman couldn't manage to get along with a big teddy bear like Abraham. Then he gave it up.

"Still a believer, huh? A Writ Reader and all of that?"

"Whole 'nother topic. Don't cotton to the Tribe, way too off-the-hook for the likes of me. Yet life in Elysian is kind of a bore. So here I am, stuck betwixt and between. But a path in the middle, that suits me right down to the ground. How 'bout you?"

"You mean, am I a believer? Well, I do have beliefs. However, gods and demons and angels and saints aren't involved. Never saw any point in trying to personify the cosmos. Sure, makes everything look more human. But it adds a layer of complexity guy doesn't really need. I mean, if you set up a god who is the founder-owner-manager of a universe, next thing, you're stuck with trying to explain his behavior. And if you want to make it credible in human terms, your job gets a hundred times harder."

"Guess I might say 'amen' to that," Abraham allowed.

"Met a brilliant guy, Roy Fisher. He got me into philosophy. Later on, I wound up teaching it. Put me on the path. A few strong, simple, clear ideas is all you need to have to get where you're going. The same way sailors use the brightest stars to navigate."

"Yeah? Give me one example."

"Life is neither good or evil, but merely a place for good and evil."

"Hmmm." Abraham grabbed the end of his nose and mulled that over. "How 'bout another?"

"You have a power over your mind—but not outside events. Realize this and find strength."

"Okay-y," Abraham said. "Where's this stuff come from?"

"The ancient Greeks. A school of thought called the Stoics, mostly. Roy was a big fan and he turned me into one, also."

"So, you're trying to keep it going."

"Why not? Our world has passed through a dark age before. And there were monasteries—compounds like Elysian—where devoted people saved copies of the old manuscripts and records of the classic thoughts. And when the world was ready, they brought all of it back into the light.

"Up in Arcata, where I'm from, we're mostly fighting to survive, just like you-all down here. But we also try to save key parts of the university from destruction, like its library. And we put effort into music and theater and film archives. Seems nearly thankless, right now. Yet future generations could truly value it. 'Hope is a choice.' That's one more thing Roy used to say."

"Huh."

"'Gold is tried by fire, men by misfortune.' And that's your bonus thought for today. From a Roman, Seneca. He was about mid-range in a legacy that ran from Zeno to Spinoza. Then ultimately on to Roy Fisher, of course."

"And you."

"Yup, I'd like to think so."

"Well, let's get you set up for the night. I take it, you don't have much in the way of bedding."

"Nada. In my duffle, I've got spare clothes and some knick-knacks. That's about all she wrote."

"Okay. Well, we can skootch together a pile of hay, and I've got a few clean saddle blankets to throw over and under you."

"Sounds just about near perfect."

Chapter 13

Frogs ratcheted in the creek. Crickets sawed away in the underbrush. Owl hoots. Breeze that soughed through leaves. These sounds and others mingled in a tranquil, native lullaby that swiftly escorted a weary Kyle off into dreams.

At first, he thought of Luz Maria as he always did when he fell asleep. As if he were trying to get back home through the power of mind alone. Luz, back there in the kitchen of Bret Harte House on the HSU campus, and their tearful farewell, a last moist, fiery, prolonged kiss before he rumbled away in the vintage Mustang—one of the few vehicles that had survived the Flare in running condition. Though it had needed a heap of work. The venerable hunk of Detroit iron had been found stashed in a basement garage, then was adapted by HSU techs with a flex-fuel engine altered to handle crude fruit alcohol. The vehicle appeared to be a wreck but ran like a champ. Initially. And the jerry cans lashed in the backseat and trunk meant that being able to pull off a round-trip without needing to find more fuel wasn't utterly out of the question. The rescue of Roy and Felicia from Woodside could be achieved, and Kyle felt determined and thus confident that it would be.

His route was simple and straightforward, even if its logistics weren't. Up over what was left of route 299 to Redding, then I-5 and south, speeding along in the dead of night, swerving around roadblocks or bashing through them with his car's reinforced front bumper—a stout V welded from railroad rails—or stopping to pay the tolls of a bribe of silver or dope or ammunition when he had no other option. He'd made it over Pacheco Pass to reach the Bay Area and congratulated himself that he hadn't needed to fight anyone off.

But he'd patted himself on the back a bit too soon.

Palo Alto was the San Francisco Peninsula town where he got tangled up in a shootout between a gang of Hispanic ex-cons and local cops—who'd formed a gang of their own, operating out of Stanford Medical Center, a compound that they'd seized, fortified, and were now struggling to retain. The battle at the intersection of El Camino and Sandhill Road had riddled Kyle's car and ruined his own gun when it took a round in the magazine. Yet he'd managed to escape with his life.

A deep and detailed replay of events that followed took a firm grip upon his dreaming mind....

A great bass boom! comes from behind. A hornet seems to sting the rim of my right ear. Rear and front windshields of the Mustang blow out across the seats and hood of the car in a loose spray of diamond crumbs.

Still, I and the Mustang win clear. Sounds of battle grow dim, then disappear. Pocked asphalt rushes below my spinning tires. No other threat seems visible, to either side. Nor ahead.

Suddenly I'm laughing in loud manic bursts. I pound on the steering wheel with my closed fist and scream, it's so hard to believe I've won through, I'm close to Woodside, and I'm still alive.

Kyle flapped a tattered map open against his steering wheel. He remembered the message Roy had managed to send up to Arcata in the hands of a sea-going refugee who'd fled the Bay in his sloop: "Go through Atherton, not Redwood City—that's owned by a vile gang called the Guardias and far too dangerous for a stranger."

The Mustang rumbled through the ruins of Menlo Park. Kyle saw a campfire flicker in the depths of a shattered storefront, a pale face that peered at him out of the shadows. Then a dark green cluster of oaks and redwoods that signified he was nearing the east-west road of Atherton Avenue. He hung a tire-squealing left.

There were more fires among the mansions of Atherton, a sylvan district that had been one of the toniest and wealthiest suburbs in the nation. Most of its grand trees were chopped down, the windows of its great houses smashed out. Kyle could see dim figures that scurried toward the road at the sound of his approach. *Should I switch on headlights? Give me a chance to spot trenches. In his note Roy said that deep slits get dug across roadways down here as car traps. Okay, yeah, hit that switch. No dome light now, can't see the map. Isn't this street supposed to go into a T with Alameda? No road signs left but that must be it.*

Kyle swung right, onto familiar turf. He went three blocks up, then left and roared on into the Coast Range foothills.

New threat. A stench of hot metal and burnt plastic wiring, wreathed in a wisp of steam, gouts out from the hood of the car. Shocked, I fling a look at the temperature gauge. Should've looked before. Dial is pegged! Must've smashed the radiator while ramming that last roadblock. Will this old 'Tang still run? Can I even make it to Roy's before the engine seizes? Yes. There's his driveway, right by the Mediterranean cypress. Mustang's engine knocks as I stop front of his house. I raise my foot off the gas pedal and my car shudders and dies. Grey steam and stinking vapors spew from the edges of the hood. I bang open the door and roll from the seat, fearing the car will burst into flames. I jump up, run a few paces, but it only continues to steam and fume.

The Fishers' two-story Tudor style home stood dark and silent. A burnt-out vehicle slumped on melted aluminum wheels and puddles of black, sticky tire ash in front of the garage—by the looks of it, a former sportscar. Intense heat had scorched a wavering brown pattern on the garage door.

"Hey! Roy? Hello! Anybody home?" Kyle called out.

"Well, finally here you bloody are. Took your own damn sweet time, I'll say. Nearly gave up on you!"

Kyle spun at that gruff and familiar voice, saw a tall, angular figure emerge from a clump of oleanders by the house. It was Roy, no mistaking that lanky form, knobby chin, hooked nose, dense pepper-and-salt thatch of hair. His grin was broad for a man draped in weaponry. In his arms he cradled a short, double-barreled shotgun known throughout the West as a coach gun; on his left side hung a bone-handled Bowie knife in a homemade sheath; on his right hip a 1911 model .45 Colt in a flapped military holster.

"Roy!" Kyle bounded toward him. "Been fighting a war, or what?"

"Matter of fact, yep, I have."

Kyle tried to hug him, but Roy fended him off with the upraised barrel of the shotgun.

"Sorry, son. None of that right now."

Kyle noted then how stiffly Roy held himself, the lines of pain engraved on his face, the weariness in those bloodshot blue eyes. "Hey. You hurt?"

"Uh-huh. Don't bother about that. Not much time. Come here."

Roy limped to the garage, leaned the gun against its wall, dug in his pocket for keys. He unlocked the door and swung it up and open. Kyle was treated to a view of a tiny Honda trail motorcycle hitched to a wheeled trailer that held a sea kayak in one of its two sets of cradles.

"Did my best to set you up," Roy said. "Your boat's packed with all the good stuff I could pull together. Road routes are all turning into snake pits now, in fact I'm astonished you made it down. So, here's what you'll use to get back up the coast to Luz Maria."

Kyle saw another sea kayak, a double-cockpit model. Its long hull was leaned up against an interior wall of the garage.

"What about you and Felicia? Two of you planning to use that?"

"Felicia's dead."

"Roy! Shit! How can you say Felicia's dead, then just stand there in front of me like a fucking ice block?"

"Hell, I grieved," Roy said, his voice a low rasp. "More than you can know. And now, I'm done. I side with Seneca. Let your tears flow—but then let them cease."

Successive waves of shock wash over me. Felicia. Luz Maria's mom. Only woman I ever met who exceeded Luz in natural warmth, despite her dignified bearing. Felicia, the one who guided me to a safe and happy landing in the family after all that time Roy treated me like some kink-tailed tomcat on a back fence, yowling for his sweet kitten. His reply to my courting: only hollered insults and flung boots. And Felicia is now gone. Both my eyes flood to release hot streams of sorrow. But I'm still jolted by how impassively Roy observes me.

"Enough!" Roy said. "Let's get you inside, and pronto." He nodded at the thickening shadows. "Be night soon. Then anything out-of-doors is out of luck."

Inside the house, Roy sat at a kitchen table. He poured scotch from a half-empty bottle of Laphroaig. He told Kyle about the attack two nights ago by a crew from the Guardias, the Peninsula gang determined to seize and loot the town of Woodside. How that gang first had fired his car with a Molotov cocktail, and while his attention was diverted, broke into their house by climbing through an upper floor window. He'd found them and fought them after sprinting toward Felicia's screams. Even though he'd killed three and forced the rest to run, it had been too late for Felicia—she was already bleeding out from her many stab wounds.

"Where is she now?"

"Dug her a grave out back. In her garden. She's wrapped, and under a tarp. I've just not finished burying her yet."

"I want to see her."

"No, you don't."

Roy's big Adam's apple bobs in his throat. He presses a thumb and forefinger against his eyes. I leap up from my chair and start over to comfort him, but Roy hears my footsteps, and his eyes snap open in a glare. He flaps both hands to herd me back, clears his throat.

"Three of 'em were standing over her. One got a shot off, but I yanked back my shotgun hammers and let 'em have both rounds of buckshot. Put all of 'em down, and two out. I finished the last 'un with my Bowie. Rammed it through his eye socket and into his skull. Gave it a twist."

He stops. A faint creak from the cooling house echoes in the silence. Roy stares at the tabletop, his big hands knotted into fists on each side of his plate.

"I'm sorry, Roy. Real, real sorry."

"Miserable low-lifes. Dragged 'em out to the street. Left 'em for the feral dogs. Now maybe those bastard Guardias will take a hint."

"Didn't see any corpses lying about when I drove up."

Roy shrugs. He opens his hands, a smile flickers on his lips.

"C'mon, got something important to show you," Roy says. "It's back in the pantry."

Roy rose laboriously to his feet, the barrel of his shotgun pressed to the floor and his hand on the butt plate, using that weapon as a cane. He limped to a corridor that led to a back room. A door made of two-inch planks on stout hinges had been newly installed over the old entrance to the pantry and secured with a galvanized barrel bolt. He opened the door.

"Go in," he told Kyle. "You need to see this. It's way in the back, up on the top shelf. I can't reach it anymore."

"What is it?"

"Go see."

Roy flicked the switch to an interior light. Kyle saw a small step ladder inside the pantry, and a bundle wrapped in black cloth on a high shelf. He went in, unfolded and set up the ladder and went up it. He had just put his hand on the bundle when he heard a clatter and looked down to see a belt and the sheath holding Roy's knife slide to a halt on the floor beside him.

Then he heard the door slam and the bolt slide home. The light went off.

"Goddammit. Roy!"

Kyle jumped off the ladder, took a running stride and hurled his body against the door. It banged, trembled, and failed to yield.

"I'd not abuse myself that-a-way, were I you." Roy's reproof drifts in, muffled by thick wood. *"Built it strong, in case I needed to keep some guy penned. Only way to get out is to hack your way through to the bolt. Just grope around till you find my Bowie. May take some time, but I have faith a mighty fellow like you will eventually be able to whittle your way through."*

"Roy! Let me out! I'm not joking!"

"Sorry, son. Can't do it," he says. *"Got me an idea you might try to impede my range of motion."*

I pound the door with my fist.

"Son of a bitch! If you don't open up this instant. . ."

"You'll what? Cry? Piss your pants? Settle down, son. You need to hear everything I'm going to tell you."

I slide my feet around on the pantry floor until I find that knife in the dark, yank out the blade from its sheath and immediately try to ram it through the jamb near the bolt. It barely penetrates a quarter of an inch. I realize I in fact will need to slice and pry out many, many splinters before I ever manage to get free.

"All right, Roy. I'm listening. So, talk."

"Good. Won't take long, 'cos I don't have whole lot of time left.

Been holding myself together best I could for a gut-shot ol' hoss."

"A. . . a what?"

"Didn't I tell you not more'n five minutes ago that those Guardia bastards got off one round before I blasted 'em? Just failed to mention where they hit me. Plugged me straight through the gut, left side."

"Roy. Please open this door. We need to try to find you a doctor."

"Waste of time. None close by, and I'm too far gone. Infection's set in. Appreciate you acting like you don't smell it, but I sure can. Anyway, shortly, I'll be far beyond hurt."

"Roy. I don't want you to do anything stupid."

"Me neither. Why I planned something smart. Out in that garden is a deep, wide hole and at the bottom of it is Felicia. She left without me being able to say goodbye, so I'm going to fix that by telling her hello on the other side. If there is another side. Which I aim to find out. I'll jump in, get next to her under that tarp, and hand Charon his fee, see what happens next. You'll hack your way out of that pantry, then I'd be obliged if you'd shovel some dirt over us before you go on your way."

"Roy!! No! That's insane!"

"Uh-uh. The opposite. A black door is forever held open. The right hour has come for me to step on through. Marcus Aurelius said, to help a man cross over, think of annoying people you get to leave behind. Like you, son." Roy's chuckle was obscured. Kyle still heard it. "Joke. Hope you realize that. And so, here's my overdue apology. Back when, I acted mean for poor reasons. As you first courted Luz Maria, it was neither right nor proper for me to abuse you as I did. See, it's always tough for us dads when young men come for our daughters. But, no excuse. Rude things I did or said, all that was over the top. Genuinely regret it. Hope I've made up for it since."

"Well, if you're really sorry, I'll only let you make up for it now by unlocking this door."

Another chuckle.

"Goddammit, Roy! Can't you drop your tough-guy routine for just one single second? Why not tell me how bad you were hurt as soon as I got here? So that I could help you."

"You've not heard a single word I've been saying? Come on now, Kyle. Inhale some good old-time coffee fumes. Wake up."

"What the hell am going to tell Luz Maria after I return to Arcata by myself? Assuming I'm able to get home. After wading through hundreds of miles of crap to come down here to get you. But do you make that worth it, or only dismiss my effort? What do I say to Luz? Hey honey, guess what, your dad was a weenie who decided to quit, instead of fighting for his valuable human life with every strength or weakness that he had? Like he always told everyone else they had to do?"

"Hey, hey, hold up there, my man. Thought I taught you somewhat better," Roy says. "Suicide can be cowardly, of course. But clinging to a life robbed of virtue surely must be reckoned as more cowardly. Suicide instead could be a besieged warrior's brave, clean finish, the painter's master stroke, that graceful diver who enters the water properly with toes pointed and who leaves nary a ripple behind. The key is, have you completed your social duty? Is leading a life devoted to the four great aretés no longer possible for you?"

God, do I ever recognize that voice. It's classic Roy Fisher, thumping on the podium with a fist, or pointing at the crowd of students with both forefingers, as he stands in front of white boards scribbled with words and phrases of Greek.

"Well, ripe fruit must fall off the tree. Always has and always will. I'm merely clipping away my last piece of ragged stem. I'm returning to the cosmos something I only got to borrow for a while.

"And y'know, back in class, the thing I always used to say—actually—was that people should live as though they had but one day left. Memento mori, the prospect of the gallows, and all that jazz. Anyway, do that every day, sooner or later you'll discover you're right. Here the Nose-less One comes! But if you choose your own exit, you get to be certain of your timing. No small thing. Seeing your final hour approach is a big stroke of luck. A chance to get your mind right.

"What I'm trying to say here, Kyle, is hey, look on the sunny side. I get to bug out with Felicia, and you don't have to lug a dying sack of shit north on a long road home. You expended effort to get your butt down here, which I do appreciate. But no point in you having to burn yet more juice to drag me back north, since I'd likely croak on you about halfway. To subtract a faltering self from that equation is best. Look at it logically, right?"

I drop the knife and pound the door with clenched fists. It shudders, rattles, comes no nearer to opening. "No No No NO!" I yell.

"Think I'll finish off with a wee dose of practicality. Plus, one last ladle of philosophy. Anyway, when it comes time to shovel dirt down onto me and Felicia, you'll see a hunk of cord coming up out of the grave. You pull on that string, and in a second or so, you'll see my 1911 Colt sliding right on up. I'll have the other end of that cord tied onto the trigger guard, and I'll have discharged the only bullet loaded in that pistol, so no worries about whether it's armed. There's more ACP rounds packed in your kayak gear, along with a few other nice surprises."

My door punches get weaker, and my yells softer as Roy's voice, steady and low and calm and implacable continues to pour through thin cracks between the planks.

"My other advice is, you want to launch in the Pacific, go up Kings Mountain Road and down the other side on Tunitas Creek right after you cross Skyline. If you prefer to launch in the Bay, just head out on Woodside Road to Seaport, but do it at the crack of dawn, when those gangbangers are all sacked out with concrete wigs from their previous night's party, okay?

"Now, here's my kicker. Always, you were the tough guy. My job was turning you into a tough guy with a functional brain. The ultimate Greek ideal is Achilles and Ulysses, not one or the other, Kyle. Muscles and wiles, both. The man of action who's also a man of thought.

"I helped you spark up your Diogenes lantern, right? Now, it's your blessed duty to carry the blasted thing. And I mean everywhere. In all and any circumstances, hold that baby up. Be a light unto your fellow man, it's your legacy, and it's your responsibility now. Wisdom, courage, justice, temperance. The sacred four. Make 'em shine. I helped you to advance, now it's up to you to help others.

"All right, then, all my love forever to you and Luz. Tell you what, son, if you learn how to love the way Luz does, you'll have the full package, okay? No treasure better than her wise and steady heart. Commit to the well-being of others, as she always does. Make a better job of it than I did. Don't seek satisfaction in trivia. Better to stay hungry. Now, as Marcus said, 'The chimney smokes, and so I must leave the room."

"Please, Roy, don't."

"Sorry, buddy. I see Socrates over there rattling and shaking a cup. Raising those shaggy eyebrows. Beckoning to me with his free hand. And I'd say that means I've got to run."

Silence.

I slide down the door until I'm on my knees. Abruptly, I feel empty. So weary. I slap the door once with both hands, then I'm done. Kneeling, arms raised, waiting, and I'd say my thoughts are whirling but there are no thoughts as such, merely a slowly revolving maelstrom of darkness with silent flashes in it like a summer storm at midnight.

And outside, only more silence.

Until there is that far-off and percussive THUD.

Of a gunshot.

Chapter 14

Kyle snapped awake, found himself lying on his side on a lumpy pad of saddle blankets. Not standing over a grave in Woodside, shoveling dirt. His heart banged away madly, wetness streaked his cheeks and his neck ached. He turned his head the other way to loosen the vertebrae, felt more than heard a muffled pop in his spine, and sensed a slight ease of tension.

"Roy," he whispered. "Felicia." Bits of imagery whisked through his mind like a strip of cinema being rewound at high speed, then faded. A theater of dreams went dark.

He sat up in the cool, still air of a forest night that had turned completely silent. *Not a creature was stirring,* he thought. *Must be the wee hours. But which of them? How long till sunup?*

He threw his blankets all the way off and stood. He hadn't undressed so he didn't need to put clothes back on. He climbed down an outside ladder from the loft and walked out into the night. He thought he might find comfort by going to visit the horses in their stalls but then chose not to disturb them. Instead he walked the path to the creek. Shadows hovered thick and black down in the canyon, but he was able to find the creek bridge by following the sound of gurgles and splashes. He sat out on the middle of its planks with his legs dangling to listen to the stream waltzing by far below.

He sought to visualize Roy jammed in a circumstantial vise like his, pinned between the aims of the Tribe folk and the Elysians. *What would he do? One thing's sure, Roy loved challenges. They're yours to confront or to evade, he would say. What's the correct move?*

Totally your call. But in any case, strive to learn from every choice made. Big challenges are sparring lessons from the cosmos.

A steady boost in ambient light began to coax shapes from the grasp of night. Kyle stood, stretched, and ambled off the bridge. As he hiked up out of the gulch, he saw a bloom of pale yellow that nodded above a clump of broad, triangular leaves. He leaned in through the twilight of early sunrise for a closer look and saw the plant itself was a deep green mottled with black. *Fawn Lily,* he recognized. *Or, Adder's Tongue. Roy's favorite for a backpacker's snack whenever we went to tramp the Cascades in spring.* He plucked a few leaves and scanned the surrounding area for more lilies of the same tasty variety.

With his pockets stuffed, he walked back to the Cuadra, moving on past the stalls to a paddock where Buck the big stallion stood moored stolidly to the earth in sleep. The horse's head hung down and his barrel chest expanded and contracted in long, slow heaves. Kyle climbed the split rail fence to approach him. He paused a few yards away to admire the muscled arch of his neck, the wide, unyielding stance of his legs, the way his grey hide gleamed like rubbed pewter in the early light.

Buck must have scented Kyle or otherwise sensed his nearness because his eyes opened as his head came up. He snorted and shied sideways, then trotted away to the far fence of his corral. Kyle held his position and stood still. The horse eyed him suspiciously. Kyle pulled a leaf from his pocket and made a show of eating it. Then he removed all the other leaves he carried and dropped them in a pile. He strolled off toward the fence, where he was surprised to see a large human shape approaching on its far side.

"Trying to make friends?" Abraham said. "A waste of time, I think."

"Yeah?" Kyle hopped the fence and turned around.

They watched Buck amble up to the small heap of green. Kyle hoped he'd try a nibble, instead, he bestowed a single disdainful sniff. Then he snapped his head up to glare at the two men who watched him. He snorted, and launched into a gallop around the corral, throwing both hind legs up in sideways kick as he passed. Those big hooves were too far off to hit them, yet both men flinched anyhow.

"See what you mean," Kyle said. "A rude way to say good morning."

"Real outlaw, that one." Abraham sighed and clapped Kyle on the shoulder. "Can I interest you in breakfast?"

"Sure! More than I was able to interest Buck."

They turned around and strolled toward the barn.

"Hear how he got that name?"

Kyle shook his head.

"Carlos thought he'd break that stud in one big go. Forced a high port bit in him by prying his mouth open with a stick, then mounted him in the squeeze chute. When we released them into the pen, that ol' boy bounced over the ground just like a jackrabbit. Crow hops, sunfish, every move you can think of! Hit the far side with a big bound and rear, then threw his hind legs up and out with a corkscrew like you just saw. It made Carlos sail off high, straight up and over the fence. That part looked graceful, but he landed awful hard. After all that, we began to call the horse Buck, and it stuck."

"What was his name before?"

"I forget."

"Hear Carlos now wants to clip his nuts."

"Yeah." Abraham shook his head. "Not everyone who works here at the Cuadra buys in. What we mostly want is to see Carlos try to ride him again. 'Cos that was a really fun day."

—

Breakfast was a round slab of bulgur wheat flatbread and a hard-boiled egg, chased by a jug of cold fresh water from the creek.

"What's your plan for the morning?" Abraham asked.

"Do you need me here?"

"Nope. Tomorrow, maybe. Tribe'll give us more horses from their remuda for hoof-trimming."

"Okay. Then I need to figure out whether I go up to bother the Tribe or back down the hill to bug the Elysians."

"Time to play detective again, huh?"

"Sounds grand for what I bring to the table." Kyle raised a leg and pointed at his river sandal. "Best to call me a gumshoe." He put it back down and stared at it. "Or, seeing what it's like to have to hike in these things, maybe a flatfoot."

"Ah. Those are Before-the-Reckoning words, aren't they? After our generation passes, people will have no idea what they mean."

"Right. Got to make my stupid jokes while I can."

"If you're wearing those pups out, we can glue, nail and clinch some tire tread onto 'em," Abraham offered.

"You mean resole my sandals the way Ephraim did his boots? No thanks. Looks like they weigh a ton." Kyle slowly chewed and swallowed his last hunk of flatbread, then gulped some water. "And speaking of Jimbo, how does that guy rate pants and shoes, anyhow?"

"Well, you're right, not many can boast of such goods in Elysian. But as a picket, Ephraim's allowed to wander the Pale as far as the Portal. It's the guard post where all our swaps happen with the Outside."

"Yeah, I heard. And what sort of stuff might that guy give his fellow wanderers in order to get?"

Abraham spread his hands and shrugged. "Don't know. But you have to feel some sympathy for Ephraim, that boy's had it rough."

"How so?"

"Well, he lost his mom when we fled north from Pharaoh."

"From what, now?"

"Guess I'd better back up and fill you in on the history. Pharaoh is what Elysians call the desert compound they ran away from. I mean, that's what they call it now. Back when we saw the place as our refuge and sanctuary, it was Horeb, or Ras-es-Safsafeh."

"Why'd they ever leave?"

"Got to back up even further, then. Did anyone tell you how the faith was founded? No? It all began as a sort of neo-Christian movement. Pentecostal, with heavy outreach to street people and convicts. Founded by Jedediah James, who was the older brother of Elder Ezra. Well, one early convert was Nathan Cooper, who had been jailed for embezzling from the U.S. Air Force."

"How'd he manage that?"

Abraham chuckled. "I'll explain by laying his full name on you, just the way he liked to. He'd be Lieutenant Colonel Nathan Reginald Cooper to you, airman! Cooper had run an air cargo wing at

Norton AFB, near San Bernardino. Anyway, he got out of jail after he got converted, became Jedediah's right-hand deacon, and more or less seized the upper hand when Jed died of a stroke. I'll grant him this, he saw way into the future. Cooper knew that a Reckoning of some kind would happen, and he prepped for it. First move was to buy a surplus base with bunkers and tunnels and even a missile silo out in the Old Woman Mountains, near the Mojave. A base that began when General Patton used the area for tank training in World War Two, and then the Air Force took it over and used it as a secret complex during the Cold War. It had a deep well, greenhouses and so forth, so it could be self-sustaining—as long as you had a force of people who would do all your work for next to nothing."

"Meaning, the Elysian converts."

"You got it."

"Including you?"

"Yep. I was on parole and working as a horse trainer for mustangs at a BLM ranch over in the Yucca Valley when Elder Ez brought me into the fold, so to speak."

"So, when did Lieutenant Colonel Nathan Cooper start abusing the young women?"

Abraham lifted his head and his lips parted in a smile of wonder. "How on earth did you know that?"

"Let's see. You've got an isolated community, an amoral yet authoritarian leader who seizes total control, then a bunch who want to rebel and split away from him. Not so hard to put together."

"Well, you're right. Cooper set his cap on having as many sons as possible by as many women as he could. He cited the Bible patriarchs to justify it, of course. Not everyone agreed, and the ones who didn't all tried to run off in a big bunch one night. He came after us with his most loyal supporters, and we had a fight near Ridgecrest. We were able to beat him back and get away, but there were casualties. One was Hagar, who was Ephraim's mom. And her death was especially tragic, because she grabbed a gun and committed suicide. See, she was terrified at one point when it looked like Cooper was about to win, and if he did, then he'd be sure to grind her under his thumb. Ephraim was only a little kid, so his mom's death was very traumatic for him."

"And he was Cooper's son?"

Abraham nodded.

"Yikes." Kyle pinched his bottom lip between thumb and forefinger as he thought about this. "And so, why did you and the Elysians migrate up here to the North Coast?"

"Well, this place was always going to be Cooper's second compound. He'd bought the whole Gilead Creek valley from a bankrupt timber company."

"Tribe guys gave me the impression they'd been here first."

"Well, they had. But they were only squatters. So, we negotiated with them. We'd done more than enough fighting by then. Peace was what we were after. And so, we ended up bound in the deal we have with the Tribe today. Which has its problems, yet by and large the knots and kinks do seem to work themselves out."

Chapter 15

Kyle rounded the last bend in the trail that led down to Elysian. He paused for a moment to study the view of a peaceable hamlet with threads of woodsmoke that twisted up from cabin chimneys, bordered by a swath of green fields and orchards. *Place truly is Tolkienesque, a kind of a religious Shire. But the slaying of Rebecca shows that one forever should fear the serpent, in any Eden. 'Look for a worm in the apple, no matter how red and ripe.' One more aphorism from Roy.* A poem by Blake that Roy loved to quote also crossed his mind. *'O rose, thou art sick. The invisible worm that flies in the night, in the howling storm, has found out thy bed of crimson joy, and in his dark secret love doth thy life destroy....'*

Laborers on the fringe of the settlement noticed Kyle's approach, and by the time he reached the Council Lodge, Samuel was there to greet him, the massive staff of his office held upright in his hand.

"Should've known you wouldn't keep off," he muttered.

"Uh-huh," Kyle said. "If I stay away, can't get my job done. So, how's Sayer Ruth on this fine day? Settled down any?"

Samuel shook his head. "Not so you'd notice. That who you came to visit?"

"Thought I'd try my luck with Elder Ezra."

"See that you're not wearing your knife."

"Didn't want to make folks nervous. 'Specially you, pal. So, I left it up at the Cuadra."

"All right. I'll check to see if Ez is interested."

They sat in the second chamber, the one with an oculus in its roof and the elaborately carved redwood chair set against a wall. At this moment the skylight presented the aspect of a huge, clear blue eye, fringed by the lashes of swaying grasses at the rim of the sod roof. Samuel had objected to leaving Kyle alone with the Elder. But when Ezra insisted that he leave, a grumbling Sam stalked out.

So, Ephraim was correct. Elders do wield a scepter here and all must do as they say. But it leaves a question. When push comes to shove, does an Elder command their last living Sayer or can supreme power surge the other way?

"You wish to talk with me, and with me only, hmm? Is it because you've made a sensitive finding?" Ezra asked. His eyes, framed by a net of bags and wrinkles seemed both amused and quizzical, an effect magnified by his spectacles. "Or do you hope to startle me and then ambush me, as you did our Sayer Ruth?"

"I'd say, option one."

"Naturally. It's what you would say, even if your real aim was option two."

"A fair point."

Kyle tried out a smile and was pleased to observe Ezra smiling back. Perhaps they *did* understand one another.

"What did Sayer Ruth tell you?"

"I insisted she relate everything. And she did, I feel quite sure. Since that's what our Sayers do. They are anointed vehicles of revelation."

"Ah. Then I have only a few new bits to add to yesterday's brief. But first, I do have things to ask about. Questions I've been turning over in my own mind."

"All right. Ask away."

"Is Samuel truly scared of water, or no?"

"I would not call Samuel scared of anything. He does like to go to the shore and wade around the coves at low tide, harvesting mussels. Knocks them off the rocks with the end of his stick."

"All right. But can he swim? Put himself in deep water? Dive?"

"Don't know." Ezra tilted his head. "Why?"

"I realize Sam's a trusted member of the Writ Readers. And he's your town officer of some kind—"

"We call him our Provost."

"Okay. So, this Provost owns freedom of movement. He can decide where he goes. Does he also decide when? Set his own schedule?"

"Yes, unless we ask him to do some specific thing. But again, why?"

"He's the searcher who found Rebecca, submerged up in Bethesda Pool. A hard thing for an ordinary person to see on a good day. I mean, that pool is deep. And she was buried under a heap of rocks."

"I've always found Samuel to be amazingly observant."

"Sure. But it's far easier for people to spot a thing if they already know it's there."

Ezra's brow furrowed. "So, you suspect that—"

"Samuel does have a violent past. His favorite tool is a blunt object. Rebecca got whacked on the head by exactly that sort of weapon."

"Why, he's one of our most devout!" Ezra looked aghast. "I've never known Samuel to engage in any act of wanton or undeserved mayhem, not ever. Not since his deep conversion to our way."

"Well I have."

"Only because I asked him to."

"I meant, even before you had me tossed into the cell. Out in front, that moment when he disarmed me. His assault was sudden, and it was harsh."

"But afterwards, he apologized to you."

"Sure. Great move. But is there any violent eruption that Sam *hasn't* apologized for yet?"

Ezra looked both puzzled and offended. "Why commit a deed so foul? To attack our Sayer Rebecca, would be—"

"Blasphemy."

"Yes. Precisely so."

"I don't mean his. Hers."

"What?!"

"Back in the day, when cops used to investigate crime, detectives would look for means, opportunity and motive. At least, that's what all the books and movies used to say, so I consider that pro advice. I'd argue that when someone intentionally slays a fellow human, then his motive must be quite strong. For instance, few people have a problem swatting a mosquito. Hey, that lil' buzzing bastard is just some annoying pest—and a pestilential one. But killing a wee, sleek, trembling mousie? Still a nasty pest, yet kind of cute, and so crushing it may be difficult. Now consider the quantum leap, when you bash some beautiful girl so hard you put her into her grave? Well that should be a rough move for everyone but a psychopath. But let's say we're not dealing with one of those. Table the psycho option. What might be some alternate reasons for an ordinary person to act in such a horrid manner?

"Let's consider the strongest human motivations. Among them, rage, jealousy, hatred. For starters, visualize rage in a true believer like Samuel. What would enrage such a man? Well, he'd never commit blasphemy himself. Yet if he saw someone else blaspheming? Could look like a summons from God to let his too-long-leashed dogs of war out for a trot. And who might seem more like a blasphemer than a Sayer that he saw breaking her vows to smithereens?"

Ezra ran the fingers of both hands through his aureole of white hair. "I think, if Samuel were in this chamber and heard you accuse him so, he'd answer with his stick."

"That's my point," Kyle agreed. "His most potent response. It's why I wished to speak with you alone. Spare myself the rod, so to speak."

A furtive rustle made Kyle turn his head to peer down one of the shadowy hallways that radiated from the chamber. He saw the bearded face of Michael looking back at him, then the dwarf spun around and disappeared.

"You've only made a case, not proved it. And what of jealousy?"

"Okay, let's move on. I do have a decent finding about Rebecca's lovers, up on the Pale."

"I shouldn't call that 'decent.'" Ezra frowned. "And you say, 'lovers,' plural?"

"'Fraid so. Which is not something I revealed to Sayer Ruth yesterday. I'll name them for you. They are—"

"When I hear my name, I wish to be present, so I know what's being said."

Ruth's voice echoed from the dim corridor. Led by Michael, she glided out of it to stand before them.

"Actually, we weren't talking about you, Sayer," Ezra said.

"But we could," Kyle said.

"In which case, I'll stay." Guided by Michael, Ruth sank down onto a bench, and he hopped up to sit alongside her.

"Well, then. We should pick up back where you and I left off," Kyle said. "Since you stalked out of the room before we were done. Let's discuss your envy of Rebecca."

Michael scowled while Ruth pursed her lips.

"Or, let's just jump ahead to the conclusion." She flipped a hand in a gesture of dismissal. "Your suspicion on that score is baseless."

"A full investigation requires that no one remain entirely above suspicion," Kyle said. "Not Michael, not you."

"Or you!"

"Naturally. It's where this whole thing started. I'm required to prove my own innocence by locating a guilty party. Right, Elder Ez? And to all the data that already exists in my favor, you must add that I had a fine opportunity to run off yesterday and make my escape on a good horse. Yet I didn't take it."

Although I very badly wished to—

"And why did you not?" Michael demanded, looking irate.

"Elysian and the Tribe would've seen it as an admission of my guilt. Then, your whole focus would be on recapturing and punishing me. Right?"

"Absolutely," Ezra said.

"Plus, my teacher Roy convinced me that everyone bears a social duty. To become a complete individual, a man must fully embrace links that go well past his mere existence as an individual."

But! Would Roy ever say that Elysian is where and how and when I ought to live up to a social duty? Perhaps not. Might give me a pass on that one.

"How pompous!" Michael scoffed. "So then, does an unbeliever like you claim to be a part of our community, too?"

"No, I'd go much further. I'd claim to be part of every human community, at least while I remain alive on earth."

Roy would have to chug a glass of whisky before he could blurt out a sentence like that. But hell, you need to work with what you've got.

"Do you realize how arrogant and prideful you sound?" Sayer Ruth demanded.

"Of course. Do you?"

The chamber fell into a moment of uneasy silence.

"You accuse me of envying my sister." Ruth's voice was cold. "Yet I did not envy her. My relationship with Rebecca had been troubled, I'll admit. But the big reason is that she's the one who took away my eyesight. Forgiving her for that deed has been a difficult practice for me."

"What happened?"

"We were children, fighting over a pencil. Rebecca always was excitable, impulsive, even as an infant. She stabbed me in the left eyeball with the sharpened lead point. Shortly after that, I lost vision in the right as well. Trauma to the optic nerves, the doctor said."

"Oh, that's grotesque. And a shame. I'm sorry it happened to you."

Ruth turned her face to him as the lid of her unveiled eye flickered up and down. "Grotesque. Yes." Two spots of color bloomed on her cheeks. She leaned forward. "You have to understand that at age seven the last thing I saw on this earth was my own sister trying to stab my face."

An uneasy silence fell again as everyone absorbed this.

Ruth straightened up. "Well, each of us has an inner battle. Forgiveness is a harder chore than most people imagine. But ask yourself, if I never revenged myself on Rebecca for inflicting such damage on me, why would I attack her for something as paltry as envy? That's a wisp, a chimera. Easily dismissed by someone who daily strives to purify the spirit."

"All right," Kyle said. "I guess we could grant you that."

But that doesn't mean we can eliminate hatred as Ruth's motive for killing. In fact, it underscores the possibility. Yet now is probably the wrong time to bring that up. She'll just bug out again, and I won't learn anything else from her.

Michael decided to change the subject. "So, you might as well tell us. Who were they—Rebecca's lovers?"

"Carlos and Red."

"Both?!"

"Apparently. Perhaps more. If there were a third lover, and he—or she, since it's the Tribe we're talking about!—wound up feeling badly excluded or rejected, well that could be a necessary motive."

"How about jealousy between Carlos and Red?" Ezra asked.

"Possible," Kyle replied, "yet unlikely. Red's a pal of Carlos, not just another Tribesman. And he's a lieutenant. I could spot no real tension between them, in any event. On an issue like this one, that would be hard to conceal."

"So, you're saying there might be a someone else, a different member of the Tribe?" Michael asked.

"Could be. But there's this." Kyle pulled the black strap of fabric out of his pocket. "Sayer Ruth told me this probably belonged to an Elysian. It apparently was used to tie Rebecca's body to a rock so that she'd sink into the pool."

"I've thought about that sash ever since you showed it to me," Ruth said. "If someone from the Tribe *did* commit this murder, why would he not try to leave a false clue? Something that would point elsewhere?"

"Nice theory and indeed possible. But for right now, let's assume that the clue points right where it looks like it points. I mean, at an Elysian. I've already made a case that it could be Samuel, I've even made a case that it could be someone acting on behalf of Ruth. But let's set both of those possibilities aside for now. Open up that question."

Sayer Ruth nodded almost imperceptibly.

"Plenty of Elysians out there wear a sash like this," Kyle continued. "Let's also posit the murderer's motive as unknown, and just look at opportunity for a moment. Who might be free to wander up to Bethesda Pool during that short span of days when Rebecca happened to be killed? Do you keep records on Elysian work assignments and so forth?"

Era shook his bushy head. "No. Nothing written. Yet we have supervisors who might recall such things. Inquiries could be made."

"Will you make them?"

"Of course, we shall. Michael, would you take charge of that?" The dwarf nodded.

Aha. He gets to run something. And it makes him quite happy.

"So, there's Ephraim, who patrols as a picket. But you have plenty of ground, and I assume the same guy doesn't cover all of it on every day. How many pickets are out there? And who was patrolling the north side during that period?"

"We have four pickets appointed to make rounds, and they rotate on days and routes, just as you suggest. Who among them was up there then should be easy to find out," Ezra said.

"Excellent." Kyle took a deep breath, then puffed it out. "Once we know, our first question to that crew should deal with whether or not that picket saw something out of the ordinary. Just because one was in the area doesn't automatically finger him as a suspect. If this killing was planned, that picket—let's call him Picket A for the moment—might been set up as a fall guy. In the same way and for the same reason that the hemp sash might've been used as a false clue by the Tribe. If a killing is premeditated, it can also be clever. Can any of you think of anything that I'm missing?"

"Gracious," Ruth said. "Now you don't sound quite so arrogant."

"Thanks so much."

"The Elysian sash you found got me to thinking about clothes," Michael volunteered. "Did anyone ever tell you that Rebecca was naked when she was pulled from the pool?"

"No. That's interesting. What clothing would she have worn?"

"Her robe," Ruth answered. "That's all a Sayer wears. We have a light gray one for summer, a heavy black one for winter. Her black one still hangs in her room."

"Her grey robe is missing?"

"Yes."

"Okay, a thing to look for. I assume it would be distinctive, if found on the Pale."

"It would. Wool is precious material. Only four such large robes exist, and we already know where three of them are."

"What shall you do next?" Ezra asked.

"Guess I'll head up to the Pale, grill the folks there a bit more. Stop by Bethesda Pool for another look-see on the way. And by the way, do you really have to chain me to another overseer?"

The three members of Elysian hierarchy glanced mutely around their tiny circle, taking stock of each other's reaction.

"No, I think not," Ezra summarized. "Go on your own recognizance for now, Kyle. But I would say, only within the Pale. As you've pointed out, any attempt by you to run off shall be dealt with. By both Elysian and the Tribe. Severely, yet justly."

"Oh, I'd expect nothing less from you-all."

Chapter 16

Bethesda Pool was a slab of blue lapis, buffed to a high sheen by a noon sun's unrelenting rays. The upstream waterfall had slowed, due to a few days' lack of spring rain. Consequently, ripples from the rapid's tumble into the pool began to fade after a run of less than two yards.

Kyle sat on the edge of the Haul Road where it curved past the pool's calm center.

Roy said philosophy must fit itself to reality, not seek to cram life into any set of notions. Philosophical tenets should be open baskets, not barred and sealed vaults. Belief should match inputs to human neurology, not try to deny what is sensed, but accept and interpret it, in whatever way existence chooses to present itself.

Remember that human neurology is made to exclude more information than it absorbs, retains or interprets. Our system was built that way to keep our brains from being flooded by data. That filtration process begins after birth, when nature snips at human ganglia until nerves fall away like vineyard canes beneath a pruning crew's shears.

This exclusionary process then continues as cultural programming. Children are taught to forge generalizations that they subsequently used to simplify and shape perception. This phase can be useful—anyway, it's inevitable, Roy said—yet it soon can turn detrimental. If learned concepts never are challenged, then such filters don't just simplify, they also stupefy.

Barriers to fresh perception also limit opportunity. Whenever one feels stuck, a solution that lies near to hand is to abandon all

*preconceptions, or at least shove them aside as far as possible. Let
your neurons handle info that you've habitually excluded.*
One easily proves the worth of this move by sitting down in any
spot, especially a familiar one, and shucking the scales of the usual
from your eyes. Examine all surroundings anew. Don't be limited by
what you saw previously. Absorb things you've not allowed yourself to so much as notice before. The key here is not to attempt it
by striving, but by relaxing.

Roy drilled him on this procedure many times as they knelt on
the dirt of a trail to study animal tracks and other spoor during
their wilderness hikes. "Make your mind a perfect blank," he'd say.
"Should be easy, a guy like you. More than halfway there."

Kyle began to sweep his gaze slowly back and forth across the
Bethesda Pool landscape, waited for it to speak. It didn't, not for
many minutes. He saw forested slopes, a jumble of rocky scree that
merged with water-smoothed boulders on the pool's far shore, the
mucky strip of churned up sand at his feet where he had battled
with Red, and turning his head, the Haul Road that curved behind
his back. On the east side reared up the knoll with the tanoak on
its summit holding the watchnest. To the west, long waves of green
hills fell away to a blue sea.

All these things he'd observed here earlier. Nothing surprised
him or seemed much changed.

Yet a phenomenon nagged from just below the porous border
of consciousness. He let this feeling prompt his gaze to slide back
over the scree slope. Broken slabs of rock here had weathered sur-
faces colored a dark chocolate, undersides of a pale beige. One
slab looked odd. Lines marking its color shift went up at a slight
tilt, as compared to other rocks nearby.

"Aha," Kyle said.

It took some boulder-hopping and scrambling to reach the far side
of the pool and ascend to his target slab. But then he had trouble
identifying it, since the perspective was different. He was forced
to go back down and squint at the slope afresh. After he had its location fixed once more, he climbed straight to it. He put his hands
on its rough edge, and—with a grunt—shoved the stone upright.

A swatch of grey cloth poked up out of a scattering of leaves and
dirt. He grabbed onto the rim of fabric and tugged. A robe that

he happened to grip by its hood came up out of the ground like a ghost arising from a grave. Kyle shook the garment and watched a cloud of duff and soil drift back to the ground.

Then he noticed something else that had been buried. A thick, polished stick with a rune carved into the end of it poked out. It looked like the handle of one of the Tribe's stone hammers. He was bending over to grasp it and pull it free when another stick flew between his leg and lower arm to clatter on the rocks and shatter into fragments.

Hm. The stick has feathers. Since it's an arrow. The thought barely had time to register before one more stick whizzed past, a yard higher. Its keen edge stung as it sliced across his forehead. *Fuck! I'm out here and up here on this slope fully exposed and a perfect target!*

His reaction was instinctive. Only later did he realize the degree of good sense his spontaneous tactic made. Kyle jumped down to the next rock while twirling the robe in his hand. He leapt again to the right while swinging the robe to his left. After landing, he crouched while bunching the robe up in his hands then tossed it ahead of him to the right while he jumped left.

Blood had just begun to slide off his forehead down into his eyes from the cut of the second arrowhead as the third one struck. This shaft whacked right into the rocks between Kyle and the place he'd thrown the robe.

Yay, I'm messing up his aim. ¡Olé!

But Kyle didn't need to matador-fake the archer any further by waving that robe like a cape, because he was now just one jump away from being able to dive straight into the pool. His body was arched in the air only feet above the water when the next arrow whizzed past his ear. Or at least, that's what he thought it was. And not, say, a horsefly.

But then he was in the pool and sliding on his belly down a skein of moss that coated the stones below the shore and thinking *I barely made it into the water, so angle those hands now like diving planes to take you out to the center* and feeling his stretched-out body move free and clear as it glided deeper into the center of the pool. He grabbed onto one of the scattered boulders that had been used to bury Rebecca's body just after he reached the bottom. This rock's weight ballasted his body's tendency to bob up. *I need to wait. He'll be disoriented if I fail to surface. He'll wonder if his last arrow killed me.... Yeah, but then when I absolutely must come up in order to take my next breath, which way do I go?* He hung onto the rock, sought to lower his heartrate, tried to tame a burning lust for more air. *Don't let yourself get any more excited, and you won't need a lot more oxygen. Ho-ho. Okay, while you're hanging out down here, trig the route of the arrows. They came from the downstream end. And their arc was dropping too, for such a short flight, so the archer must be on top of the berm on the far side of the Haul Road. If I surface by the waterfall, I'll be furthest away from him. And if I surface slowly, I'll...what? My head might resemble a rock? Get real. But you've got to surface anyhow, so might as well try to resemble a stone as you do it.*

He swam upstream at the bottom of the pool, and when it sloped to the white rill of foam at the base of the waterfall, he followed it to the surface. Kyle spun around so he was facing downstream and eased his head up just far enough to blow water out of his nostrils and suck in a breath. His eyes were drawn to a flutter of movement, he saw the limbs of a bush shake, then nothing. *Bet he thinks he nailed me. But lack of movement over there now might mean he's taking off. Not sticking around to make sure. I hope!*

Kyle dove under again, swam to the strip of sand, then cautiously clambered out. He sprinted across the road, going over to the bush he'd seen move. He was surprised to find a path behind it, not much more than a game trail. It looked like it took a route that ran straight up to the head of the canyon, cutting off every leisurely switchback formed by the road. *It's the path deer use when they want to get somewhere in a hurry, and not meet any human while they're going.*

As he looked around, he took a moment to tear a strip off the bottom of his shirt and knot it around his forehead to slow the bleeding from the arrowhead slash.

As he did, in a bare patch of dust on the path, he spotted a footprint made by a tire-tread sandal. The toe was pressed deeper into the ground, shoving up a small ridge of dirt. *He's running uphill. If I'm to follow, I'll need a weapon.* He gazed longingly across the pool, toward the spot where he'd dug the 'whacker up. *Take me too long to get it.* Searching for an alternative, he spied a pair of baseball-sized rocks, snatched them up and shoved them in his pockets. *Lot of good those'll do against an archer if he spots me coming. And what sort of fool won't take a gander back down the trail from time to time?*

Kyle began to jog up the hill. He alternated between watching where he put his feet and glancing as far ahead as possible, trying to discern any sign of an ambush. But he topped out of the canyon without difficulty then paused on the north-south reach of the Haul Road. He stood, looked, listened, yet could detect no further sign of a nearby human presence. *Now what? Did my attacker even cross over at this point? If so, where's his footprint? What's he heading for, and why?*

—

The collection of arboreal huts he came across was neither as large nor as elaborate as Treetown One. Yet it was substantial, about twenty trees were garlanded with cabins. Kyle supposed that it made no difference which door he knocked on first; in a community as tightly bunched as this place, all inhabitants would know within seconds that he had arrived. However, he didn't even need to knock. As soon as he put a foot on the nearest set of stairs, a window above him swung open and a head with dangling red dreadlocks leaned out.

"It's the dick from Elysian! Hey, what's up man?"

"Hi Red. This the place you call home?"

"Nah, I call all our Towns home, depending on who I aim to visit. You looking for me? After a rematch?"

"No time to fool 'round. Got some heavy news. Nearly had another killing at Bethesda Pool today."

"Yeah? Who?"

"Me."

"You dishin' it out, or takin' it on?"

"On the receiving team."

"Well-l-l, I do see that rag headband of yours shows a lil' color."

"Yeah. Worse news would be if I had brain matter leaking out. Can't spare me none o' that."

"You 'n' me both, brother. Come on up. Jade's here, she can doctor you."

At the top of the stairs Red held open a door, and Kyle entered a small room with its walls supporting an array of deer and elk antlers. From these horns hung furs, baskets, leather bags, and horse tack. The space was redolent with the smoky resin of cured hides. Sleeping hammocks were suspended from an oak limb that penetrated one wall, crossed the length of the room, then disappeared through the rough planks of the far wall. Hammock chairs—slings with woven armrests and woven backs—swung a foot or two off the floor, dangling from ropes knotted to ceiling joists. The door post had one thick peg jutting out of it, and from it hung a quiver made of otter fur that held an unstrung, sinew-backed bow and a half-dozen willow-shaft arrows fletched with barred hawk feathers. Kyle consulted his memory. The first arrow that had bounced off the rock in front of him had feathers of a pure black, taken off a raven or crow wing most likely.

Jade sat on the furs of a sleeping shelf and smiled at him, but a furrow of concern also nested between her dark eyebrows. Sally had completed Jade's "do" of tight braids and cornrows, and that plus her mix of African and Asian genetics gave her an exotic appearance that was multi-ethnic yet elusive as to origin. She could be as easily from Ladakh as Hawaii or Turkey.

"You hurt?" she said. "C'mere. Let's have a look."

She *tssked* after she unwound his impromptu bandage. "Now, that's what I'd call a close shave," she said.

"Right. Any closer, and I'd have a stick poking out of my eyeball. And I probably wouldn't be walking around too well. If at all."

"Well, any deeper and I'd try stitches. But I think I've got stuff that'll work, not quite as intrusive. Fish-skin glue and some sinew threads to hold it closed."

"You've done this before."

"Damn straight. I was an ER nurse in Ukiah before the Flare. And now being with the Tribe gives me tons of practice. Guys up here get hurt all the time."

While she worked on him, Kyle briefed her and Red about the recent attack on him at Bethesda Pool.

"You score a peep at the rascal who fired on you?"

"Nope. All I know for sure is he wears tire-tread sandals and ran up here to the Pale."

"Plus, he's a lousy shot."

"Thank God."

"Hey, thought you weren't no kind of believer."

"It's a figure of speech," Kyle said. "So, how many people up here are shod in tire-tread?"

Red shook his head, and his dreadlocks swayed. "Not many. We mostly favor mocs, like this knee-high kind I wear. Better for riding." He squinted at Kyle. "Tell me 'bout that 'whacker you found under the rock. Said it had a rune? 'Member what it looked like?"

Kyle thought about that, sketched a line with a triangle attached to one end in the air with a tip of a finger.

"Hmm. Wunjo-like. That'd be Ol' Deek's, maybe."

"What would Ol' Deek have against me? Or what might he have had against Rebecca?"

"Not much. Big thing to know about Deacon is the guy truly *is* old. Like, pushing eighty. Can't hardly see, nor hear so good, or even get around. But he done got plenty of stuff filched out of his place, over in Treetown Two."

"Yeah? Like what, and when?"

"A 'whacker. A knife. A bow. Mocs." Red arched his brows. "And... that would be a month ago. Back when your pal the scarecrow was spotted skulkin' around. Like I say, that boy is 'bout as popular up here as snakebite."

"The scarecrow?"

"Oh crap, you know who I mean—Ephraim."

Chapter 17

"How are you at tracking?" Kyle asked.

"Oh, I get after it," Red replied. "Not as keen as some rangers, but I do manage tolerable well."

"He's being modest," Jade said.

"Didn't know he had that in him."

Red shrugged.

"Seems to keep track of *me* pretty well," Jade said. "Don't hardly get time to myself."

"That's 'cos you motor-vate me," Red said. "Don't want no one else sniffin' after you too near."

"Except for Carlos and Sally," she reminded him.

"Well, yeah, them," he affirmed. "Goes without sayin'."

"Look, we need to light out after that guy who took a pop at me. Because when I consider the 'why,' I think he's got to be the same asshole who murdered Rebecca. Hated seeing me uncover clues. And when we look at the 'who,' it's most likely Ephraim. So, now I want to catch him, hold him down and beat the snot out of him until he tells us 'why.'"

"Count me in! I'm way on board with that," Red said.

"Me too," Jade said.

"Well, the only weapon I'm toting right now is a rock. Need to up my game. May I borrow your longbow, there?"

"Can you shoot it?"

"I've bow-hunted deer. Elk. Got a black bear, once. And you and I have a similar wingspan, so the draw should be good."

"'Kay. But where's that scary Arkansas Toothpick of your'n?"

"You mean, my Bowie? That's got a clip point, a Toothpick has a spear point, which is how you tell the difference. But anyhow, I left it up at the Cuadra, so I wouldn't scare the good folks down in Elysian. So, just loan me your bow until I get my survival rifle back from Carlos. Then I'll feel geared up."

"Carlos don't have your gun."

"Where is it?"

"Samuel and Ezra made us leave it with them, down in Elysian, that same day you met us."

"Shit."

"They told us that we've enough guns."

"And do you?"

"Not hardly."

"How many?"

"A few."

The sound of many thudding hooves rapidly approached, then ceased. There came a whinny of horses, then a shout: "Red! Get your bony ass down here! Need to talk to you!"

Red flapped open the window, and the heads of Kyle and Jade peered out right beside his. Carlos and four rangers appeared below them, all mounted on horses that snorted and pranced about, their bay coats striated by dust and sweat.

"What's got you bunch in such a godawful lather?" Red asked.

"Outsider weirdness," Carlos said. "Had some dude on a motorbike approach the Portal. Picked up a guy who jumped out of the brush, then turned around and scooted off without even talking to us."

Red and Kyle looked at each other.

"Ephraim," they said at the same instant.

—

A horse was found for Kyle. He felt disappointed it wasn't Penny, but it turned out to be a perfectly serviceable Morgan gelding. He rode along at the rear of the pack—and even some way behind, to keep rising clouds of dust out of his face. The otter fur bow quiver softly bounced against his spine.

They rode pell-mell for Treetown One, turned east down an access road that led to the Portal. Kyle loved the exuberance of a gallop, a chance to view some new terrain. But part of his mind continued to churn over what he knew and what he suspected about Ephraim. *Always felt that kid was furtive, mean, had some type of scheme working behind those shifty eyes. If he did slay Rebecca, now got to figure out why. Probably the usual reason! Wanted her, but she wouldn't have him. Found out she was inviting others to take a crack and it drove him nuts. Don't forget, he just now tried to kill me too! Death's his major solution. 'Course, he never took a shine to me. Antipathy ran both ways, as per usual. Yet it's clear the kid had big issues with social humiliation. Hyper. Not far from rage. If it was indeed Jimbo who rode off on the back of that motorcycle, where's he planning to go? Who will he be with?*

The Portal seemed barely worthy of the name. It wasn't much more than a flimsy board shack and a counter-weighted pole on a pivot that formed a barrier gate which could be dropped down to block a dirt road. Behind this shack a rickety picnic table lurched next to a rock fire ring with a scummy grill of blackened steel thrown over it. A large, speckled enamel coffee pot sat on the grill.

The rangers rode up, dismounted, and moored their horses to a hitching rail. A man posted to the guard shack exited the structure and walked toward them. "Moe and Jeff went by, ridin' hell for leather," he told Carlos. "Yelled out that you'd sent 'em down the road."

"Yep," Carlos said. "Did that. Won't catch up to any motorbike that's worth a damn, but maybe they can figure out where it's going."

"Strange as it is to see one a' them things," Red observed, "be even stranger if it was travelin' 'round up here on its own. Got to be part of a bigger passel of folks."

"Did you see the guy that bike picked up?" Carlos asked the Portal guard.

"Yeah, but I couldn't make him out real good."

"Kyle here," Carlos jerked a thumb in his direction, "had the thought it might be the scarecrow, Ephraim."

"Could of been. Gawky and thin, just like him."

"He took a few shots at me at Bethesda Pool little more than an hour ago. With a bow. Right after I found the 'whacker someone probably used to hit Rebecca, buried under a rock. Then he scampered over the ridge. Thought he was just running off. But maybe he's got something else in mind."

The face of Carlos clouded over. "Used to think the scarecrow was only an annoyance," he said. "Your suggestion that he's a lot worse, I find troubling."

"Makes sense to me, Chief," Red said. "Some barrels have no bottom to 'em. We've got us a real shit-u-ation. What you want us to do 'bout it?"

"Not much *to* do, till we figure out what's what."

"Send a rider to Elysian, maybe? Clue the Elders in?"

"Wait. After our scouts come back, we can send a more full and complete message." Carlos pointed a finger at the battered coffee pot. "Any go-juice in that thing?"

"The last of it," the Portal guard said. "And I added water to stretch it out. So, it's weak, kinda. Wouldn't so much as float a railroad spike."

"Might as well put it out of its misery, then. Got a cup?"

—

After Kyle grew bored with sitting around, he decided to string Red's bow. He pulled it out of its sleeve in the quiver. It looked to be made of Osage orange, with a laminate of deer sinew to award it more rebound power over a shorter length. He tucked the end of a limb in front of one ankle, stepped over it, and pushed back with his calf on the grip while pushing forward on the other limb. and slid the string up until the top serving popped into its groove. The amount of energy this took made him estimate the bow's pull weight as around seventy pounds at full draw.

He plucked out an arrow. It felt light, flexible. The business end was a flat wedge of sharpened steel lashed into the shaft with a winding of sinew threads gobbed with glue. He wondered if that flat head would plane in the air, throwing off his aim. Then as he examined the arrow's hawk-feather fletching he saw all three vanes were set at an angle to make the shaft spin. If the blade tried to plane, it should average out. *Good enough.*

For a target he selected a dry knothole on an old valley oak that stood about fifty yards off. He nocked the arrow and assumed a stance. Then he realized the chatter around the picnic table had faded to silence. He glanced back over a shoulder and realized all the rangers were openly watching. *Crap.* He groaned inwardly. *Just what you need—a highly critical audience.*

He took a deep breath, exhaled, raised the bow above his head and as he lowered it spread his arms to draw, taking in another breath as he did so. He sighted along the shaft, lined the head up with the string for windage, and used intuition to calculate the elevation. *Remember the big tip from Roy, you never choose when to shoot. You let aiming itself decide when to open your hand...*

His hand flew open and the whirling dot of the feathers leapt from the bow. A split-second later a few shards of wood spurted from the oak's knothole as the arrowhead buried itself dead center. Kyle heard footsteps.

"Aha. So, you suck at that too," Red said. "Let me see you do it again, with a lil' side bet. My bow against your knife. What do you say?"

Kyle gave him a tight smile. "You kidding? Dude, I plan to quit right now, while I'm still ahead."

———

They heard the rhythmic thunder of galloping horses drifting up to the Portal gate. Then the pair of mounted rangers who had ridden away to scout appeared. They slowed to a trot, hauled up at the hitching rail and hopped off.

"See anything?" asked Carlos.

"Caught up to 'em! And the bunch they're traveling with."

"Really?"

"Yep. And you just ain't going to frickin' believe it."

"Try me."

"That biker's with Cooper. And he's here with a whole goddam convoy."

"What?! Y'mean, Lieutenant Colonel Nathan Cooper, that bitch from the Elysians' southern compound?"

"Uh-huh. Him, exactly."

The mouth of Carlos formed a wide O of total astonishment. "You've got to be shitting me!" he exclaimed.

"No sir. Wish we was."

"Christ on a crutch. What's he after up here?"

"Didn't say. Only thing, he wants to meet us tomorrow morning at the gate, have a palaver with you, like."

Carlos narrowed his eyes. "How many people with him?"

"Thirty, forty men, that we saw. Hard to get a count, they were inside these big vans. Maybe women, kids there too."

"Huge honkin' vans, they was," the second scout confirmed.

"His boys armed?"

Red snorted. "Of course, they'd be friggin' armed, Chief! Never would've gotten their tails up here, otherwise. Their desert home is what, eight hundred miles south? That's a helluva stretch of bullshit to stride through, comin' up to us. Lotta roughnecks out there."

"Did you see Ephraim with them?" Kyle asked.

The rangers glanced at each other, then looked back at Kyle, puzzled.

"Y'mean, from Elysian? How'd he be out there?"

"Might've been the guy the motorcycle picked up near the gate."

"No, didn't see the scarecrow. Saw that scooter though, parked by the vans, that one the guard described. More of 'em were buzzing 'round. And yeah, all the guys had long guns slung over their shoulders. Semiautos, by the look. Big magazines sticking out of 'em. And sheathed machetes on their belts and whatnot."

—

As the sun set that day, the Tribe members gathered to confer at the base of the mighty oaks of Treetown One, high up on the ridge. They dined on roasted deer carcasses, and waved the succulent, dripping ribs of venison around to emphasize conversational points.

"That asshole and his whole damned crew didn't come up here just to visit, I'll 'test to that!" Red waved his rib vaguely eastward, then poked it back under his mustache so he could tear off another bite of venison with his teeth. "He sees this place as his, always done so." he asserted while he chewed. "Now I bet he plans to claim it."

"Yeah, but if he's just after a takeover, then why's he trying to talk?" asked a ranger with a long black braid hanging down his back. "Force that size and that mobile, could've just rammed the gate and slid on in. Surprise attack, like. What they used to call a blintz."

Carlos turned his hard, grey gaze on the man. "You really think that's what they used to call it, huh?" he scoffed.

"Well, he's asking for a talk to minimize casualties, probably," Kyle said. "Not your casualties, his. If he swept straight in, yeah, he might take over for a short while. But then he'd be surrounded by a lot of unhappy people. Any crew member he lost while bashing his way in couldn't be replaced. Then the sheer numbers of other folks here might make themselves felt, no matter what weapons he's got."

"So, what do you think? He's going to try to score the whole ball of wax by just yacking at us?" Carlos asked.

"He'll politely ask you to surrender."

The clump of Tribe leaders who sat cross-legged on the dirt swayed as they erupted into raucous laughter.

Carlos held up a hand. "Okay, so we don't. Then what?"

"He'll explain why you lose if you try to fight him. And throw in some other stuff, like he's an original follower of the Readers cult, and he bought title to this land himself years ago, and so forth. To establish his legit claim on the surface. But all of that's really just to put doubt in your mind."

"Nah, that's horsepucky!" Red shoved his rib through the air as if he were impaling someone on a spear. "Use it or lose it, you son-of-a-bitch. You ain't been around, for shit. All of us sure have. For a full ration of shit, 'n' more."

"It's called usufruct," Kyle said. "Land users acquire rights."

"What our college boy said." Carlos smiled. "Nowadays, possession is nine hundred and ninety-nine percent of everything. There's no law but that. And guess what, there's no sheriff in town but us."

"So, you *do* intend to fight the guy, then?" Kyle pointed his own rib at Carlos. "Because I agree with Red, Cooper did not drive a big convoy some eight hundred friggin' miles just to turn around and scurry back home at the first sign of trouble. In fact, Cooper might not have anything down there to go back *to*. Could be, his water at Pharaoh ran dry. Could be, his place recently got overrun by a much bigger, meaner bunch. What I'm saying is, he might not be feeling disposed to take 'no' for an answer."

Carlos nibbled on his rib for a moment. "Way I see it, there's one of two ways to go," he said. He shot a look at the black-haired ranger. "Either we *blitz* his ass at sunrise, tomorrow. Or we hold off and yack with him, just like he wants. I mean, we hit him with his 'no' right away, or we postpone long as we can, then lay it on him later."

"Buying time would be smart," Kyle said. "Gives you a chance to stage your response. Napoleon claims that in mountain warfare, defensive ops always have the best advantage. You've got mountains, so you may as well use them. And I bet you know this ground way-y better than Cooper does, so you ought to use that too. Need to offset his stash of weaponry somehow."

Carlos wiped drippings off the ends of his chin whiskers with the sleeve of his buckskin jacket. "Listen to this egghead!" he exclaimed. "Boasted that he taught philosophy. Now, what? You brag you're some kind of army history prof, too? Tell me, there anything you're not an expert on?"

"Not a brag. It's just that the main guy who taught me all my stuff had a great class, 'Logic in Warfare.' He said that military strategy ought to really be called the science of saving lives."

"Hell, yes. Just what we want! But our lives only, not his," Carlos said.

"Name of the game, exactly. And Cooper sits on the opposite of the board. Or as Patton said, you don't win a war by dying for your country. You win by making that other son-of-a-bitch die for his."

Red whooped and brandished the now-bare bone of his rib, then flung it over his shoulder and reached for another.

"How many guns do you have?" Kyle asked.

"Some," Carlos hedged.

"Like what?"

"With ammo? A Winchester 30.06, and a 12-gauge pump. Mossberg."

"That's it?!" Kyle made a face. "Okay, how about your guns without ammo, then?"

Carlos looked at Red.

"A .22 lever-action rifle, a .22 six-shooter, and a lil' .22 auto pistol," Red said. "They got used to a fare-thee-well, back in the day, once we had to feed ourselves after the Flare. No more goddam truck-runs to the store, know what I mean? But we done run plumb run out of bullets and parts. Stuff's real hard to trade for now, no matter who comes through."

"All right. I had a virgin brick of five hundred .22 longs in my duffle. But that got taken out, and Ezra likely has 'em along with my survival rifle down in Elysian, right?"

Red nodded.

"Have you sent a rider to Elysian yet?"

"Sure," Carlos said. "Had to clue 'em in sooner or later."

"And?"

"And what?" He looked irritated.

"You didn't ask for anything? Like, having a mob of those guys snatch up their farm tools and head back up this way?"

Carlos snorted. "As if rubes like them would be of any use at all in a fracas with Cooper's crew."

Kyle shook his head. "You people hope to keep this place? Need to make an 'all-hands-on-deck' style of response. Otherwise?" He turned the palms of both hands up and shrugged.

"Y'know, we might could send one more guy," Red suggested. "Beckon their men. And if he grabs those bullets of Kyle's, well then, we got us three more guns."

"Four," Kyle said. "I'd ask Ezra to send my AR-7, too." He looked at Carlos. "Even so, that's not enough. But I have an idea."

Carlos replied with a smile, but it was thin. "Guess you're full of 'em," he said. "Or, it."

"Hey. It's your fight. I'm only giving you my two-cents' worth."

"Either that, or you're now serving up your complete and entire three-penny stash. But go ahead." Carlos sighed. "Lay it on me."

"Your chat with Cooper goes well? Good. It'll buy us more time. But say instead, if it all turns to shit in a hurry, I'd suggest you have your best mounted rangers hidden out in the surrounding trees and brush with lances. At your signal, they charge. But they only gallop through his formation once, and when they do, they target guys holding the semiauto rifles. Your second wave is your quickest runners, male or female. They're right behind your cavalry horses, and their job is snatching up those rifles. Arm them only with knives, I'd say. To finish off the wounded, if needed. But their main aim should be to nab those guns. Get that weaponry back behind your lines, pronto. Every gun they lose is one you gain. It's a quick way to adjust the odds."

"C'mon! Thought you said that we should just take defensive positions, way, way back in the hills. Like Napoleon."

"Yes, you should do that. Right afterwards. But as you do, you'll need something to be defensive *with*. Because the paltry crap you've got for armament now just won't hold a line. No matter where you make a stand, he'll slice through like a hot knife through lard."

Carlos put one elbow on a knee and propped his chin in his hand. "Sounds like you want us to sacrifice our people right away, that's what it sounds like to me."

"Don't want it. Yet, if fighting breaks out, it'll happen anyway. Losses may have to occur for you folks up front. But do it in a way that means you lose many fewer, on the back end."

"Why should you care about it, either way? You're not one of us. What do *you* risk?"

"Whatever. Just let me point out one other option. You can make a decision that avoids wounds or dying for any Tribe member or Elysian. Which is, talk to Cooper tomorrow, and say that you'll turn over everything or anything he wants. Just lay down on your backs, stick your paws up in the air. Let him scratch your fuzzy little belly. Put a collar on you. But—let me ask—is that how you guys do business? Is that really the way you're made? That really how you want to go down?"

The Tribe men within the sound of Kyle's voice all looked at each other. He observed as their individual senses of outrage rose in might and fed upon each other's grunts of objection and looks of anger and so mingled and mixed together and began to almost assume a palpable shape, like a rising ocean wave. The Tribe was not only growing more unified, it was becoming far more intensely pissed off.

Chapter 18

Lieutenant Colonel Nathan Cooper sent a different message the next morning, via motorcycle. He demanded now that their meeting occur at the spot where he'd already set up his camp, a mile east of the Pale and its Portal. Carlos countered by insisting Cooper still drive up to the Portal gate, the first proposed site. Carlos threatened, if Cooper failed to appear there at the time Carlos set, the Tribe would not agree to any future meeting.

At first, it looked like Carlos won this gambit round. Cooper came up the road as if humbly displaying an intention to comply. But it soon grew clear he'd devised a show of force as a statement of his own. He came with his whole convoy, led by a growling trio of all-terrain trucks—Mercedes Unimogs with giant van bodies bolted onto their beds. These trucks rumbled up to the gate escorted by outriders on whiny dirt motorcycles. Those riders displayed rifles strapped in U-shaped mounts on their handlebars, near to hand and ready to grab. Bringing up the rear was convoy's most impressive vehicle, a fuel tanker truck, and in its cab the man riding in the shotgun seat cradled in his arms a literal shotgun. He had its barrel poking out of the window.

Kyle had planned to take a position with Red and the mounted Tribe rangers hidden back in the brush, and so observe all proceedings from afar. But Carlos surprised him by insisting that Kyle come to the table. "Some of what we'll try was your damn idea, guy," he said. "So, I think you ought to have a close-up view of how it works out. 'Sides, I want your opinion on Cooper. Sounds to me like you've got an opinion on just about everything anyway, and your take's bounden to be at least somewhat different from mine."

Up at Treetown, Kyle had borrowed a set of worn buckskins so he could blend in better with other Tribe negotiators at the table. He slung his small AR-7 across his back and threw the fringed jacket on over it. His gun would be close, just difficult to grab in a hurry. As he strolled up to the table with Carlos, he took mental stock of the force concealed in the woods behind him. *Calling it an order-of-battle would be a tad grandiose though, wouldn't it?* There was Red mounted on his favorite bay, with a lance slung across his shoulder on a strap and the Mossberg pump 12-gauge in his hand. The Tribe's best shooter had snuck across the road and was now posted at a hide on the hillside with the scoped 30.06 deer rifle.

Kyle's retrieved brick of .22 LRs had been broken open and he'd given a hundred rounds each to the rangers holding the Tribe's small-caliber arms, keeping the remaining bullets for himself. It wasn't much of a show, in comparison to Cooper's firepower. But a lot of other Tribe horsemen also held those long and keen lances. *Which could seem real goddam scary if they came right at you during a mass cavalry charge. Though we've got to hope there's not one. Should it happen, the massacre of the Light Brigade might look like a spring picnic.*

Carlos had assured them, one and all, that he saw use of force on Cooper as a last-ditch option, selected if Cooper sparked a fight off and left them no other choice. "Even then, I'd show everybody a signal that'll be clear and definite," he said. "I'll wave both arms at you-all, not just a hand, okay? And if you *don't* see that, then I want you just sitting tight and way out-of-sight, get me? Agreed? Everyone on board?"

A few yards away from the table Kyle and Carlos paused to watch the tanker truck driver gingerly fit its obese bulges into the last open patch left in the lot before the Portal gate.

"Likes to travel equipped, I'd say," Carlos said. "A man with his own gas station!"

Kyle watched the driver jump out of the cab. His passenger, however, did not step down, but up. He planted a foot on the hinge of his open door, levered himself up onto the truck's hood, then sat down on the roof of the cab. The butt of his shotgun rested on one thigh while its barrel pointed casually up toward the clouds. It was a prime shooting perch for someone armed with a riot gun.

"And that's not all," Kyle said, pointing. "Got their man positioned right there, to prevent pigeons from flying over to speckle all their shiny stuff with any bird crap."

"Roger that," Carlos said.

"Still content, are you," Kyle inquired, "to head into this talk unarmed?'

"I'll take my 'whacker and my blade." Carlos shrugged. "But my real plan is to intimidate 'em with the power of my stare."

Coopers' outriders stopped their bikes. A few men clad in mismatched bits of camo uniforms dropped out of the doors of the parked Unimogs as their diesels ceased to rattle at nearly the same instant. The sudden onset of silence called attention to itself, like the opposite of a trumpet blast.

Two men strode in loose cadence toward the Portal's guard shack. Then an older man swung down from the cab of the lead truck to walk along in the wake of this marching pair. The whole trio was directed by the guard to go around to the picnic table. As they approached, the young men in the lead did not appear to be armed. But the older gent who followed them was distinguished by more than a confident stroll and his solid-black fatigues. The butt of a large pistol with ivory grips projected from his left hip in a cross-draw holster supported by a Sam Browne belt.

His escort personnel separated, moving to either end of the plank table. Lt. Col. Nathan Cooper came forward with his hand outstretched.

Carlos didn't even stir an arm. "Let's save handshakes for afterwards, Colonel," he said. "I mean, when and if we get near to something we agree on. Otherwise let's just sit and yack. Hear what you've got to say for yourself."

They sat. Cooper laced his fingers and plonked his paired fists on the table. "That's not such a kind greeting," he said. "Sad way to treat a man who's been your landlord for many years. And never in that time has he tried to dun you for compensation, or a payment of any rent."

Kyle studied him. Cooper had a narrow face, huge schnoz, cupped ears—the man indeed did look like Ephraim's sire. *Guess the genes for that appearance aren't just dominant,* Kyle thought, *they're protuberant!* But Cooper had done his level best to reframe the visual curse, growing out a mane of black-dyed hair that had been gelled and feathered back around his wing-like ears, and a salt and pepper beard shaped to produce the look of a stalwart chin, something that might counterbalance the mighty prow of his nose.

Carlos smiled at Cooper's gibe and shook his head. "We're in a changed world. Once upon a time, a guy could buy a hunk of ground and keep hold of it without living on it," he said. "What, ten years ago? Different reality now, dude. Any piece of paper you got that says you have rights here would be best used to light up a cigar. If you handed it to me, I'd use it to wipe my butt."

Cooper emitted a long sigh of forbearance. "You look at this in the wrong way, my friend. It's not simple human affairs that we discuss here today. This concerns the Writ Readers' covenant with our Lord. All land is ultimately His, to distribute as He sees fit. No mere mortal may ever deny His promise of sacred ground to His Chosen."

"A fantasy like that carries even less weight than a sheet of paper." Carlos chuckled. "Might sell a fairy tale to your troops, but we're a mile off from ever buying in. Sad fact for you to face is that you went to the trouble of making such a tail-busting trip up from the desert for absolutely friggin' nothing. Now you've got to turn about and go home. Sorry, but we just can't help you."

Kyle shifted his gaze to Cooper's guards standing at ease at each end of the table. Maybe they were unarmed, but over their camo shirts they wore vests that looked like they held ballistic plates—either steel or ceramic. He tried to read the expression on their faces: stern, emotionless resolute. They saw him looking yet refused to meet his eyes. *Hey. They both resemble Ephraim. So, are these Cooper's sons, too? How about all the other troops? Is that even possible?* He turned his attention back to Cooper. His back, shoulders and chest seemed bulkier than was likely for a man of his slim build. *He's wearing a vest too,* Kyle decided, *something lighter, under his fatigues. They want to appear as if they've come to talk. Yet they also look prepped for a rumble. Is that because they plan to initiate one?*

"Hate to say this, but you're an awful negotiator, friend," Cooper said. "We come, hands out in greeting, prepared to offer our support to all that can be achieved up here. We're ready to get along with you in a brotherly way. Yet instead of gratitude, we find suspicion. Instead of a hospitable response, we get hostility. You should pray over this, then rethink your position."

"Y'know, the colonel's kind of right," Kyle said.

Carlos turned an astonished face to Kyle. He raised an eyebrow while giving Kyle's ankle a sharp kick beneath the table.

"We should open our talks with a small issue, not try to decide right away whether or not they can begin to live within the Pale," Kyle continued. "I mean, that's a tough topic! So, what if we try to make headway on something else? An ice breaker. A trust-building exercise." He looked at Cooper. "For example, we believe you have a person in your convoy who may have killed a young lady from Elysian. He ran out past the Pale, looks like he joined you people yesterday. We want to question him, a skinny kid by the name of Ephraim James. Do you have him?"

"If you refer to Ephraim Cooper, my son, yes, he is now fully under our protection." Cooper's face hardened. "And he's told us *quite* a tale about how all of you here have attempted to frame him for this so-called murder. No wonder he ran off! The way you've been trying to railroad that poor lad is shameful. Gross miscarriage of justice."

"Well, then. Sounds like there's grounds for some type of debate or hearing on the matter," Kyle said. "Hey, so, what if we had one? Can you bring Ephraim out here now for that?"

Cooper went wide-eyed as he opened and closed his mouth a few times, stunned by the impudence.

Carlos grinned, finally catching on to what Kyle was up to. Pin down Ephraim as the probable murderer of Rebecca, and the validity of Cooper's claim of any right to enter the Pale would shrink. His outfit could stand revealed as a gang of self-righteous thugs, nothing more.

"Great," Carlos said. "Let's get that settled, then we can toss out a few alternatives I mean, our turf just isn't a great fit. Elysians, well, they're all just a bunch of leaf-munchers, while you guys are total carnivores by the look of you. And our lot up on the Pale, well, we lack discipline. Never much cottoned to it at any point in our lives. While you guys look as if you try to impose military order up and down the line. Know what? You ought to go and hit places that have stuff you want. Not us. We can't even refuel your trucks. Got us no metal here, or guns, bullets. Nothing in the way of canned goods. Can barely eat decent. Hey, I've got it! While you're at peak strength, why not take over some town in the Sacramento Valley? A place where you can rule over a big swath of farm or ranch land. Put it back in production. Do that, and I think you'll end up way happier."

The flummoxed look on Cooper's face became replaced by a flush of anger. He had just opened his mouth to reply when a loud clang and a pained yell came from the lot by the Portal gate. A motorcycle and its rider had fallen over. He thrashed on the ground, as if wounded.

Cooper leapt to his feet. "What the hell?" he snarled. "Ambush? Under a flag of truce?"

"Hey, no worries," Kyle said. "I bet that idiot just forgot to put his kickstand down."

He glanced at Carlos and they both stood up as well.

"Truce?" Carlos looked puzzled. "We didn't even declare—"

Cooper swiftly drew his white-handled automatic, snapped its slide with a swipe of his left hand and aimed the cocked pistol's sights at a point between the silver eyebrows that garlanded the forehead of Carlos.

Carlos flung up both arms and yelped, "No! Don't shoot!"

"Wait, don't, that's your signal!" Kyle said, alarmed.

A spatter of small arms fire broke out. One more motorcyclist flopped over. A startled, dumbfounded look spread over the face of Carlos as he realized his error and instantly dropped his arms back to his sides. But Cooper mistook that move as a grab for a weapon. He pulled the trigger, his handgun boomed, and a .45 slug plowed a tunnel through the skull of Carlos, blowing a geyser of red and grey and black and brown out across the turf as the man himself was swatted over onto his back.

Before the body of Carlos even completed its transformation into a limp heap, Kyle launched himself at Cooper, tackling the colonel around his waist. They hit the ground together and began wrestling for control of the pistol. Kyle got both hands around the wrist of Cooper's gun hand and whacked his knuckles hard against the bench. The gun flew out of Cooper's grip and sailed off. But then the pair of guards were on top of Kyle, punching and kicking him. The toe of a boot thumped into his head. His vision narrowed to a fuzzy, wavering dot.

After what seemed like a long while, his senses cleared. He heard the beat of galloping hooves and a cacophony of gunshots. He found he could scarcely move, then realized the plank table had been flipped over on top of him and he writhed out from under its weight.

He emerged into chaos. The Portal area was a mad swirl of dust cut by the sharp reek of burnt powder, a roar of engines, the whinnying of horses and the sharp cries of men. Kyle whipped off his jacket, unlimbered the AR-7, snapped its bolt and looked for targets. The distinctive boom of a shotgun drew his attention to the tanker truck, and he put four rounds into the shooter on top of the cab.

A horse thundered by almost at his elbow and he saw Red flash past with his lance lowered and a woman sprinting right behind his horse. Amazingly, she held onto the end of that horse's tail and ran with such high, gliding steps that she seemed almost to levitate. Red skewered a man holding a rifle who stepped around a Unimog truck to confront him. The woman let go of the tail and snatched up that fallen man's gun while Red wheeled his mount around to gallop back the way he'd come. He hooked an arm and swung the woman up onto the saddle behind him.

Kyle waved at Red, who seemed to recognize him despite the enveloping murk of smoke and dust. He reined and spurred the horse his way. Kyle knew a good trick once he'd seen it perform well in action. He slung his AR-7 back over his shoulder and seized the horse's tail as it went by. In a second, he was running over rough terrain at the same speed as the animal. He stumbled and nearly dropped off, but then saw the right technique was not to try to make strides, but simply bounce up off the ground and let the horse yank him forward.

They made it back into the fringe of trees, where Red pulled his mount up. As the foam-flecked horse rolled its eyes and snorted, Kyle let go of the tail and the horse spun around and danced right past him, nearly stepping on his foot. Kyle jumped back and saw that woman behind Red on the horse was Jade. Her face was tawny with dust, striped by sweat, and her whole body trembled. Her eyes darted about even more than the horse's. Just one part of Jade remained still—her fists. She gripped the semiautomatic rifle she'd snatched out of the dying hands of the Cooper guy Red had speared, clutched it with whitened knuckles as if it were the holy grail or the key to the future and the Tribe's lifeline or perhaps all three. An object on which everything depended. A prize that had made the bloody attack worthwhile.

Then Kyle saw another reason why Jade's gaze shifted back-and-forth at such a pitch. She was watching other Tribe men and women coming up through the woods past them, some sprinting themselves or bent low over the backs of vigorously leaping horses. Another pair on foot appearing toward the rear, one staggering along as he leaned on the shoulders of a stumbling other, both these people clearly wounded.

"Where the hell's Carlos?" Red shouted as he fought to keep his horse from galloping off again.

"Dead! Cooper shot him!"

"Fuck!!"

"Let's get out of here! Get further up into the Pale. We need to regroup."

"What about all these others?"

"When they see us go, they'll follow!"

"IF they see us!'

"Put up a yell, come on all three of us shout, fall back, fall back, fall back!"

Chapter 19

On the road that led from the Portal up to Treetown, a sweeping curve cradled a broad log-landing, fringed by a grove of blue oaks that cast a lacework of shade. Here, survivors of the Tribe's impetuous charge gathered to take stock of the results.

Jade slid down off the back of Red's horse and stood there, gripping the black and silver rifle while she watched the Tribe's survivors assemble in ragged knots on the landing around her. She seemed frozen in place until Red tapped her on the head and beckoned for the gun. She made a brief, embarrassed grimace, handed him the rifle, then jogged over toward the closest group of people.

Kyle had endured too many attempts to bound up rock slopes, leap through brush and over fallen logs while trying to cling to a horse's tail. Levitation that seemed easy on level ground became an insuperable chore in the woods. He'd let go of the tail a hundred yards back, and now jogged up over a berm and into the clearing. He saw Jade walk over to another horse that stood with quivering, crimson-streaked haunches, then watched as she helped slide a limp Tribesman off that animal's back.

He saw Red swing a leg off his bay and drop to the ground and loop his horse's reins around an elbow. He went up to him.

"Red! That a total shit-show, or what?"

"Why'd Carlos give that goddam signal right then?" The cheeriness that had been Red's most reliable characteristic was not in evidence, displaced by grim rage. "You guys had just started your palaver. We got took by surprise. And I mean, total!"

*Should I tell him Carlos made that signal by mistake? That he for-
got it was even a signal? Oh, what's the point...no one ever knows
how he'll act if some nutcase aims a cocked and loaded gun at him...
like that boxer once said...we've all got a plan till we get punched in
the face. And what Carlos did and why he did it makes no difference
now. Whole scene was a powder keg. Any spark could've blown it sky-
high. Result would be the same as what we confront now. As Roy told
us, if you don't face the facts, you're looking in the wrong direction.*

"Doesn't matter," Kyle said.

"Hey, Kyle." Red's eyes were bereft and beseeching. "Know what?
I keep thinking Carlos will ride up here any sec' now to say what
it is we have to do next. Crazy, huh?"

*Man, I beat you on that feeling by weeks. Roy only visits me now
when I try to dream him up, or if he decides to haunt me.*

"Well," Kyle prompted, "what do you think Carlos would say, if
he were here?"

"He'd..." Red's eyes watered. "Well, he'd prob'ly say, 'Got to fling
some crap back on these apes!'" He gestured wildly. "Ram a damn
pick handle right through their wheel spokes. Bring 'em up short."

"And what's the best way to do it?"

"Well." He pondered. "Those big-ass rigs they drive. Need roads
for 'em. Even their bikes. Can't handle much else. So, block our
road." Red cocked his right arm and dropped it from the elbow.
"Just fall some trees over it."

"Don't imagine you've got chainsaws. But plenty of axes, right?"

"Few."

"And some guys to swing 'em?"

"Uh-h-h..."

"Best to tally whom you've kept and those you lost. Who needs
a splint and bandages, and who's still able to fight. Count 'em up
and that'll help you decide what you have to do next."

"Oh, act like I'm in charge."

"More than act, Red. You've been a great number two. But your
Tribe has no number one now. So, down to you. Time to step up."

Kyle's eyes were drawn to a movement. A long black feather twirled as it fluttered down from an oak. A raven had cawed
and taken flight, dropping a tail feather in the process. Red's eyes
tracked Kyle's, to see what he was staring at. Red looked forlorn,

as if hoping fresh answers might also float down from the oak branches like that spinning, indigo plume—or as if he longed to sprout wings himself, leap from a perch and fly off from the brutal mess. *He's jittery, unsure. Red's sweet spot might be his emotions, but right now they just won't settle enough to give the man any purchase. He needs to focus…. Well, that's him. And me? How do I feel? What's this grand screw-up and pile-on doing to me? Oddly enough, I'm enthused, exhilarated! No, that's not it. There's a power, but it's something calm and clear and fierce, and it's very much like no emotion at all. A total absence of them, a presence of what…. Resolve? I don't itch for conflict, but I won't knuckle under to these goons. Must I dominate them, then? Sure. Sounds arrogant yet doesn't feel so. It's just that I refuse to be beaten in any way, shape or form by a gang of such nasty bitches. But do I want to dive into a mess with the Tribe and the Elysians and scrum with Cooper and his crew? Might be bad for my health. Instead, I could seize upon this moment of chaos quite easily, snag a horse and a bunch of gear and simply light out. Ride for home and Luz Maria. Be lo-o-o-ng gone before anyone missed me. So, why should I see this as my fight? Maybe I shouldn't.*

Red leaned the silver and black rifle against his leg and pulled the pump shotgun off his back by its sling. His movements were slow, deliberate, as if he just needed to be doing something with his hands and wished to make a mundane task last for as long as possible.

Kyle pointed at the Mossberg. "Why didn't you use that down there?" he asked.

"Did. Got one round off, then the sucka' jammed."

"Let me see."

After he handed it over, Kyle pushed the release button and tried to work the pump. It didn't move much, but enough for him to spot a ring of green corrosion on the base of a shell in the magazine. "Hell yeah, of course it jammed," he said. "Where'd you keep this ammo, in a barrel of saltwater?"

"We saved stuff for a 'mergency," Red mumbled. "But I guess we didn't save it so well, huh?"

Kyle handed it back.

"Might work, you clean it all up. Now let me look at that rifle she grabbed…. Okay, this is a Ruger Mini-14, stainless works, synthetic stock. Tough piece, what they used to call a ranch gun. Short barrel, iron sights, looks like a twenty-round magazine. And, jeez, got a live round chambered and the safety's not on. Can't believe Jade rode with it that way. Good she didn't blow your damn head off! See this blade at the front of the trigger guard? Pull it in and the safety's good. Anyway. Wonder how many other Minis we managed to snatch out of their hands."

Kyle handed the rifle back. Red hefted it, shouldered it, peered through the sights at an oak trunk. "Pow, pow, POW!" he exclaimed. He suddenly looked happier. "Y'know, you're right. We got us a few of these, we're in better shape. I should go count 'em up."

"Great."

"What about you?"

"Let me take your horse. I'll scoot up to Treetown. Where I left the longbow I got from you. Still a use for it. Might be able to snipe from the brush, take a bastard down without tipping off another. And I'll grab some axes too, so we can knock down trees, make roadblocks in just the way you said. Plus, I'll send a messenger down to Elysian, let those people know what happened, and maybe find out what the Elders have for a plan. Or IF they have one."

"All right." Red peered at him. "And it's what you'll do, for true, Kyle Skander? Not just scoot your tail off to any place else?"

"It's what I'm going to do."

"So, Asshat Cooper. What's he up to?"

"Like us, licking wounds. Regroup, take stock. Figure what might work best for him." Kyle shook his head. "My big don't-know is how Cooper managed to score his giant assets, kept his mitts on such awesome crap for so long. Okay, once upon a time he embezzled from the Air Force. But damn, *what?* The dude sold F35 software to the Chinese? But I'd say this, if he keeps trying to force his way in, it's because he thinks he's got no place else to go."

"Nah. I'd say, he reckons it's his already. Claim's been staked, man. Up to us to persuade him otherwise."

Chapter 20

Red's bay was nearly as excitable as its owner. Keeping the horse pointed up the road and its mind on business was a chore that consumed most of Kyle's attention. *'Course, he's still jacked up from that galloping charge and a battle, plus I'm a strange rider. I'd bet, Red loans him out almost never. Feels like I'm trying to keep my seat astride a squirmy lightning bolt. Might spook at anything, leap in any direction. As likely to go over the berm into a gulch as to jump uphill or off into the woods.*

But Red's bay also was nimble and fast. *I'll get there in minutes.* As Kyle thought this, the horse did abruptly spook, performing a high buck coupled with a sideways crow-hop. For a second he was weightless, afloat, only vaguely connected to the horse by the reins in his left hand and a handful of mane hair clutched in his right, a purchase that he'd been able to snatch at the last split-second by pure instinct.

But he could pull himself somewhat closer to the horse's back by hauling on its mane. Then *bang!* the animal came down hard on all four hooves and Kyle's butt slammed back into the saddle. Next came a frantic dance as the bay tried to sprint away either up or down the road and Kyle fought to defeat that impulse by keeping the horse spinning in circles. Soon, the horse—either tired of making all the turns or growing dizzy from them—just halted in its tracks with snot drooling from its muzzle and its ribs heaving like a bellows.

Which is when he finally saw what spooked the bay—a grey-haired woman who was clad in a buckskin dress stained dark with blood from neckline to hem. She stood swaying up on the road berm, then stumbled as she came down to the road surface. Her bloody right arm dangled uselessly. With her left hand, she dragged a silver rifle by its barrel.

Kyle dismounted, wrapped the reins around a forearm, led the horse toward her.

"Sally?" he asked. The woman appeared as if she might be Carlos' wife and Jade's partner, whom he'd met on his first day at Treetown.

She sank wearily to her knees, released her grip on the gun. She offered him a wan smile that included a tiny nod of recognition. Then she flopped over and planted her face in the dirt.

———

Kyle entered the grove of Treetown One, jogging beside Red's bay and leading the horse with a hand through the cheek strap of its bridle. He'd tried going in front and holding the reins but kept getting his calves and heels clipped by the front hooves of the excitable animal. Also, jogging by the horse's neck, he could push Sally back onto the saddle whenever she began to slip off—which had been often.

Many Rangers had galloped all the way back to Treetown amid their retreat. Some of these now ran toward him as soon as they saw him approach.

"Get a blanket! Bring Sally inside!"

"Bound her up as well as I could," Kyle told them. "But she must've lost a ton of blood. Be great if you could get her to drink some water."

A huge, dark shape loomed at his elbow—Samuel.

"Some fightin' already, huh?" he said. "My ass shoulda been out there!"

"Don't worry," Kyle assured him. "This crapola is not going to pass anyone by. It's just starting. What's happening in Elysian?"

"Elders been chewing over all the sketchy reports. Sent me up to fact-find."

"They plan to send a force, too?"

Samuel snorted. "What? Bunch of field hands swinging rakes?" He pointed at Ruger Mini-14 that Sally had brought, now slung beside Kyle's survival rifle on his back. "Against that? Stuff I just heard Cooper's guys are armed with? No way in hell!"

"So, what's another option?"

Samuel walked beside him as Kyle led the horse toward a watering trough, a V of rough planks fed by a pipe that led down from a spring. Samuel moodily swung one end of his staff at clumps of grass.

"Elysian has a contingency plan," Samuel said. "A refuge spot we call Forest Camp. It's a hideout in the woods, up on the Gilead middle fork. Place was set up, with supplies, just in case a day like this ever came."

"Okay. But still just a temporary solution," Kyle said.

"Right."

"Ephraim probably knows about it."

"He does."

The horse plunged its muzzle down into the water trough and began to slurp in several gallons without ever coming up for air.

"We can guess what Cooper has in mind," Kyle said. "His outfit is built for movement in a block, centered around his vehicles. Must stick to roads and trails. Main goal must be seizing structures. He came from a long time spent at a compound. So, that's the kind of thing he knows and sort of place he'll want to go to. My bet is he plans to seize Elysian and use it for a base. Reach out from there to strangle your ensuing resistance. No matter where you're hiding."

"We might not make it so easy for him. Never seen people in Elysian lookin' so pissed."

"Yeah, we're down to all or nothing. Big mess to dealt with, 'fore it ever resolves."

"Need to stick that mess mostly on him!"

"Exactly. But 'how's' the hard part."

"Always," Samuel said.

Roy's military strategy class, 'Logic in Warfare,' was our last class on Fridays—his last to teach and my last to take. Afterward, we'd squint into the afternoon sun as while we strolled a causeway bridge that ran from campus over to Arcata's old downtown district. We'd go to a familiar green bench beside the statue of President McKinley in the town square. We'd sit, Roy would haul his traveling chessboard out of his coat pocket, unfold the thing, snap its magnetic pieces into place, plop the board down on the bench between us and then hold out both fists, in one of which nested a white pawn, and in the other a black.

No matter which I picked, whether I opened our game or didn't, he'd whup me up one side of the board and down the other. Not for a second did I ever consider it likely I might win. Roy beating me at chess was a universal constant, our personal law of gravity. Only way I hoped to improve was to advance in the max number of moves I made before I got crushed. Getting at least one move further along in the game, like anywhere past a dozen, felt like a type of victory to me.

My grand improvement in play came on the day that Roy told me, "Y'know, Kyle, you think way too hard about not making a mistake. That's an important part of any struggle. But it mainly belongs in Part One. Basically, where Sun Tzu hangs out. With chess, you're already in Part Two. Then it's time to commit, to execute. And then, too much thinking proves a liability if it slows you down. Be defensive, if both your terrain and your situation suit you, as they did Henry at Agincourt. Otherwise, consider that a bold offense can be a strategic theme. Think, boxing technique. Keep your enemy rocked back on his heels and you need not worry about what he might be thinking. Make him so busy reacting to you he can't think...straight, anyhow! This was part of the usual game plan for Alexander, Hannibal, Napoleon, Sherman, Patton and Rommel.

"A key for making boldness work is not letting yourself get all worked up about the chance of making a mistake. Don't fret about that during the execution phase. Because there always shall be mistakes, and the faster and harder you go, the more there'll be. If you make a mistake and you get paralyzed by the thought you might make another, then, brother, you are toast. Instead, always follow a parry with a thrust. Make an opponent pay for your mistake by forcing him into still more mistakes of his own. But never expect or even hope for a game of zero mistakes by anybody, you especially.

"Y'see, in chess, the winner is always he who makes the next-to-last mistake."

"Kyle? Kyle? Hey, you with me here?"

"Uh-h sure, Sam. You were saying?"

He looked up. Kyle realized he must've been staring a long while down at his own feet. Red's bay was tugging on its reins, watching him with eyes wide and ears up as a long pink tongue licked drops of water off its muzzle.

Samuel was looking at him with both eyebrows raised on a wrinkled forehead. "I was asking you if the Tribe had made a plan? You know, anything I can tell Elysian about."

"Right. Well, Cooper's force is strong. Well-equipped. But it's relatively small, so he must hope to keep it united. Which means, we want to make it split. One way is to let them get up to Treetown, then lure them to send some people south toward the Cuadra while keeping part of the force at Treetown, or—best case scenario—lure some north on the Haul Road. Pull that off, and we can maybe pick a few more of their guys off. But they'll try to regroup, and their main force must come into Elysian on the Haul Road, no way around that. A natural choke point on the road is formed by that rock knoll above Bethesda Pool. Where the watchnest is? Great place to roll some boulders down on them, slow their trucks, maybe inflict casualties."

Kyle paused, looked back down at his feet. He sketched a curving line in the dust with his toe.

"But we still want them to come into Elysian. Make it look deserted. Let them take it over. Allow them to relax. Let them think, goal won, victory achieved, all of that."

He tapped his toe on the ground.

"Which is the moment when we attack. We not only have Tribe rangers and Elysian people concealed in the woods and hollows around the village. We even have top fighters hidden in secret spots in buildings within the village. Trojan Horse in reverse, see? That way, we can hit 'em from two directions at once. A pin and a skewer. Total surprise." He tapped his toe again, looked up at Samuel. "Our best and biggest chance. It works? Game over!"

Samuel had an eyebrow arched. He looked skeptical, not bewildered. "Red. He done come up with all of that?"

"Nope. I did."

"Oh. 'Scuse me for asking, but who put you in charge?"

"I'm *not* trying to take charge, Samuel. Those are just logical ideas. Doesn't matter who voices them. We should do what makes the most sense. Right?"

"Right. But how 'bout, did Red agree to it?"

"Haven't told him. Thought it up just now. Been rather busy. Still am! Got to gather some axes and hatchets and whatnot, send a crew down to fell trees across the access road. Pick up my bow quiver. And speaking of weapons, you want to check out this bad lad?" Kyle swapped the reins to his other arm, lowered his shoulder and shrugged a rifle sling off his shoulder. He handed Samuel the Ruger Mini-14 that a severely wounded Sally had dragged up onto the road. "Can you shoot one of these pups?"

Samuel propped his staff against the horse trough and took the rifle up reverently in both hands. "Well, shit-howdy!" he said. He looked at Kyle. "Course," he said. "Y'know, I was in the Marines a year."

"Just one? What happened?"

"Other-than-honorable." He rolled his massive shoulders. "Had me a fracas."

"So?"

"Guy that lost, ranked. Wore more stripes." His scarred lips bent in a smile under his dented nose. He eyed Kyle. "Truthfully? A bunch more."

"And?"

"Pissed me off. I kicked his behind."

"How come you could bail out of the Devil Dogs then, 'stead of being tossed in the brig?"

"That, uh, incident…took place in what Popeye would call a house of ill repuke. Brass just wanted to make it go away."

Kyle cocked his head. "Kind of miss that, don't you? Kickin' ass, takin' names."

"Well…yeah."

"Okay. Here's your new weapon, rifleman. Take it down to Elysian. Hide till they get there, then jump out. Shock the utter tar out of those idiots."

"Wait. You're giving me this gun?!"

"Why wouldn't I?"

—

Kyle galloped back down the road to the log landing, heading up a herd of many other thudding hooves. A squad of Tribe rangers rode right behind, each man with an ax lashed abaft of his saddle. They found a landing crowded with equine and human bodies. Yet the space also boasted an aspect of organization that it'd lacked earlier. People on impromptu pallets were now lying in an orderly row in the shade. Any that lacked bandages so far on their wounds were undergoing treatment by Jade and a roaming team of care givers. Red and another ranger moved through the people still up and able-bodied to divide them into groups.

Kyle hauled the bay down to a walk, whoa-ed him to a halt right next to Red, got off and handed him the reins.

"Your dude is quite the handful," Kyle said. "But we got it done."

"Glad things worked out for you. See, he don't play all that nice with all that many."

"What's his name?"

"Spooky."

"Fits as tight and right as your own handle does! So hey, look here, brought you some faller-fellers." Kyle gestured to the handful of rangers behind him. "Ought to get 'em chopping away soon, I'd say. What's your story here?"

"Three dead or missing. Nine wounded, but Jade says they look like they're all going to pull through."

"Boost that figure to ten. I ran across Sally, up the road. She managed to grab one of their guns, but she herself didn't look so good. They're trying to patch her back together up at Treetown."

Red looked grim. "Sad to hear it. Sally done good, snatchin' us a gun. Takes our tally up to four Mini rifles! Reckon that means, least four a' their shits won't be a bother us no more, too."

"You had time to think up a battle plan?"

"Bits 'n' pieces. You?"

"In general? My idea is, always give Cooper the opposite of what he seems to want. Slow him down if he tries to speed up, and vic-ey-versa. Wants to stick together, break him up. Tries to split up, push 'em back into a clot."

"How?"

"What it comes down to, huh? First is the slow-down. Blocking the road will help. But I think, we need to fall the tree *crowns* onto road, not the trunks, since those'll take him longer to saw through. After that, got to tempt him. He'll have a hair up his butt about coming after the Tribe due to this morning's fight, no question. I think the bad news is, we'll have to let him take Treetown. Because he'll really, really want to. But as soon as he does, lure his guys away. Like the Indians did. Display some easy targets who retreat. When his guys give chase, ambush 'em, and use a U or L formation. I'd say, work your first fade over in the direction of the Cuadra, because he'll never get his big rigs over that footbridge. Gives you a natural escape route.

"Next, we need to tempt him north on the Haul Road. It's the direction he'd prefer to charge anyhow. Let him run free as far as the knolls above Bethesda Pool, but roll some rocks into the road to slow him down there. After his folks emerge to clear those, roll some more down on his head. I still expect they'll get through and try to occupy Elysian by nightfall. And...I just saw Samuel up the road, not ten minutes ago. He said the Elders plan to evacuate to Forest Camp, on your creek middle fork."

"Know it," Red said.

"I suggested Sam and a few buddies hide inside Elysian. Everybody else sneaks up and surround the town after Cooper takes it. Then at a signal, we all attack from the inside and outside, at the same moment. Let's say, sunset."

"Cool." Red nodded vigorously and his dreadlocks swung, seconding the motion.

"Great." Kyle eyed him. "Well?"

"Well, what?"

"Will you give those orders?"

"Me? Those ideas are yours!"

"Yeah. And I try to lay 'em on your guys, they might get rejected, 'cos they come from an Outsider. Job is yours, pal. Not only that. Not just about the actions. Morale is a huge item, too. You need to mix in a big rah-rah speech, along with your orders. Get everyone jacked up. Don't only tell them how they're going to win, explain why they've got to give it their all."

"Durn. What should I say?"

Kyle rolled his eyes. "Red! What do you think? You folks are fighting for your homes. Game is for all the marbles. Look at the prospect of losing everything you've labored for, year after year. To a pack of goons like Cooper's band. What's your heart tell you?"

"All right, all right. I get it." Red took a deep breath, heaved it out as a sigh. "What're you going to do, then?"

"I'll run down with the falling crew to block the road." Kyle tapped the otter-skin quiver that he'd retrieved and slung over his shoulder beside the AR-7 during his quick visit back to Treetown. "Then I'll scout out Cooper's bunch, see how they're shaping up. See if I can make them nervous by ventilating one or two. And that'll start our payback for Carlos.

"Get that done, I'll come find you and report. After, you want to arrange the ambush toward the Cuadra, I'll bring some of your guys north to set up the ambush at Bethesda Pool."

"Deal." Red thrust out his hand. "And by the way, here's something you're going to like. Dale got shot in the knee. Jade says he'll live, be okay, but right now he can't ride."

Kyle looked mystified. "Come again?" he asked, as he gave Red's hand a short, firm clasp.

"Dale? He's the guy what owns Penny. Says it's all jake with him, you want to use her as your mount now."

—

After frenzied bouts of ax swinging, the ranger crews dropped a half-dozen oak, bay and manzanita crowns across the access road between the Portal gate and Treetown. But they heard a grumble of Cooper's Unimog trucks draw closer, and they withdrew much further up the road.

Except for Kyle. He perched in concealment on the hillside above the first roadblock, with the chestnut mare tied up in a clump of brush nearby. He had his bow strung and an arrow nocked. Both the bow and the AR-7, which had a full magazine clicked into place, lay in reach at his feet.

He observed as a pair of dirt-bike riders whined up to the leafy barricade, looked it over and then scooted back to the trucks. The whole convoy came to a halt. Camo-clad men wearing boonie hats jumped from the trucks to deploy with their guns, forming a loose perimeter around their vehicles. Kyle remained stock-still, although he did use his monocular to scan through that ring of deployment to see if any of the armed guys happened to be Ephraim. They looked so much alike he couldn't tell. But one thing was clear, none of 'em were Cooper. He'd apparently chosen to stay inside a vehicle. *Wonder if his trucks are armored. Bet his rig is totally pimped out.*

That moment he'd awaited then arrived. A man who held a chainsaw walked up to the obstruction. He set the machine on the ground, yanked its starter cord a few times and then pushed its whirring bar onto the first bough he wished to cut. Kyle had already raised and drawn his longbow. He let the aim settle and released. His arrow strike landed a bit higher than he'd hoped. Still was a decent shot. The man dropped his snarling, stuttering saw, clamped a hand onto his neck, and wheeled around, squirting jets of arterial blood every which-a-way.

A second of horrified silence held around the convoy, then the men with guns began to shout and to shoot at once. The bangs of their shots echoed and collided to blend in a continuous roar. Bullets whacked and whirred, ricocheting all over, but none came near Kyle's hideout. He calmly unstrung his bow, slid it back into the quiver. He picked up the survival rifle, gazed through its peep sight, picked out a target and emptied its magazine via eight rounds of rapid fire. One of Cooper's riflemen jumped up to his feet, both hands clasped to his face, then fell over backwards. Shooting by Cooper's riflemen redoubled, although they still hadn't located a target. *Bang away, damn fools. Quicker you run through your ammo, the better we like you.*

Kyle slung his weapons, lay prone, then writhed on his belly through the brush toward Penny. *Check in with Red, then go to the knolls above Bethesda.*

"Cooper has a machine gun!"

The bulletin was blurted out by a ranger who'd galloped down the Haul Road to the knolls above Bethesda Pool. There, Kyle was hard at work with a handful of other men and women from the Tribe, struggling to pry boulders from the hillside and roll them down onto the road. A half-dozen sizeable rocks were already in place. But clearly, many more would be needed if they were to have a prayer of stopping or even pausing Cooper's convoy.

Kyle shaded his eyes with a palm as he gazed down at the shouting rider and his lathered horse. "What the hell happened?"

"Red tried to hold Treetown. Just long enough to make it look like we was all dug in. But Cooper's motorcycle guys rode around us to the road and set up his damned artillery on a tripod and hosed us down with it, for real. Took a lotta hits! So we beat feet for the Cuadra, and they come after us, setting up and firing all 'long the way. Everybody then run across the bridge and yanked it down and seemed to stop 'em. But no one's gonna be able to come back this way now to help you. Us, I mean."

"Shit. No good news to mix in with that?"

"Well, ol' Larry used one of their Minis to shoot out a radiator on a truck, so that un's stuck up on the ridge. But they set a big hunk of Treetown on fire. See the smoke?"

Kyle raised his eyes to the ridgeline, where puffs of black were being striated and stretched to the east by the onshore breeze. "Yep," he said.

"Red sent me back, long way 'round past 'em, to clue you in. But you best get ready, or clear out, one. I saw 'em startin' to come this way as I galloped by at full tilt to get here ahead of 'em."

"Gotcha." Kyle thought for a moment. *If Cooper's gang shoots a machine gun, like what, an M-60 or something, they could turn this clump of exposed rock up here into a shrapnel factory. No place to hide. Trying to hold them or even snipe at them in this bottleneck would turn into a suicide mission, awful damn quick. And it's still way too early to have us one of those....*

"Let your horse water at the pool," he advised the ranger. "Give the guy a break. Then ride fast through Elysian and back up to the Cuadra, till you meet Red. Tell him I'll try to send everyone I meet, from the Tribe or Elysian, up to that Forest Camp on the middle fork. Me, I'll go down to Elysian, hook up with Samuel. If Cooper attempts to occupy the village, I'd still recommend a counterattack, *en masse*. Right at sunset."

The ranger touched a hand to his hat's broad brim, simultaneously showing that he understood and agreed, while giving Kyle a salute. Then he trotted off.

"Did everyone hear that?" Kyle asked. The people working beside him looked at each other and then awarded him a collective nod. "If we stay up here, we're likely to stay permanently," he continued. "Till the ravens tote us off, bit by bit. Which wouldn't give much of a boost to your cause. Now, I'm not the boss. Can't tell any of you what to do. But I'd say, at this point, getting our butts away from here quick might be the best part of valor. I'd strongly recommend anybody with a horse ride down the road to whatever route is best to reach that Forest Camp. Mount up and ride double, if you can. Anybody left on foot, well, there any sort of path you can use, or can you bushwhack right across the watershed?"

"Yes," one woman said. "In fact, I'd much rather go that way."

"Great. Try not to leave too many footprints. Or hoofprints. We want Cooper's boys to be intent on scoring just one thing. When they get it, we'll have 'em pinned right on a bullseye. I'm going to ride down to Elysian now myself, see what the Elders have got cookin'. Meanwhile, you all keep safe. Hope to see you again at some other point in our lives."

Chapter 21

Penny pricked up her ears as she watched Kyle approach. She could tell he was agitated. Scent of stress hormones he emitted alone told her that. She herself felt aroused by the grand milieu of equine and human excitement. But she felt especially moved by this human whom she already liked so much, who rode bareback with such confidence and was sensitive to her own subtle messages back to him.

She felt more than ready to take him on a fast canter down to the sea and Elysian. When he bounced on the ground and vaulted up to mount, she dipped a shoulder to shrug him on board close to her withers, the position which by now she knew he favored. She felt his toes hook her a little bit just behind her front legs. That told her his seat was secure.

Kyle rode the mare hard through the cool and fragrant drift of a breeze past deserted fields and quiet village outbuildings. He stopped near the final structure, the domed Council Lodge, set back tightly against the hillside. Two people, one tall and one quite short, stood just outside its entry as they engaged in a hot, arm-waving argument. They were Michael and Sayer Ruth.

"We have to leave *now!*" Michael shouted.

"I must stay to protect our sanctuary," Ruth asserted. "My duty is sacred. It may not be sloughed off on others. It can never be disregarded."

"You'll be a hostage," the dwarf warned, shaking a finger at her. "Cooper will use you as a bargaining chip. Saving you then shall put more of us at risk."

"I've been saved, and far beyond their ken. Or—as I'm sorry to say now, Michael—perhaps beyond yours. Know that they cannot harm a hair on my head," Ruth said. She drew herself up to her full height, slipped her hands into the sleeves of her robe. "Not while I take my refuge in the bosom of my Lord."

Kyle halted Penny near the gong, dismounted, tied her to a leg of the wooden tripod that upheld the sawn-off acetylene tank. The debaters at the doorway paid him scant heed as he approached.

"Sayer, they've already begun to shoot people. Men and women, both."

"Surely an exaggeration. If Nathan Cooper comes such an incredibly long way to visit with us, it must be that he's ready to talk peace. He's always aimed to unify our sect. But even if he does not see a way for us to reunify now, I shall use the charm and power of the Spirit to convince him that a pathway truly might exist. It can be that simple, Michael."

"No. You can't really be that stupid," Kyle said, as he drew near enough for both to hear him. "He in fact *is* shooting people. I saw the bastard do it! And I was just told he machine-gunned the Tribe at the Cuadra bridge. That man's after conquest, not dialog."

"Kyle Skander, do not dare to intrude on our discussion," Ruth fumed. She turned her face toward him, though her sightless blue eye still roved the landscape at random. "You've been nothing but a source of woe since you came. I would not be in the least surprised if any trouble that's happened with Cooper occurred because you provoked it."

"Well, Kyle's the one I believe now," Michael snapped. "Writ Readers ran off from Pharaoh years ago because Cooper was an abusive asshole. Right? Stripes like that, a tiger doesn't change. Must've come up here because he ran out of people to screw down there and had to locate a fresh supply. More of his folks ran away, or he ground them into the dirt. In any case, welcoming him into Elysian is begging for more of the same. I won't be a part of it!"

The sound of a full squad of revved-up dirt motorcycles blended into a tenor snarl that drifted toward the compound.

"Shit. Here they come," Kyle said. "Bikers are his outriders. Must've squirted right past the boulders." He glanced at Michael's short legs. "I'd say, run for it, but it seems late."

Sayer Ruth snatched up handfuls of her robe, swept the fabric around her, and stalked back into the Council Lodge. Evidently, she planned to stay.

"What's up with Ruth?" Kyle asked.

"Can't begin to tell you," Michael said. "Been acting truly strange, ever since—"

"Since Rebecca died?"

"Sure. I guess."

"Interesting. Never mind. Here's what's important. Have you seen Samuel? Anybody else today, looking for spots to hide in Elysian?"

Michael's face warped in puzzlement. "Why would I?"

"Crap."

"What?"

"Somebody needs to stay inside Cooper's ring. We've got to get the colonel looking over his shoulder, if we're to beat him. But you. You don't have to do it."

"Do I have a choice?"

"Can you ride a horse?"

Michael gave his head an emphatic shake. "No."

"I'm going to jump up onto the lodge roof. Way I see it, your options are, you can come with me, or go hang out with Ruth, or surrender immediately to Cooper's guys and see how nice they treat you."

Michael deliberated. "Roof," he said. "Maybe I'll help you distract Cooper. Don't know how, though. Fling dirt at him?"

"Good man. If I think of a way, I'll suggest it. Meanwhile, wait here. I'll be right back."

Kyle ran to Penny, untethered her, slipped off her halter and whapped her on the rump. She bent her neck around to peer at him, baffled. "Hah!" he shouted as he gave another hard slap. Penny decided to take his travel suggestion. She trotted off amiably in the direction that she'd been pointed.

He hoped that seeing a rider-less horse amble off into the woods wouldn't prove of much interest to any of Cooper's goons. He didn't want to see that sweet mare get shot. And he also didn't want those men to think very hard about where she'd come from or why.

He ran back to Michael. "Okay, let's get around to the hill side of this place, hoist ourselves up on top so we can hide in the sod. Don't worry, I'll give you a boost."

Together they scooted away from the entry apron, moving into a niche between the first domed chamber of the lodge and hillside. The weathered end of a log roof beam projected from the eaves, low enough for Kyle to grab. He yanked the otter-skin quiver off his shoulder and tossed it up onto the roof, soon followed by the survival rifle. He turned to Michael, laced his fingers together, bent and nodded. Michael stepped up into his hands and pushed off with that leg as Kyle pitched him upward. The dwarf landed astride the log beam with a pained "Oof!" but scrambled up into the grass and out of sight. Kyle spun around, leapt up and grabbed the beam with both hands, then contract-ed his stomach muscles as he performed a reverse somersault. He wound up lying with his legs on the grass and his chest on the beam. He writhed backward, picked up his weapons, and crept on elbows and knees up to the high point of the dome that roofed the chamber, stopping right by its smoke hole.

Michael was already there. He pointed with a stubby finger off into the distance. One of the Unimog trucks was pulled over next to the farm fields, and a figure dressed entirely in black stood atop its cab. A glint of afternoon sunshine sparkled off binocular lenses that he held up to his face.

Meanwhile the dirt-bike riders were moving ahead, churning up dust then pausing, and then charging forward once more as they leapfrogged each other.

"Enjoy the view?" Kyle asked.

"Not much." Michael looked at him. "Just a large gang of men holding guns."

"Unfortunately, yes."

"So, I didn't quite get your plan. Let them sweep into Ely-sian. And what?"

"They declare victory, wonder where we've run off to, and mainly relax. That's when we attack." Kyle glanced back at Michael. "So, it was important to me whether or not you saw Samuel. He was supposed to put a few other tough guys to-gether and hide out here in the village. Then at sunset, as Tribe rangers and the Elysians charged, our role was to hit Cooper's guys from behind, confuse and terrify 'em. I mean, in theory.

"But say, you and I get stuck on this roof. And we don't happen to see an attack ever occur. Well...I'd say, we hide till around midnight, sneak off, go find our people, work up a Plan B. Whatever the hell a Plan B might look like. Just now, I haven't the foggiest."

Michael nodded curtly. "Don't mind me asking. But why is Kyle Skander still within a hundred miles of a mess like this?"

"Don't want those bastards to win," he said. Michael looked skeptical. "Well, really, I just never want to lose," he added. And Michael smiled.

"You could've been long gone, though," he pointed out. "Several times."

"Sure. So, why not?" Kyle shook his head. "Might make me look stupid to someone else. But what I see happening all around me now is just...fascinating."

Michal shook his head and opened his mouth to reply.

It was the moment when Cooper's men opened up with their big machine gun. Its bass cackle sounded off in long bursts as heavy slugs tore through Elysian. Most buildings caught at least a sample of its fire. By the time their sweep reached the Council Lodge, the shooters had ineptly raised their sights. Shreds of grass and sprays of dirt hit Michael and Kyle in their faces as they frantically backpedaled down the far side of the dome.

"Damned idiots!" Michael exclaimed. "That's a hell of a way to find out if people are still indoors."

Kyle stopped just short of dropping back off the roof and lay flat at its edge panting, with his fingers tangled in the grass. He felt startled by a surge of panic. It was one thing to deal with an enemy who acted on a basis of logic and restraint. But firing through a village without knowing or apparently caring whether it held combatants didn't just show abysmal stupidity, it also displayed a wanton savagery. The combination abruptly struck him as terrifying to an overwhelming degree.

What have I gotten myself into? Michael was right, I not only could be a hundred miles away, I should be! Resting at home with my head on the lap of Luz Maria right this instant. It's far from being my fight. Why be sucked or suckered in? Pride? Ambition? Weird lust for dominance? Some idea of measuring myself against Cooper by pitting myself against him? If so, I'm a fool, a moron!

Emotions boiled and churned. Every nerve in his body felt scorched and aflame. Contradictory thoughts surged and collided and combusted in his brain. He realized then that he was right on the verge of losing his grip on himself. He lay there, face pressed down into the sod, his breathing shallow and ragged. And then Roy's voice whispered in his ear.

Anyone can pose as a philosopher if times are easy. But when things turn fraught you discover what you're made of. It's the big conundrum men have been forced to confront throughout the run of their days on earth. Which core beliefs are a key to virtuous behavior in hard times? And yet, since all men search, some men find. Whence comes the poise that's no superficial or fragile pose? An answer must run deeper than words, although some words point the way. Such as these, from the Bhagavad Gita.... "Prepare for war with peace in your soul. Be at peace in gain or in loss, in victory or in defeat. In this peace, there is no sin..." or this, from Emerson, "If the red slayer think he slays, or if the slain think he is slain, they know not well the subtle ways I keep...."

Kyle turned these phrases over in his mind. Terror eased its grip. And then he realized that Michael was speaking loudly to him, back in the physical realm.

"We need to do something, go somewhere! We shouldn't be sitting ducks right here on the edge of the roof."

"No, no. All right. They've stopped shooting. Let's crawl back up higher."

They wriggled their way back through the grass, hearing the motorcycles snarl up to the Council Lodge and sputter to a halt. Kyle and Michael finally regained the spot where Kyle left his bow and survival rifle by the smoke hole.

"Have you shot guns, ever?"

"I grew up with the Tribe, remember? Back then, we had tons of ammo. Right after they pulled a binky out of a kid's mouth, they'd put a gun in his hands."

"Okay. This thing is a semiauto. Small caliber, so go for head shots. Or aim for the groin. They've got vests, so a torso hit won't do a damn thing for you. Peep-sight, eight-round clip is in it, and I have two full magazines and a bag of bullets in my lower pockets, here."

"You'll use the bow?"

Kyle nodded. "Not that I plan to aim for anything, yet. It's not clear there'll even *be* a sunset attack. However, if Cooper's guys do try to find us and to capture us, that won't be a freebie for 'em. I guarantee."

Michael's eyebrows rose, but he replied with a brief, decisive nod.

The Unimogs grumbled up to the lodge entry, maneuvered across its broad fan of bare clay and shut down. Atop one van body the heavy machine gun was set on a tripod, surrounded by a low ring of sandbags, with the gunner himself sitting on a short stack of two bags. As Kyle peered through strands of grass, he saw another goon with a rifle climb a ladder up to the top of the other Unimog. Then its front door swung open and Cooper clambered out. The colonel was followed immediately by Ephraim, clad in a suit of freshly ironed black fatigues—almost the spitting image of his dad.

Hey, why's Ephraim get to play dress-up, while Cooper's other kids don't? Rest of 'em just look like run-of-the-mill lil' green men. What makes Jimbo an apple of daddy's eye? Prodigal son clasped once more to his family's bosom?

They heard an indistinct conversation at the entry to the lodge, one that concluded with Cooper's voice barking out commands. Then motorcycle riders roared away, fanning out in teams of two to award all other Elysian buildings a closer search. Kyle leaned his head over the smoke hole, saw a shadowy shape of a pair of men pass by below. They disappeared, then jogged back through the domed chamber again. He heard one shout, "Sayer Ruth's here! But otherwise—all clear."

"Hsst," Michael whispered. "Cooper and Ephraim are going into the lodge now."

"Well! *This* will be a don't-miss-it chat," Kyle whispered back. "Ruth's probably waiting for them in the second chamber, huh? I'll crawl over there. You cool where you are? Great. See ya."

The oculus-skylight for the second chamber presented a difficulty that Kyle instantly discerned. The sod roof here sloped down to the opening, feathering to nothing along the rim of the hole. And that slope looked awfully steep. Grass grew all over it, but he didn't know how stable the soil underneath might be.

He writhed through the bunch grasses at the upper edge. Voices came from below. He needed to get closer. He spun around and tested his way downward, looking for sturdy tufts and clumps where he could brace his feet. *Go just a little further.*

"— It's not the welcome we looked for, and certainly not the one we expected." That was Cooper. "I admit, I based my ideas on just those few messages sent between us. But what the hell happened?"

"The Elders. I did tell you that would be our hardest problem, and it was." *Ruth is talking!* "They failed to see, reunification was the measure we had to take to make our faith secure, so it can long endure. A confessed sin always must be forgiven, no matter who the sinner is, or his crimes. Thus sayeth our Lord. And yet they still refuse to give any heed to his Sayer. I will admit to that. And the Tribe stays rebellious. My power has been insufficient. We all are imperfect vehicles."

"Amen to that, Sayer. May the Spirit's power win through for us in the end," Cooper said. "But I'm afraid that I can't stay inside another second. Must leave you two alone. Certain matters must be seen to, and they can't wait. For peace to reign in the valley, security must be a first. Anyway, you and Ephraim have an important item or so to discuss. Do you not?"

Kyle reached the slope's base. He braced a foot on a section of log that formed one part of the rim of the octagonal oculus. A tiny spray of dirt went over that rim as he slid to a halt. He hoped that it wouldn't be noticed. His memory of that chamber was, well, the place always had a little crap scattered across its floor, a few leaves, a feather or two, or some dusting of anonymous granules from the outside...so to see any particular item dripping in shouldn't seem far out of the ordinary.

"What have you told the colonel about Rebecca?" That was Ruth. If Cooper had left, she'd be talking to Ephraim.

"She resisted...your authority. As the Elders did. Just like you told me." Yes, it was Ephraim's reedy voice.

"But how did you explain her death?"

"Someone acted on your orders."

"I did *not* order Rebecca killed!"

"You said I should follow her. I did. You said her lack of morals should be exposed. Her broken vows should be revealed. And she should be harshly punished for it. Punished in a manner that no one could mistake."

"Public exposure. It's what I wanted, and it should've been enough. All we needed was for the truth of her sex gluttony to be revealed to all in Elysian."

"You surprise me, Sayer. You know, you're not the only one to whom the Lord speaks! When I saw Rebecca stroll down to wash herself at the pool, fresh from all her sinning, all naked and shameless, even singing and humming to herself...."

Kyle felt his foothold on the log shift. The bare wood where his sandal had been planted was soft and rotten. Its fibers were spreading apart, and a kind of brown ooze had begun to seep out. He wound the fingers of both fists more deeply in the grass.

"And she mocked me! Called me awful names. Said that I was stupid and ugly, and that no girl or woman wanted me, or would ever have me. You see, Rebecca had turned cruel, too. Deeply unworthy of being a Sayer. Just revealing her evil was never going to be enough. Wrath had to be brought down on her. Instantly! I could feel the Lord's fire in me. And so, His holy retribution was delivered."

"Ephraim. This deed is one that you must confess. To everybody. Take full responsibility. Explain how and why it happened. Even claim that you were the Lord's channel for justice, if you must, and that you sought to manifest His will. But leave me out of it! Or you shall diminish my authority and harm any chance to unify our community, quite severely. And so, promise me you...."

The log split apart, Kyle's foot skidded off it, the grass in his hands tore loose from the soil and he suddenly found himself out in open space and tumbling as he fell off the roof and dropped into the dark maw of the oculus.

Chapter 22

K yle's first sensation was that his whole back felt as if he'd been worked over by a pack of goons with clubs. The next problem he discovered was that he couldn't move an inch. His wrists were bound, as were his ankles. Then those bonds had been bent toward each other and hooked up behind him—effectively hogtying him. The straps used to make these bonds were so thin and hard, they felt like they sawed into his flesh. And he promptly discovered a few other problems. He'd been blindfolded with multiple windings of a rag so he could not see, and he couldn't complain about it either, since he'd also been gagged. He bit down experimentally, found his gag was a wooden stick, pulled into corners of his mouth by a string that ran around the back of his neck. In addition, his brain felt like it was trying to crawl out of his ear in order to escape a throbbing headache, an agony of migraine-like proportions.

The good news is that my fall didn't break my spine. The bad news is that they didn't take kindly to me dropping by to interrupt their chat. Must've called in Cooper's thugs to truss me up. And they certainly did a swell job.

His most useful news was that at least he could still hear; they hadn't plugged his ears. And the gist of sounds he was picking up told him that the conversation between Ephraim and Ruth had devolved into an enraged argument.

"You used me to get rid of Rebecca. Now you plan to use me again just to deflect blame away from yourself!"

He heard the sharp impact of a blow, as if a face had been slapped, and a near-simultaneous gasp.

Kyle craned his neck, moved his throbbing head around and tried to see if there was a way to rub the blindfold against something, get it to pull off. But the chamber's bare floor provided his sole opportunity. He moved his forehead up and down, rubbing it against the dirt. He felt gratified when the bandage slid up enough that faint light came to one eye. He turned his head the other way, rolled his eye downward and won a slim, crescent-shaped view of the room that came to him above his left cheekbone.

"Think you can use me, then just wipe your feet on me, huh? Think you're *so* superior to everyone? Well, those days are done. There's a new boss in Elysian. And guess what, Ruth, it's not you!"

Sound of another slap.

Kyle bent his neck to an especially awkward angle. Now he saw that Ephraim had Ruth shoved up against a wall of the chamber. He had a wad of her robe gripped in a fist and was delivering blows to her face with his free hand.

Then something remarkable occurred. Ruth pushed her hips against the wall and brought her forehead down onto Ephraim's face in a head-butt. Her blow was neither particularly strong nor well-delivered, yet it stunned him. She was able to wrench free of his grasp and run to the firepit at the center of the room. She snatched up a thick hardwood stick that had been used as a poker and whirled around with it just in time to get rammed in the chest by Ephraim's shoulder. She fell over into the firepit—which at this point held nothing but cold ashes—and he yanked the stick out of her hands. Kyle didn't see what happened next but he heard it—a loud *crack!* as Ephraim broke the stick over her head.

Ephraim dragged her limp body out of the ashes and over the floor, closer to the spot where Kyle lay. Kyle mimed a lapse back into unconsciousness; he didn't think Ephraim would note his small adjustment of the blindfold.

Ephraim freed the sash from Ruth's robe. A sheathed bayonet hung from a canvas military belt buckled around Ephraim's waist. He pulled the blade out and cut her cincture in half, then used a piece to tie her ankles together and her hands behind her back. He rolled her over and stared down at Ruth for a long moment, then reached down with both hands and yanked her robe open, exposing her bare chest. He knelt beside her and began to knead and kiss her breasts. Kyle wondered if he shouted out, whether that would make the situation any better or far worse.

At that moment, another man wearing camo strode in from the outside. He happened to be one of the few Kyle had seen who did not resemble Cooper.

"Heard some commotion in here," he said. "What's going on? Ah—"

Ephraim blanched, looked up. "I just interrogated the Sayer. She was a traitor. In league with that Outsider." He pointed at Kyle's trussed up body. "That's when she attacked me. But I subdued her. Now I need to check her for weapons."

"Um-huh. Looks like what you're doing, all right," the man said. "Hey, the boss wants your ass outside. We're trying to figure out where everybody went. It's like they just melted into the woods. And you know this place."

"Sure. Have an idea."

"Well, come on then."

Ephraim stood and began to follow his cohort out of the chamber. Then he paused next to Kyle. He hawked up a glob of phlegm and saliva, then spat the gob out forcefully onto Kyle's face. Yet Kyle didn't flinch and so appeared still dead to the world. Satisfied, Ephraim stalked out.

—

Kyle calculated the angle of sunbeams that slanted down through the chamber's oculus. He concluded that little more than an hour remained until sunset. He tilted his head back to check on Sayer Ruth. She stayed exactly as Ephraim had left her. *I don't see anything anywhere 'round here that I can use to cut through my straps. However, if I can get over to Ruth, maybe I can untie her. Which won't do me any good unless she comes to, then frees me. Still, that could be my one chance. Makes it well-worth a try.*

He wondered if he might be able to stretch and contract his torso enough to move over the floor like a caterpillar. But that didn't work. His sole alternative was to rock back and forth enough to roll.

He wasn't looking forward to having his weight land repeatedly on his bound wrists and ankles. He already felt pain as blood pooled in his hands and feet. *At least I have a stick in my mouth, something I can bite down on if things hurt. Kind of 'em to provide that.* Each flop over made the bonds dig deeper and swelling in his extremities worsen. By the time he reached Ruth, his hands were in bad shape. His fingers felt like bratwursts. The upsides were that the blindfold had finally fallen completely off his head, and the string holding his gag in place had snapped, allowing him to spit out the stick. *Now I must force my fingers to move. Otherwise, everything I've already accomplished here shall be worthless.*

He couldn't figure out how to flip Ruth over to get at her hands, so he started on her ankles. The knots were square knots, yanked tight, but once they gave way they released quickly. One more sign of hope came from a quiver of movement that he felt in her legs. Maybe she was waking up!

"What...what are you doing?" Her voice was faint.

"Setting you free. Soon as I do, you need to return the favor. Okay?"

"What happened to me?"

"Remember your visit with Jimbo?"

"Who?"

"Ephraim."

"Oh. Yes." She shuddered. "Where is he?" Her voice gained strength.

"Went outside. But he could be back any minute. Let's work fast." She glanced down at her bare chest. "What's this?"

"Um, Ephraim said he had to check you for a concealed weapon."

"Wish I had one. I'd gut him with it." Her voice dripped contempt.

"Oh. Feeling a change of heart are we now, Ruth? Here, roll yourself over so I can get at your hands."

She did so. The agony of his fingers nearly made him faint, yet he got her loose enough that she was able to wiggle the knotted sash off her wrists.

"I...don't know how to untie you," she said. "These feel like plastic strings or something. They don't have knots."

"Oh, knock it off, Ruth. I know you can see. Shit-can your blind lady shtick, okay? It's gotten tiresome."

She was silent.

"And now I know that you worked on a plan to bring Cooper up here, too. So, don't even try to pretend otherwise."

"I thought you were knocked out. How much did you hear?"

"Enough. So, are you going to get me loose or what, dammit?"

"I have scissors in my room. I'll go and get them."

"Well, hurry! My hands are about to explode."

While she was gone, Kyle struggled to distract himself from the pangs in his head and limbs by looking around the chamber. He saw one of the plank benches smashed in half. *Must be where I hit. I broke it, but it broke my fall.*

Ruth came back, began to cut away his ties. His legs flopped down and his spine straightened. "Ungghh..." he said. Then his hands were free. "Son-of-a-bitch. Ouch goddamn fucking crap." She did his ankles.

"Can you stand?"

"Not yet."

"What should we do?"

"Me, I'll just lie here for a second. But you, you should scamper on out there right now and inform Cooper that you've changed your mind. He's not welcome here in Elysian anymore. So, he should pack up all of his goddam clones and goons and get the hell out of town."

He saw her gazing down at him. There was a sizeable and colorful lump on her forehead, right at her hairline, and a rivulet of drying blood that ran down her cheek. Her eyepatch had gotten knocked off during her short but furious bout with Ephraim, A wizened eye socket threaded with pale scar tissue was on the left side of her face. And on the right, an earnest blue eye had largely ceased its endless wandering. No point in trying to maintain that ploy anymore. At least, not with Kyle.

"Cooper brought no women with him," she announced, as if that explained everything. "None."

"He didn't?"

"No. Ephraim just informed me, rather gleefully, the colonel left all women behind. Their Mojave compound was about to be overrun, by a gang that runs an oil refinery. Where I guess they'd been buying fuel. So, Cooper brought away with him only the personnel he considered important. Figured there'd be enough women up here. To help him make his grandkids. And populate the world with new young saints all made in his image and likeness."

"Who told you?"

"Ephraim. He said that he originally wanted Rebecca to be a wife to him. But was more than willing to settle for me."

"Hey, one heckuva opportunity there. You think about it?"

"I said, I'd prefer to decline. That's when he went off on me."

Kyle rose up to his hands and knees. He rested there briefly, then managed to stand. He wavered away from the vertical a few times, then steadied himself. He put his hands up and massaged his wrists.

"So. Other than your scissors. Or that broken poker. Got something that looks more like a weapon?"

She shook her head.

"I need to get back up on that roof."

"How can you do that?"

"Know where any ladder is?" he asked.

"No."

"Darn."

He dragged an intact bench over to a spot beneath the skylight. He went over to the shattered bench, picked up the longest piece of plank and propped it on the intact bench, making a ramp.

"Well, here goes nothin'," he said, backing up to the far wall of the chamber.

"Wait. What should I do?"

"Run into your room. Lock the door. If it doesn't have a lock, brace something big against it. Get under the covers. Wait there until things go quiet. Add another whole day, just to be sure, then come out."

"No! That's silly."

He shrugged. "Suit yourself."

Kyle sprinted toward the bench, kicked a final stride into the center of the leaning plank, and shot upward. He aimed his outstretched hands at the crib of logs that framed the oculus and was able to slam his fingers home into a gap between the logs. His big question was whether they all were as rotted as the one that had split open and let him fall. And the answer was: mostly. He clawed at the crumbling wood in a fury, switching hands, tossing away loose shards until he finally gripped a firmer section. Then he did a chin-up, swung a heel so it also caught on part of the crib, and mantled his torso upward until he was able to roll onto the lower part of the sod slope. He laid there for a moment, panting. He glanced down through the skylight and saw Ruth looking back up at him, her hands clasped together at her chest, and one bright blue eye agleam in the shadows.

Chapter 23

The thick carpet of roof grasses undulated slowly in an evening breeze. The sun was a glowing orange orb, its lower curve balanced on a line of purple mist that spread over the sea and limned the entire horizon.

Kyle parted the grass strands at the top of the dome and looked around. He saw no sign of Michael. He wondered if Cooper had sent men up to check for any infestation of more interlopers on the roof after he'd plummeted down through the skylight, and if so, whether Michael had been caught. He hoped not. A further forlorn hope was that the searchers might've missed finding his weapons over by the smoke hole of the first chamber. But when he crawled over there, he saw that both his bow and the survival rifle were gone. *Shit.*

He heard an electric generator crank up. Someone threw a switch, and the apron in front of the Council Lodge began to blaze with stark white light. He could see the Unimogs had been repositioned. The one with the machine gun nest atop its van body was now parked tight by the lodge entry, while the other had been moved a hundred yards away. A sandbagged rifle pit had been installed on top of it, to provide overlapping fields of fire. The tanker truck had been parked cheek-by-jowl near that more distant Unimog.

As he studied Cooper's set-up, Kyle saw that any chance of a successful attack by a force of Tribe rangers and the Elysians appeared to be remote. Then he noticed a section of the roof grasses waving a bit more than the others. He saw a hairy face raise up to peer at him. It was Michael. He crawled steadily on up the dome and soon reached Kyle's side at the smoke hole. The dwarf was dragging the bow quiver and survival rifle along beside him.

"Wow," Kyle said. He punched Michael in the shoulder. "Good to see you. I thought sure that Cooper's guys had busted your tail and hauled you off."

"They sought, yet they did not find," Michael said. "There's advantage to smallness. Not always, but sometimes."

Cooper's guys clearly planned to make the Council Lodge the core of their main defensible space. Yet their preparations lacked intensity or focus. Some men leaned against the vehicles, smoking hand-rolled cigarettes. An outer ring of sentries lounged by their parked motorcycles. A yammer of their conversations blended with the hum of the generator. They looked as if they did not perceive themselves as under any threat that could be genuine or imminent. *Most likely, they weren't.* Kyle looked back over his shoulder. The sun was half-sunk into the purple mist, charging a section of it with an amber glow. In another five minutes or so it would be fully down.

Then he caught a hint of movement out of the corner of his eye. A dark lump of sod moved slowly along the edge of the roof. Kyle nudged Michael with an elbow and pointed. That creeping lump seemed to be a rather large one, but nobody on the ground was paying it any mind.

The lump had a head. Kyle recognized that it was Samuel's. Otherwise, he was fully draped in a cloak bristling with grass stalks, like some kind of ad hoc ghillie suit, and he seemed intent on reaching a point above the entry. Kyle badly wished to try something to draw Big Sam's eye up to the dome's summit, yet he feared adding any jot of movement that might draw unwanted attention from below.

"Should we..." Michael muttered.

"Let's wait and see what he has in mind," Kyle cautioned.

Direct sunlight faded. All of Elysian became curtained by the vague blue gauze of twilight, except for that stark circle of electric glow in front of the lodge.

Kyle saw Samuel slip off his ghillie cloak and adopt a crouching stance at the edge of the roof. He noted a reason why Sam had crawled along so slowly—he gripped his big oak staff in one hand. He wondered why he hadn't brought the Ruger rifle.

Samuel bobbed up and down twice. Then he sprang off the lodge roof and landed on the top of the Unimog. The gunner, who'd been sitting idly on his sandbags, cross-legged, arms on his knees, turned his head to gape at the new arrival and received a smack of that staff across his face for his trouble. He fell over backward. Samuel lunged ahead to take his seat. He racked the charging handle on the weapon, aimed it. But before he triggered it, he took a second to boot Cooper's gunner off the roof of the van with a hearty kick.

Men in fatigues standing by the side of the truck looked up to see the source of the ruckus above them and were rewarded by seeing the body of the gunner flail through the air and crash onto their heads. That vision was succeeded by a spear of hot flame from the barrel of the M-60 and the thunder of full auto fire as Samuel directed a hail of bullets at the other Unimog.

"Come on!" Kyle jumped up, grabbed the bow and ran for the edge of the roof.

All around the Council Lodge a flood of dark shapes erupted from the shadows. The Tribe rangers and the Elysian ad hoc militia had chosen to stake everything on a mass charge. He saw waving farm implements and stone hammers, thrashing bodies, a few bright splashes of muzzle flash. The tactic seemed to work well. Cooper's men were being swarmed before they even had a chance to use their guns. Kyle nocked an arrow, tried to draw his bow and shoot, but he couldn't identify or isolate a target.

And then he could.

Out at the edge of sphere of light, Ephraim stood in his black fatigues and pointed a silver rifle back toward the lodge. As Kyle drew the bow and tried to aim he heard Ruth's voice scream, "No, no no no, stop it, this is all madness!" Waving her arms, she ran out from the lodge entry into the circle of light. Ephraim instantly shot her. As her body crumpled to the ground a stunned Kyle opened his hand, but he botched his release and could not tell where his arrow had landed. He speedily nocked another shaft, but Ephraim had vanished back into the shadows.

The Unimog at the entry began to crank up as if the operator planned to drive it off, but Samuel stopped all that nonsense by yanking the machine gun from its tripod and sending a stream of fire down through the cab roof and engine hood. Then he put the gun against a sandbag, stomped its barrel into a curve, rendering it useless. He snatched up his staff and leapt off the van to join the melee.

The other Unimog had burst into flame. Meanwhile, the tanker truck began to drive away, but no one did anything to stall or halt its departure. If that rig blew sky-high, Elysian's inhabitants and its invaders alike would all go up in smoke right along with it.

Kyle saw bodies fall to the ground, some in pairs or trios that savagely tussled with each other. However, the violence already was winding down. Cooper's men had been whelmed by sheer surprise, swarmed by a crowd of Elysians and Tribe rangers who'd crept up through the shadows to jump them.

Kyle looked around for Michael, but he was nowhere in sight. He unstrung his bow and jumped off the roof of the lodge himself, prepared to swing the stave of his longbow like a wooden sword. But the fighting was already over. Cooper's men were either beaten to the ground or standing with their arms up in the air, surrounded by knots of angry farmers and rangers.

Then Ephraim staggered out of the darkness, with one shoulder bloodied. Michael walked behind him, poking him in the tailbone with the muzzle of the survival rifle.

"Hiding under a bush," Michael announced.

"Nice work," Kyle told him.

Then Kyle began to shout. "All of you need to hear me! Ephraim said it. He's the one who killed Rebecca. And just now, he shot Ruth too!"

Samuel dropped his staff and went right across the clearing in two bounds. Kyle never imagined the big guy could move so fast. Samuel grabbed Ephraim by the neck with both massive fists, and then, like a crane raising a debris bucket, hauled the youth up into the air.

Ephraim writhed, kicked and struck at Samuel with his hands. It availed him nothing. He might as well have been a moth fluttering against an iron lamp post. Holding Ephraim's body aloft, Samuel bore him into the center of the ring of light.

Michael slung the survival rifle over his shoulder, then he scampered over to that gory, huddled mass that was the fallen body of Ruth. Two other Elysians helped him to turn her over. Michael checked the pulse in her neck, mournfully shook his head. "She's passed," he said.

"Mistake! Accident!" Ephraim gurgled. "I was trying to hit him." He pointed at Kyle. "Him! The Outsider. He killed Rebecca, not me."

"Jimbo betrayed all of you to Cooper, then ran off to join him," Kyle said.

"He did 'zackly that." Red came into the light looking much the worse for wear, his face battered and dreadlocks askew. "And so, this damn scarecrow good as got Carlos killed too."

"He attacked Ruth inside the lodge, before he came out," Kyle said. "Right after he talked to her about killing Rebecca. Then he knocked Ruth down and I saw him start to rape her. Only one thing stopped him. Cooper had him called outside."

A preternatural silence fell.

"Any last words?" Samuel growled.

Ephraim's eyes rolled frantically as Samuel tightened his grip. He spluttered, gasped, and gave a few feeble kicks. Then his eyes stopped moving and bulged, their whites all agleam except for black dots that stared down, transfixed by the wrath on Samuel's face. A dark stream of urine coursed the length of Ephraim's pant leg and disappeared into his boot.

Then Samuel appeared to relent. He lowered Ephraim till his feet hit the ground, where they scrambled for traction. But he shifted his left hand to the back of the youth's skull, slid his right up to cup his jaw. He grunted and gave Ephraim's head a violent jerk first to the right, then to the left.

A gristly *snap!* His body sagged in Samuel's hands. It began to vibrate and jerk. Samuel tossed Ephraim's twitching corpse to the ground as though it were a soiled rag.

The big man stood there for a long moment, his chest rising and falling while air whooshed through his broad nostrils. "Now, I must go seek forgiveness," he said finally. "Somewhere."

"Both of us," Michael said. He glared at the limp heap that had been Ephraim. "I still hate him."

Out beyond the edge of light, a shape moved that drew Kyle's attention. A dirt bike's engine sputtered, caught. He heard the motorcycle accelerate, saw it pass through a stray beam of illumination. It looked to him like Cooper rode on its seat, twisted its throttle. The bike bounced away toward the trees, then its headlight illumined a swatch of dirt on the trail to the Cuadra.

"That's the colonel!" Kyle yelled, pointing. "He's getting away!" Samuel and others glanced at him.

"A truck is stuck up on the ridge. More men and guns there. Must be where he's off to. Where's another motorcycle?"

"Here!" someone yelled.

Chapter 24

K yle ran and saw two bikes, painted black and olive drab, leaning beside each other on kickstands. They appeared battered by hard use. Both had keys sticking out of consoles near their handlebars. He leapt on one, twisted the key, and thumbed what looked like a starter button. It ground away but nothing happened. He saw a kickstart lever near his leg, swung it out, twisted the throttle open and pumped the lever up and down with his foot. The motor huffed and popped but did not start.

Samuel strode up. "You've flooded it," he growled. He threw a leg over the next one, turned the key and pushed the starter. The engine turned over, but also did not catch. He got off the bike to examine it. "Cooper!" he exclaimed. "He busted my spark plug. Hammered it with something before he ran off. Broke it on yours too, prob'ly."

"Damn." Kyle cupped his hands behind his ears. He heard a whine of Cooper's fleeing motorcycle as it climbed the path to the Cuadra. Then he heard another sound, the snort and hoof clops of an approaching horse. He saw the outline of Abraham, leading Penny out of the thickening darkness.

"Lose somebody?" Abraham asked.

"Maybe not," Kyle said. All the mare had for tack was a rope that lay looped around her neck. "Let me at her. Sweetheart, you good to go?"

The mare nickered. Kyle took the rope and vaulted up on her back. Michael came churning up to them on his stumpy legs. He

thrust the survival rifle at him. Kyle dropped his bow, grabbed
the rifle by its sling and threw it across his back. "Thanks, man.
Much better."

He gripped the horse's mane, put his heels to her and they took
off. He soon realized that he'd have to steer the mare toward the
trail by leg pressure alone. Luckily, Penny was fully responsive to
his wishes. He could feel her body surging rhythmically between
his thighs, her eagerness to accomplish his aims. As well as her
enduring love of any chance to run at full tilt.

A headlight beam whipped about on the hill above as the fleeing bike swerved quickly through switchbacks. Kyle saw he had
zero hope of catching up to Cooper. Still, he wondered if Cooper
knew that during the morning's battle the footbridge over Gilead
Creek's south fork had been yanked apart by the Tribe's retreat-
ing rangers....

The mare's hooves pounded up the trail and Kyle rocked in synch
with every surge of Penny's haunches. He felt no worries about
needing to guide her; this was a chunk of local terrain that every
horse within the Pale had to know by heart. He crested the knoll
above the saddle where the Cuadra was, and a stray puff of breeze
brought the smell of the barn to him—mingled aromas of grain
and hay and old manure, accented by the acrid tang of equine pee.

Thump!!

The hollow noise of a distant impact echoed in the night.

Penny galloped right past the barn and shadowy pens of the
Cuadra, churning on toward an inkier darkness below the trees
and the downhill approach to the creek crossing. That was when
Kyle realized the mare had no understanding that the bridge was
gone. No bit and bridle meant he had no means of hauling her
down, and he didn't think a mere "Whoa!" would cut it. It only
took him a split-second to make the call. He leaned back, swung
a leg over her withers and hopped off. He was able to take one
running stride as his feet whacked the ground but then stumbled
and rolled, gradually slid to a halt with his skin pin-striped and
torn by pebbles.

"Ow, ouch, crap!"

Just as he'd hoped, Penny took a sudden loss of her rider as a
signal that she ought to do something different. After three more

galloping strides, she braked and turned, craning her neck around to try to see what had become of him.

BLAM!!

A heavy caliber gun went off. The mare gave a terrified whinny as she leapt past Kyle and back up the trail toward the Cuadra. It seemed to him that she suddenly had a hitch in her gait. He felt desperate to come to her aid and grieved he couldn't. Because whatever else may have happened to Cooper during his crash in the creek canyon, he still had a gun and wanted to use it, whether he could see what he banged away at or not. Making him quit now had to be a priority. Or there was no telling how long the bullshit might go on. Or who else might land in his sights.

Of course, Kyle also had a gun. That is, he still had one if his tumble off the horse and onto the trail hadn't wrecked it while the rifle itself had busily been inflicting more trauma on his bruised spine.

He rolled up onto his knees, unslung the survival rifle, ran his hands all over it. No part of it seemed busted or loose. *Probably a great idea though, to swap out its present mag for a freshie. Can't know how many rounds Michael might've fired, back down in Elysian.* He groped in his cargo pockets for the spare magazines. *Gone. The bag of bullets, then. Also gone!* He rocked back onto his heels. *Naturally. Cooper's goons, the ones who trussed me up, also checked my pockets and snatched out the ammo for themselves. Why wouldn't they?*

With care, he popped out the small rifle's magazine and swiped its top with a finger. He felt at least one round still in the mag. So, he likely had another in the chamber. That is, if Michael had fired the weapon at all. *In that case, I've got a minimum of two bullets. Can't check its chamber or empty the mag and count any other rounds now without a risk of fumbling some away in the dark... And over across from me now on this gameboard, I can't know how many bullets Cooper might've fired, or how many he's got left.*

He slapped the clip back home. *Looks like this could turn into q-u-i-t-e the chess match. So. What's my next move?*

He realized his current spot out on the trail's long stretch of bare dirt, even amid the darkness, made him more visible than he should be. He scooted himself off to one side and put his back against the trunk of an oak. Then he waited, mouth open to sharpen his hearing, and sought to pick up any stray sound. Anything that might not be a frog or a cricket.

Crunch-crunch of footsteps. That wasn't somebody on the trail, it was a person walking in the woods, over leaves and twigs and forest litter. There, on the far side of the trail—that flicker of a darker shadow. Heading for the Cuadra. *Why's Cooper going there?* The black shape paused, moved, paused still longer, moved again. *Doesn't have his bike anymore. He aims to grab himself a horse.*

Chapter 25

K yle rose to his feet and crept along the trail, moving in the same direction, tracking the shadow. *No worries about him catching sight of me, long as he stays ahead. And me shuffling along on this trail's dust means that my footfalls are much quieter....*

As Kyle glided through the night, he considered the quintessential math problem of the unknown bullet ratio. *I'll never find enough light around the Cuadra, not any time soon, to be able to count my rounds. So then, what? I plan to fling a few puny .22s at a guy who's blasting away with .45 slugs? Doesn't seem too smart. Roy? Got anything to say?*

Kyle recalled slouching in his seat in a classroom of HSU's Behavior & Social Sciences Building, as Roy went on and on about the morality of various types of weaponry, from flung rocks to dropped nuclear bombs. But appealingly, his hand-out was a photocopy of an op-ed from a Texas news columnist named Molly Ivins, and in his mind's eye Kyle could still see that swatch of copy paper on his desk, could still hear himself chortling as he read Ivins' lead, *"Taking a Stab at Our Infatuation with Guns—Let me start this discussion by pointing out that I am not anti-gun. I'm pro-knife. Consider the merits of the knife. In the first place, you have to catch up with someone in order to stab him. A general substitution of knives for guns would promote physical fitness. We'd turn into a whole nation of great runners. Plus, knives don't ricochet. And people are seldom killed while cleaning their knives...."*

Right. Of course. Sure. Roy's Bowie knife! Now, where did I leave that? Well, I hid it under a grain sack up in the barn. But hey, if it's crazy for me to chase Cooper with just a couple tiny rounds of .22, wouldn't it even more insane to go after him with a knife?

Roy during that day's lecture: "Way best thing for you to get about a blade, though, is that one never has to reload the damn thing. Plus, Miss Ivins, totally right on this, notes that one must really close in on a target in order to use that sort of weapon. So, your aim might not turn out to be such a big issue, either."

Kyle found Cooper grew easier to observe after he left the darker shadows of the woods. But he still demonstrated strategy. Agile as a bat, Cooper flitted from wall to fence post, always waiting and looking around himself before shifting rapidly over to the next shaded spot. *Sucker's moving that butt of his 'round pretty good. Must not have gotten hurt so bad as he dumped his bike. Well-l, lucky him!*

Kyle halted, froze, when Cooper reached a corner of the barn, then swung his gaze all around the Cuadra to ensure that no one there observed him. He vanished inside. A moment later he came back out, bearing a halter and a bridle.

Okay, pal. Go pick your horse out. And right afterward—s'il vous plaît—I'll take my shot.

As the colonel went off toward the corrals, Kyle moved in on the barn himself. He padded up the staircase and went over to a suspended plank shelf where Abraham hung his sacks of grain, to keep rats away from them. Those sacks were necessarily small since dry grain had grown precious—as Abraham had told Kyle— and tended to be fed now only to sick horses who looked like they needed a boost or to pregnant mares. So, the sacks didn't get moved often. Kyle had stuck the coiled belt and the Bowie knife under the final sack in the row—but that sack was now missing. Roy's knife was gone as well.

Under his breath, Kyle cursed eloquently.

Then he noticed something odd about the wood beam above his head. It had a broad black strap dangling off one side of it. The end of a belt. He reached up and found the knife on top. *Abraham knew it was my knife, moved it someplace safe. But why'd he move that sack? Doesn't matter. Maybe he saw the belt too, sticking out from under it.*

As he buckled the belt on, a shrill neigh and the impact of a powerful hoof whacking into a plank echoed throughout the Cuadra. Kyle calculated the distance and bearing of these paired sounds. He figured out a point of origin. *Oh, my goodness. For fuck's sake. Dude's trying to mount himself on Buck! Oooh, that poor bastard.... Well, both of 'em, actually.*

Kyle scooted back down the steps, then hustled in the direction of the stallion's paddock. He heard a thunderstorm of hooves clomping into dirt, shrill whinnying, a man's shout.

He reached the fence in time to see the big stallion galloping around the perimeter of the corral as the shadowy shape of a man pushed himself back up onto his feet in the center.

Kyle gave him credit. Cooper had the smarts and guts and patience to just stand there and let Buck wear himself out by making furious and speedy circuits of his pen.

But since Cooper offered himself as such a still and steady target, Kyle was almost involuntarily forced to raise his AR-7. He put the peep sight's bead just above the occipital ridge on the back of the colonel's skull. *Guess we're 'bout to find out what a mere .22 LR bullet can accomplish here.*

Nathan Cooper took a step forward. Kyle lowered his gun as he sought to determine what Cooper's movement might signify. He noticed that Buck had quit running. The stud now faced into a corner, sweating and shivering and stomping the earth, while also craning his neck around and rolling his eyes to see what the colonel would attempt to do next.

Kyle put the rifle's bead back on Cooper's head. He let the aim settle, then squeezed the trigger. Nothing happened. *Shit! Michael really didn't shoot off any rounds. But, great. Means I've still got eight.* He pinched the tiny bolt and racked the slide. *Now one's in the pipe....*

Cooper walked steadily, confidently and smoothly toward the stallion, reaching a point where it looked like he might have the big horse pinned. Kyle could hear the colonel speak to him, calmly but with force, trying to assert a measure of dominance by vocal power alone.

Oh, be still my beating heart. This is going to be so-o-o interesting...

Approaching the horse from behind, Cooper swung the bridle aside while placing a calming hand on Buck's croup, just above his tail. Whereupon the stallion launched the colonel into low orbit. Both of this big horse's hind hooves whacked into Cooper's abdomen and proceeded to roll the colonel's ribs up on both sides while ripping apart the intercostal muscles between them as if they were made of crepe.

During this instant of brutal surgery, the colonel got lifted off his feet to an altitude of three yards and was then sent airborne and back about another six yards. He whumped down into the dust and slid to a halt, making a limb-tangled heap that after ten seconds managed to utter a single pitiful gasp.

Kyle hopped over the fence and strolled up to him.

"Bad luck, Mr. Cooper," he said. "Or your bad karma, maybe. You picked the one horse good and ready to treat you the same way the Tribe and Elysians just did. See, nobody here wants to end up with your leg over 'em."

The colonel groaned and wheezed. Kyle wondered if stretching out his crumbled body and reordering his limbs a bit would help him breath. Maybe not. But anyway, Kyle pushed the safety on and slung the rifle over his back. He grasped Cooper's legs and tugged them out straight, then dragged his torso straight. He moved an arm out straight on each side. But he could do nothing about the lopsided ball that was the colonel's shattered chest. *Lots of dislocation and breakage in that lump.*

"Thank you," Cooper whispered.

"Sure. Now, I can't do a full check. But here's your brief for tonight, colonel. Don't think you're going to make it."

"I know." His voice sounded feeble, tinged with resignation.

"You might, if we called for an ambulance and had you run off to a hospital. But that option is oh-so ten-years-ago, right? Can't find help like that pretty much anywhere, nowadays. Don't know as to how we'll ever see it again, either."

No answer.

"However, I'm willing to offer you a kind of a deal, right now, right here in this situation where we find ourselves." Kyle knelt beside him. "You clear up a few matters for me, and I'll do whatever I can to ease your way out the exit. Deal?"

The colonel seemed to nod. The darkness made it difficult to tell.

"Okay, good. One thing I don't know, why'd you ever think to leave your desert compound in the first place."

"Well dry. Food out," the colonel wheezed. "Gangs in. All signs. It was time."

"Uh-huh. How the hell'd you manage to put together such an amazing convoy?"

"Bunkers. Kept in bunkers. Ready."

"And then you heard from someone up here, that it would be a good idea to come? Who was that, Ruth and Ephraim?"

He nodded.

"And why was that?"

Fingers of one hand fluttered against the dirt as Cooper struggled to make a gesture. "Our faith." he said. "Ezra stole flock, stole Hagar, Ephraim. Must save."

"And how'd you communicate with Ruth?"

"Trystero mail. Travelers, Ephraim."

"Hey, y'know, as links go, your Ephraim's kind of a weak one, right? I mean, your kid's just not right in the head. Murdered a Sayer here, and tried to kill me, too. So, you made your big move based on his totally crap intel."

No answer.

"'Course, none of your big-nosed, bat-eared boys have struck me as all that bright. Kind of wacko, really. Wonder where they get that."

"Beloved. I...well-pleased."

"Caused a ton of death and damage up here, in a real short time."

"Make omelet...break eggs."

"That right? Well, your shell's kind of cracked, too, colonel. What's your pain level?"

"High. I...horrible...."

"You know, you sparked our war off the instant you shot Carlos."

"No, no." Cooper sucked in a tortured breath. "You. Shoot first."

"Nah. One of your idiots on a motorbike just got all crossed up and fell over. But you had to put your pistol to Carlos' head, making him fling both arms high. Oddly enough, that was a signal for an attack. But Carlos *still* might've called off our rush with a few yells. But only if you hadn't shot him. Way I see it, most or all this mess is due to your screw-ups. Otherwise, maybe there could've been some sort of fruitful negotiation."

No answer.

"All right. You're a believer. Don't need me, since you've got a God to explain yourself to. That'll be your next chore, and I probably should let you get on with it. Only question left is how, and how soon. Now I've got a .22 I could plug you with in the brain, but that's kind of an iffy method, and I don't wish to add to your suffering."

"No. Use my .45."

"Great idea." Kyle felt around the colonel's waist, but his holster was empty. Buck's moonshot had rearranged Cooper's clothing and redistributed his gear to a considerable degree. His pistol had to be out lying around in the corral's dust somewhere. Wouldn't be easy to find till after sunrise. "Sorry, it's gone."

Cooper sighed.

"I do have myself a big blade here, quite keen. I know right where to strike. I've done sheep, goats, calves, even horses. Might sting a bit, very briefly, but then you'll bleed out quick. How about it? You ready?"

Cooper nodded. The fingers on both of his hands trembled.

Kyle hauled out Roy's Bowie. He reached out with his free hand and gently pulled down the lids of the colonel's eyes and held them closed so that he couldn't see the death blow come. Then he raised his arm and drove the knife hard and deep into a hollow V where the collarbone met the side of Cooper's neck. He angled the strike to sever the carotid artery, and as soon as he jerked the blade back out of his flesh a jet of black blood spurted from his neck. The spray fanned out over the dust and then began to settle and seep down into it.

Kyle picked up the hem of the colonel's fatigue shirt and wiped his blade off, then returned it to its sheath. He stood. The colonel's body shuddered and sagged down into the corona of dark fluid that ran down from his neck. His black garments made it seem as if he was melting into the earth.

Man, he sure croaked quick. Did he have a heart attack, too?

Anyhow, I guess that's what it looks like when your luck totally runs out.

Kyle heard a clop of horse hooves against dirt and stone, then a mutter of men's voices.

"Hey!" he shouted out. "We're over in here."

—

The lean line of Red and the big, dark blob that was Abraham shuffled toward him out of the darkness.

"What' chu got there?" Red asked.

"Cooper. Well, what's left of him."

They came closer, peered down. Red whistled. "You're right. Not much goin' on in that ol' blood slick. Man's kind of mushed out. What, you do some hat dance on the dude?"

"Buck performed that service. I just administered a *coup de grâce.*"

Kyle looked around. Where had that stallion gone? Buck had backed himself into a far corner of the paddock and stood there, a bulky shadow, stock-still, ears pricked, eyes slightly agleam. He seemed aware he'd accomplished something big yet wasn't quite sure what it might be. He also seemed to be awaiting consequences.

They all heard a brief burp of radio static.

"The hell's that?"

"Don't know." Kyle bent over and felt around Cooper's uniform. In a cargo pocket of his torn fatigue jacket he located a small, handheld radio. He held it up. "Eureka," he said.

"Who's he talk to with that thing?"

"Must be his boys on the other vehicles, I imagine."

"Well, there's one truck left out there." Abraham pointed upward.

"Yep, I know. Stuck on the ridge. Likely he kept a few guys with it, to guard it and the materiel inside. Probably what Cooper was trying to reach. The last ditch. His last gasp."

"Well, maybe use that dingus there to give 'em guys the news. Underline that 'last' part."

"Good idea."

Kyle studied the radio handset for a second, then twisted up the volume and turned down the squelch control until he heard light static emerge continuously from the device's sound speaker. He keyed the mic.

"Breakitty-breaker," he said. "Any you bozos with Colonel Cooper can read me, it's half-past high time to wave a white flag. Your force sent on down into Elysian is defeated. It's kaput. And your colonel is dead as a doornail too, which I happen to know for a fact, on account of because I'm the guy who just finished him off. Don't know what you've got planned, if anything, but let's stop all bloodshed. Right now. This minute."

He slid his thumb off the key and waited. The radio crackled, and a man's voice came out of it.

"Who *is* this?" that voice demanded.

Kyle thumbed the mic. "Doesn't matter," he said. "But this isn't a fancy attempt to fool you. Not at all." He glanced at Red. "In a while—around sunrise?—you'll hear a squad of horsemen ride up and call out to you." Red nodded. "What you must do then is file on out of your truck. Put your weapons on the ground in a pile. Walk away from them. Go stand by the van body and spread your legs. Lean toward it, put your hands on it, and wait for further instructions." Red gave Kyle a thumbs-up.

"Oh, bullshit!" the voice responded.

"How do you think we got Cooper's radio? That man didn't just hand it to us. Think it over."

The voice did not answer. Red beckoned for the radio and Kyle handed it to him. Red keyed the mic.

"Listen up, doofus. We didn't merely pop a giant can of whoop-ass on your raiding party, we also snatched your party's guns. All of 'em. Surrender to us, and we'll show you mercy. Don't, and you'll get none. Want to see what a holey hunk o' metal Swiss cheese we can turn that truck of yours into? Just ignore me and all of you ignorant cracker goat-fuckers are gonna find out!"

The radio handset emitted several bursts of static and a few fumbling noises. Then a new voice came from its speaker.

"Roger all," it said. "Understood. We will comply."

Red grinned and handed the radio to Kyle.

"Nice work." Kyle switched it off and handed it back. "So, you'll lead your lads up to the ridge early tomorrow, and round 'em up?"

"Yup. Wanna come with?"

"Not particularly. Do I need to?"

"Nossir. Take yourself a break. We got it."

"Hey, did you happen to pass Penny on your way here?"

"Sure," Abraham said. "She had a limp. Head down. Big wound above her right shoulder. I considered stopping, but figured you likely needed us more. She did perk up when she saw our mounts. Could be, she turned around and followed us up."

"Let's find that sweet gal, see what we can do for her."

Chapter 26

Kyle sorted through his gear in the loft of the barn. He overheard Abraham greet a person who approached the Cuadra. A moment later Samuel made every board in the stairs creak as he shifted his bulk from step to step and came up.

"Hey," he said.

"Ho."

"Looks like you're fixing to go."

"Sharp eyes, man. Ain't no fooling you."

"Don't plan to leave behind anything important, now do you."

Kyle peered at him. When Kyle had first arrived in Elysian, he would have described the gleam in Samuel's eye as malignant. Now he mainly saw it as deeply mischievous. As far as Sam's impulse to dominate physically anyone in his vicinity, well, that just happened to be a basic part of the man's psyche. A boulder on his personal landscape. If you never pushed back, he just rolled over you.

"Tell me what you're really trying to say."

"Some of the Elysian kids found your kayak. Yesterday."

"Great, no shit! Where?"

"Lil' cove. In kind of a notch of its own. Just to the north of that beach where you wound up."

"Huh."

"Want me to bring you there?"

"How can I put this? Abso-goddam-lutely."

"Guess I should take that as a yes," Sam rumbled.

The end of his staff *bonked* on the hard ground as Samuel probed for secure footing and led Kyle down a steep slope frizzed with dry brown grasses. A good trail ran across the top of the bluff, but a spur leading downward had vanished into a trackless crust of shattered rock garlanded with clumps of stiff brush. Below them, Kyle could see horns of stony land that thrust out into the ocean, with a steep and narrow niche in between them. Here blue ocean breakers became compressed into wedges of foam that collided and churned as they shot in toward shore and then went out of view. But all the *crumps* and sloshing noises that rose up from below told the rest of their story.

"*Here?!*" Kyle asked, disbelieving.

Samuel rolled his shoulders in a shrug. "So I'm told." He turned his leading foot sideways and began to drag his stick behind him, leaning on it so he could use its hard point as a brake. Kyle dubiously followed. If he slipped and fell onto Samuel, they'd probably both take a winger over the crumbling cliff's final edge. And another thought nagged at him—*How could kids ever play in a spot like this? Seems so unlikely.*

Samuel ground to a halt. "Hey. Right down there. See?" He pointed with the end of his staff.

Walls of the niche where the waves foamed ashore to smack the cliffs cradled a small, triangular beach. The stern of a fiberglass sea kayak poked up from its gravelly sands. Apparently, all the rest of his boat had been either broken off or buried.

"Well, well. Thar' she blows," Kyle said. He looked at him. "I'll be damned."

"Sure," Samuel said. "I'd say so." He pointed his staff at him. "'Specially if you don't manage to mend those worldly ways of yours."

"Right. But that slot down there looks a deathtrap. No way to that beach. I'd be doubly damned if I even tried."

"Oh, there's an easy way down, sure enough. But then, I don't think you'd be in any kind of shape to find a way back up."

—

Kyle sat on the broad beach where he'd washed up as a castaway, mere weeks before. He listened contentedly to the mumble and sigh of low surf while he waited for the tide to drop.

The day after he'd glimpsed his kayak's forlorn carcass, Samuel had informed him that, remarkably, a good way to reach the boat *did* exist. But it had taken the kids a while to reveal their little secret: a sea cave that pierced the rocky point at the north end of Elysian's beach cove.

It tunneled through far enough to reach the niche that held the shards of his kayak. The route was usable only at times of extreme low tide. The most rambunctious children of Elysian knew the path through the cave and had used it a few times in the past. They'd found his wrecked kayak while cavorting about during a recess break. Some ripples of their playground gossip had caused rumors of their find to leak out to adults. After more hours passed, the story of a secret path that led into the narrow cove managed to dribble out as well.

On receipt of this fresh news, Kyle had retrieved the wetsuit from his gear stash up in the barn. Now he sat on the sand on a roll of his suit's tattered neoprene, waiting for the afternoon's minus tide to take hold.

He observed gulls pick through a line of seaweed and wrack that wavered across the beach toward the brackish lagoon. He studied the shorebirds that fluttered along the lagoon's rim, from the reach where waters of Balm of Gilead Creek smoothed out into blue glass and flowed into an emerald ring of reeds, displaying all the vivid color of a Tiffany window. On the beach side of the lagoon, a beige, algae-stained slump in the sand revealed a spot where the lagoon likely broke loose to drain amid the storms of winter. *Guess that's when the salmon, if there are any runs in this creek, can swim out of the ocean and fight their way up Gilead Creek to spawn.... And speaking of that mighty urge, damn, am I ever ready to complete my trip upstream and home to Luz Maria! Would've gotten my butt to Arcata a long time ago, had I not crashed here.*

An outsize wave hit the beach below him, making a dramatic *whumpf,* then a long and sinister *hiss,* as the great fan of water it had cast up onto the sand folded back onto itself and receded. *Mmm, that wave was big. A rogue. But the one that wrecked me? At least ten times that size. Or even more....*

As Kyle considered this topic, the bright physical world around him faded to nearly nothing. And the trauma of his shipwreck reared back up out of memory as if it were a kind of mental kraken, one that reached out with long and strong arms to entangle all his nerves in a reconstruction of that night, yanking his attention to the black hole of a champing beak in order to devour it whole.

The onrush of events in Elysian had rushed him along with them, had not granted him enough mental space or energy to review, much less really process, his memories of the wreck. That is, not till this moment. And now, his mind insisted upon it.

It's foggy and overcast on that day, the sun is setting, but I've seen no safe place to land during my entire last hour of paddling. The shoreline seems to consist entirely of corrugations of black wet cliffs. I listen to hollow booms of waves that slap into vertical rock. I see pale tapestries of foam tear as they slide off those steep ramparts. I see no option to land safely.

Swells surge up beneath my kayak, and the hull twists and flexes under my seat. These are potent suckers. I need to travel just outside the zone where the largest waves break. But I also must be near the shore to ensure an accurate view. Can't miss a sheltered nook, any spot where it might be safe for me to sprint in and try to seek a landing. An error either way comes with a harsh penalty. If I can't land, I must try to spend a whole night out on a storm-tossed ocean. But if I do attempt to land in a bad place and get smacked into those cliffs, my boat and I will be broken up like a crab on a platter.

I gaze westward and out to sea, looking on a rumpled, wide-wale corduroy of big swells, a vast marine quilt that flaps ceaselessly westward to disappear under a violet haze. A little above that haze, a blob of sun releases its final rays in a riot of autumnal colors, as the dim orb itself inexorably slides down into mist. If I didn't need to make a life-or-death decision I could just sit here, bobbing up and down, and lose myself in admiring such a rare and lovely view.

But, no. Need to focus to the east. Where there's suddenly a pale and motionless gleam of sand. A beach! And damn, does it look steep. A cloud of spume exhaled by exploding surf hovers above it. Waves must be breaking there in long and hard close-outs, the kind that create a high-risk LZ.

My smart move is to keep going, get past one more rocky point, see if there's another cove, better sheltered, with an improved angle for receiving the incoming seas. If there isn't, I can always swing around, paddle back, roll my dice, and try to land at that first beach.

I push on, round the next point…and never see the subtle but sweeping approach of the long-period mound that gives birth to a huge rogue wave that soars up out of the sea to my left. The kayak's hull jolts and tilts and flexes as it accelerates. I realize my tumbling dice have just now been flung onto the craps table and not by me. A black, shimmering wall holds me on its steepening curve, and looking up I'm unable to spot any top to this bastard, just a gleaming black expanse that looms high above my head. No chance to turn off, no evasive action possible. My slim hope is to take some measure to minimize the inevitable carnage.

The sea kayak bounces and skips down the face of the rising swell like a water-sprite, a nimble thing. Not the heavily overladen torpedo that I know it to be. My heart pounds as I fight to slam the rudder right and aim my bow downward so I can regain a measure of steerage. The boat fishtails, straightens, and glides ever faster. I'm just starting to win control when the wave jacks again. It's too steep and there's no time left to navigate or negotiate with the monster. My kayak's bow is about to "pearl" and then it does so, driving deep into the inky waters of the trough. I pull up knees, push hard against both rudder pedals and the underside of the deck, bracing my body tightly inside the cockpit. I bring the paddle alongside the hull, suck in a deep breath that I know might be the last one I get for a bad long while and lean forward, helmet pressed against the top of the deck, contracting all muscles in my abdomen as fiercely as I can.

The kayak pitchpoles forward. A moment of weightlessness, of vertigo. Then I slam into the water. Then the water slams into me. The shock that envelopes me as the wave breaks is a detonation of hydraulic force much fiercer than I ever imagined it could be. The tumultuous beating that ensues is far worse than any surf zone crash I've endured before. As the wave thunders and churns, my kayak does cartwheels and spins. Whirling water tries to yank the helmet off my head—or snap my head off my shoulders. The paddle is yanked from my grasp and flops wildly at the end of its leash, the cord so taut and strained that it threatens to sever my hand at the wrist. I'm knocked out of my defensive crouch in the cockpit, and my spine is rapidly bent, twisted and jammed with unthinkable force in many undesirable directions.

Worse, I feel the sprayskirt pop loose from the cockpit rim. Icy seawater floods inside to immerse me up to my waist and my boat becomes an even more ponderous fiberglass log.

My lungs burn, I ache to take a fresh breath. The grip of contradictory currents eases, next I feel a rapid sideways drift of my overturned hull. I realize that I've been driven right into the impact zone of most of the waves. Roll up now! I retrieve the paddle and fumble it into position to make an eskimo roll, perform the sweep, and bring my face up out of the water just in time to see a new wave wall shoot up beside me, streaked with brown plumes of sand it has sucked off the bottom. I try to brace into it, but its power just knocks the paddle blade over my head and spins me upside down again.

I feel my helmet bounce off the bottom, feel a shock in my hands as the paddle hits and twists. There's another long moment of chaos. I set up to roll again, but my hand just slides off the broken paddle shaft.

Busted! Now I must bail out. This fighter plane's now twirlin' down in flames, baby! Hit the silks. Pull that red lever and Martin-Baker. I and the kayak now must go our separate ways—that's my only hope.

I let go of the broken paddle and grab my bail-bag—a small waterproof duffle I carry between my legs in the cockpit—push against the cockpit rim with the other hand, kick with both feet against the pedals.

I'm free of the boat. My head and shoulders burst up to the surface just as another wave strikes. The bail-bag is almost torn from my grasp, but I pull it back and curl my body around it. That wave bats me like a shuttlecock up onto a small, dark beach formed of coarse sand and rock. I'm astounded to see that a beach even exists here, a tiny triangle hemmed in by cliffs.

Suck of a potent undertow wraps around my legs, starts to drag me back toward deep water. It trips me and I fall, but dig my fingers, toes, knees and elbows down into the gravel as receding water wraps all around me. I manage to stay high enough that the next wave pushes me further up the narrow beach. And I see my boat too, being shoved up mere yards away. I think about jumping over to it, seeing if can at least rescue one more stowage bag. But the sea has other ideas. A new wave hustles in. It's the mightiest one so far. By a lot.

My world collapses into a pit of sheer chaos, a pinball game where I am the tiny spinning ball, and powers beyond my ability to perceive or respond to dribble me off submarine courts of sand, fling me into stadium walls of rock, sluice me down channels of stygian darkness where I have no concept of up or down, left or right, or any notion of a move I could make to improve my chance to survive.

And that's the last impression my brain records.

Until the following morning, when I awaken from a coma-like sleep on a broad beach, only to find a weird-looking lad from Elysian groping around in my waterproof duffle. And my whole next phase of—what would Roy call it?—this FUBAR Fantasia, kicks off.

The low surf grumbled and sighed.

And memory released him. Then receded into his mental background, grinning and dusting its palms.

Kyle eased out of reverie and returned to a different day.

He blinked, shaded his eyes with one hand, and peered at the sun. Quite some time had passed. He looked down at the beach. The water had retreated below the belt of sand to unveil a zone of small boulders blotched with purple seaweed.

Kyle noticed that the falling tide also had drawn water away from a notch in the cliff wall at the north end of the cove. He saw a dark spot where wave action had battered the base of a crack that ran several yards up the face of the cliff.

He got up and walked toward the notch, treading across a flat stretch of wet sand, then a shelf of rock speckled by white barnacles. A black aperture lay at the base of the notch, with seawater sloshing through it—apparently from some big source on a different side. It showed more movement than mere backflow could explain. And that hole did appear large enough for a human body to pass through. *A kid's body, maybe. But mine? Bet even kids wait till the tide drops lower before they try to squeeze through. But I don't feel very patient. So, it'll be a wet, cold trip. Better put on my wetsuit.*

After he zipped up his suit, he re-buckled the Bowie knife belt around his waist. Then he took a breath, dropped to his hands and knees and squeezed himself into the crack. The water came up to his chest as he crawled, but he found a band of air wide enough to breathe in hovered above that. Even though he had to keep his neck bent so he wouldn't bang his head on the jagged roof. *If another big wave sweeps in here, though, I'm going to get swamped AND thumped.* But the passage soon widened. Now he crept over slimy boulders in absolute darkness, cautiously feeling his way along with an outstretched hand. A dim grey light shone when he rounded a bend. A dank, briny wind fanned his face, and he could hear a new bash and seethe of wave action, like the rhythm of a stick and wire brush on a snare drum, occurring at a slightly different tempo than the ocean sounds he'd left behind at the bigger cove.

One more turn, and he was able to stand upright. He found himself looking at a tawny, pebbly beach, breaking surf and a lozenge of blue sky, bracketed by the steep cliffs on each side of the niche. And there, directly in front of him, the stern of his shattered kayak poked out of the sand like a colorful tombstone. He felt a medley of emotions well up as he walked up to the wreck and laid a hand on its bent aluminum rudder. *Regret? Nostalgia? Relief and gratitude for survival? Don't really need to pin it down, I guess. Focus on the practical.*

Clearly, the boat itself could not be salvaged. Cracks on its hull were so deep that flakes of gelcoat had popped off. As to what dunnage might be left within, he'd have to return with a pick and shovel and a few spare hours to discover that—assuming the rest of the hull lay beneath the sand, which might not be correct. But he thought up a way to check on the stern compartment right now. He backtracked to the base of the cliffs and picked out a lump of rock the size of a softball. Back at the wreck, he drew the knife and used the rock to hammer the tang at the end of the hilt. That let him drive the blade into one of the cracks. Soon he was able to saw open the fiberglass and peel a swath of it back.

The hold was clotted with sand and pebbles. But he also felt a cold, sharp-edged metal shape. He scraped with the knife blade, dug with his fingers, was able to reach the handle of a steel ammo box and haul it out. He sat on the sand, popped its latch. A slight sucking sound as the lid released. An odor emerged that he hadn't smelt in a while—Roy's garage.

He dumped the box out on his lap. A stout Ziploc bag holding about eighty rounds of .45 ACP landed first. Kyle sighed. *Can't believe that Roy even imagined I'd haul up and take with me the pistol he used to shoot himself. No way, man! But hey, if Abe ever finds Cooper's 1911, and wants to give that gun to me, then I'd have a nice piece to carry north—with plenty of bullets.*

Various wool articles had been crammed into the ammo box for padding—a balaclava, a Basque beret, gloves, a scarf. *Good warmth accessories.* After them tumbled a white plastic tube of surprising weight, and a large waterproof case of green plastic. Kyle sliced the tape off the tube and found that it held 30 one-ounce gold coins, Krugerrands. *Aha. My allowance. Or inheritance. Hey thanks, Roy.*

He turned the green case over. It had the word "comfort" scrawled on its top in black grease pencil. He popped the latches with his thumbnails, opened it and saw a silver flask with more scrawled black letters on it that read, "Everclear 151." Also, a cloth sack held a pipe of Irish briar, a pouch labeled, "Bugle & Hounds Tobacco Mix", and a handful of matchbooks saved out of military MREs. *Damn, man. You sure had an eye for pre-Flare leftovers. Who else in California owns any stuff like this? Almost nobody.*

He returned all the items to their respective containers, snapped them shut, stood up and carried the ammo box back toward the cave. Before crawling through it again, he paused, looked at the high and crumbling walls of the triangular amphitheater, then turned to look out to sea, where low waves collided and churned at the points of land before shoving a mix of water and foam into the niche and up onto its tiny beach.

What the hell happened to me, that night? Did I get rinsed out to sea and then washed back in at the big beach cove? Or did I somehow get sucked through this cave without ever realizing it? A miracle, either way. But why would the cosmos care about me that much? Hard to call what happened just dumb luck. Rarely does good fortune get dumped out in such a humongous dose. 'Specially since I did fuck-all to earn it. Elysians would most likely label it an intervention by Providence. Not sure I could muster a good argument against 'em.

Chapter 27

Kyle ambled on up to the Council Lodge. He paused to observe the denizens of Elysian as they streamed back into their settlement. Some clutched tied bundles balanced on their heads, others shoved handcarts piled high with goods, a few led packhorses, but all seemed chatty and lively, broadcasting an air of collective ease—if not outright merriment—that he hadn't seen in them before.

At the lodge entrance, a burly Latino man who wasn't Samuel—although he held a quite similar ceremonial staff—welcomed him with a nod and a smile, then held aside the entrance flap.

"I'm here to visit Sayer Michael," Kyle told him.

"Yes, I know. Go right on in," the man. "You've been here before; guess you can find your own way."

Elysian views of themselves seem to have shifted...maybe their opinion of me, too.

Kyle passed through the council chamber, down the hall and into the oculus room. The skylight dropped a bright puddle of sunlight on the floor that initially made it hard for him to see who or what might be present along the shaded walls, but then he did. His eyes went straight to Michael in his robe, who sat up high on the carved redwood chair. A short flight of steps had been nailed to the front of this throne to enable him to ascend and take his seat.

"Looking good up there, Michael. Did it astonish you to get the nod?"

He grinned at him, but Michael only raised an eyebrow and appeared dour. Kyle suspected it was an attempt to look regal.

"No. Why would I be? I felt prepared. I was next in line. And I served Elysian well. Quite well. Which was recognized."

Kyle studied him. It was easier to do, since their eyes were now on the same level. His first impression was that the companionable link they'd forged amid the fight had receded, while a measure of Michael's former truculence slid back and locked into place. *Ah, well. Cut this guy slack. He needs to acclimatize to a quick lift in status. Uneasy the head that wears a Sayer's cowl, I guess. May take a while to really own it. Was I comfortable when I was made prof? Not right away.*

"It was the Elders who elected you as Sayer, I hear."

"That's right."

"Is it the way the pick's always been made?"

"No. Our first Sayer was Judith, the mother of Ruth and Rebecca. She was anointed by Jed James, our founder. Before she died, Judith selected Ruth to succeed her, and then Ruth selected Rebecca to join her."

"Ah-h. Now there's a complicated relationship."

"All guided by the Spirit. Any assessment you try to make of our procedures is irrelevant. All right?"

"No, no. I meant, between those sisters."

A bemused smile gradually replaced the stern look on Michael's face.

"Oh. You think?" he said.

"I wonder if Ruth sought to elevate Rebecca, or really, just wanted to bring her close and keep her under her thumb."

"Oh, I'd say, the latter. But hey, good luck to anyone trying to control Rebecca, right? Ultimately, that was never going to work."

"I've thought about it. I imagine that mutual jealousy was a key part of their dynamic. Rebecca resented Ruth's power. Ruth envied Rebecca for her youth and good looks. Maybe hated her for taking Ruth's own beauty down a peg with that pencil stab when they were kids. Add in her anger and envy that Becky had been scoring herself major lovin' up on the Pale, and you wind up with the toxic cocktail."

"Yes. And as you've reported, it appears Rebecca was physically active with Red and Carlos, both. Possibly at the same time. Talk about thorough show of rebellion!"

Michael shook his shaggy head. Kyle noted that it was less shaggy than it had been. Evidently, becoming a Sayer qualified the guy for some quality time with someone in Elysian with a good set of shears.

"But we shouldn't really be talking about that sort of thing. Not in the sanctuary."

"Nevertheless, you just can't stop yourself."

Michael emitted a chuckle. Then he grunted, leaned forward, and rubbed himself on the small of his back with the knuckles of one fist. He looked up. "Want some tea?"

"Sure."

Michael rose onto his stubby legs, made his way carefully down the steps.

"What? Abdicating your throne, and so soon?"

"Darn thing's not really that comfortable."

"But it's not like you feel a strong yen to shuck the robe and go back up onto the Pale again. Or do you?"

"No."

Michael walked to one of the radiating halls and called out, "Rachel?" Then he went over to a plank bench by the fire ring, where he sat and then patted the wood next to him. Kyle approached and sat, astraddle the plank so that he could face him.

"I agree with your analysis, excepting for that 'looks' part," Michael said. "Appearances were not important to Ruth, of course."

"Oh, come on. You knew she could see, right?"

Michael frowned and his own eyes danced. Then he sighed. "Well... I must admit, at times, I did suspect it."

A robed girl with an elfin face and a mane of thick brown curls that tumbled down her back all the way to the cincture at her waist, entered. She looked vaguely familiar to Kyle, but he couldn't quite place her.

"Sayer Michael?" she said.

"Could you please bring mugs of hot tea for myself and our guest?"

She made a graceful move that mingled bow and curtsy, spun around and left.

"Don't blame you, at all. Ruth was quite convincing," Kyle said. "Only had a slight suspicion myself, till I watched that battle between her and Ephraim right here in this room. She sprinted over the firepit to snatch up a stick and got ahold of it with a one fast swipe of her hand. That's when I knew, for sure."

Michael sucked in his lower lip, bit it for a second, then let it pop back out.

"We should speak no ill of Ruth. She strove to be a worthy servant of the Lord. She died a martyr for peace."

"That's one way to look at it. Another is, she made the dumb mistake of running out into the middle of a firefight, where she hollered out some nonsense and drew attention to herself."

"She was trying to stop it!"

"If so, she tried to reverse an event she herself had set in motion. And it came rather late."

"Yet her effort was sincere. And she paid a high price."

"Okay. Granted. Let's say she had the virtue of sincerity, as well as its opposite. She was a complex creature. Most people are. Her act was one of the most interesting things about Ruth, was it not? I mean, not only how good she was at pretending to be blind, but *why* she did it. I'd pick three reasons. One was to be sure Rebecca kept feeling guilty, another was to keep everyone remembering Rebecca's awful deed. But her big clincher was that Ruth could gather a ton of information and then pretend she got it all from her psychic powers. She could claim to possess the Sight. The prophetic gift. And thus, appear to be favored by heaven."

Michael sighed once more and lifted his eyes to the oculus. "But I have to tell you," he said. "Ruth actually *was* psychic. Really. I mean okay, yeah, sure, maybe she cheated too. But that aside, she could make guesses about things that were amazingly accurate. Things she shouldn't have known, couldn't have known, even granting her the one eye that worked." Michael looked at Kyle. "Didn't she ever pull something like that on you? In any of your visits with her?"

Kyle thought about that. "Yep, come to think of it, she did. Said something about my wife, Luz Maria—"

"There! You see?"

"See what?"

"That we live in Spirit. A Presence, one that we can serve, and which can serve us. Though we be imperfect vehicles for its glory."

"Yeah. We're all rusted-out vehicles with flat tires, busted spark plugs and a burnt-out clutch."

"Do not mock. I know that you judge harshly. You think we're deluded."

"No. Actually no, I do not. If you people wish to personify the cosmos, go on ahead. Have at it, see where that gets you. I'm awestruck by your commitment to the process. Folks build the road that they walk upon, and as long as they don't harm others, they've got every right to construct it as they wish. But what I object to, are any religious types who seek to lay their trip or their judgment on me. See, I'm already committed. Made my choice a long while ago. I prefer to deal with a cosmic essence that is *not* personified. And I don't wish to be bugged by people who don't or can't or won't accept that. When it occurs, I push back. Naturally."

"But do you gain nothing from Writ, then?" Michael persisted. "Since you've read it? Have you no longing to rest faith in our Lord?"

"Hey, I've gotten a ton from holy writ. Almost as much as I got out of Shakespeare. But as far as Christianity goes, I'd second my teacher Roy on that. He said it was a splendid idea and humanity really ought to try it sometime."

Michael's chortle had a rueful tinge, as though he didn't really want to laugh at this. Yet he did anyway.

"Our sole glory lies in our striving," he murmured.

"Roy said the only true worship of Christ is the imitation of Christ. The rest is mere jabber."

Michael rubbed his jaw. "Well, then I'd say, there might a point or two we can agree on."

"Okay, here's another. It doesn't bother me a whit that you folks study your so-called holy books and discuss them, or that the Sayers try to interpret what's read. It does give people something to think about. That process brought western civilization through one dark age, and maybe it'll carry us through another. Still, I think it would be best if many additional books were toted along during that journey. Which in fact is what happened in most of those monastic communities of old."

Michael's eyes gleamed. "Good idea. Why don't you stick around, then, and help us build our library?"

It was Kyle's turn to laugh. "These days, there's some real joy in Elysian. All you folks are flush with victory. Still, I don't think it would be long before burning me at the stake would start to look like some sort of reasonable entertainment. And here's the big reason—I think that guy I read about in the Bible would much rather be called 'brother' than 'Lord.' I mean, you folks can claim the opposite all you want, but I will never, ever buy it."

The slim girl Rachel arrived carrying a pair of earthenware mugs that had curlicues of fragrant steam rising from them. She handed one to Kyle and one to Michael, smiled and departed with a swish of her grey robe and a swing of her mane of long hair. Kyle realized she had been the one to bring his soup that morning of his first long chat with Ezra.

"Bottom line, I think I'd be a lousy fit here, long term. That is, if I decided not to go home to Arcata. And there's zero chance of that."

"I see your point."

Kyle took a sip. The flavor was herbal yet earthy. He couldn't quite name the tea's ingredients, but he liked it.

"Anyway, I think the Elders made a shrewd call when they named you Sayer. If anybody can improve communication between the Tribe and Elysian, it's you."

"Thanks."

"In fact, several times, I felt surprised by how well that already works. I mean, stuff known in Elysian got known up on the Pale awfully darn quick. And that info flow also seems to work nearly as well going the opposite way. Almost as if someone was managing it."

Michael was poker-faced. "I have no idea what you're talking about."

"I'm sure you don't."

They sipped their tea in silence for a moment.

"And I must say, one aspect of your appointment I find totally amusing. Had *no* idea you were a virgin."

Michael sighed. His eyes twinkled. Two pits deepened under his cheekbones as he compressed his lips. "Well," he said finally, "I guess I am one now."

Chapter 28

Kyle slid a palmful of a salve mixed from sulfur and lard into the gouge above Penny's right shoulder. Since the night a slug fired from Cooper's gun drilled a trench through her hide, a week had passed. Her wound had largely closed and steadily healed, yet it still needed a smear of Abraham's custom horse-care goop to forestall infection and keep the flies out.

As he worked on her, the mare bent her neck and eyed him, then tried to nibble on his leg. "Be still," he admonished. She straightened up but danced a little on her hooves. "Sweetheart! What's gotten into you? Chill."

He walked around behind her to put the pot of salve back on a shelf, and the mare shifted her weight from haunch to haunch, lifted her tail and swished it aside. He wondered if she wanted to kick him. That would certainly be a surprise. But no, she had something else in mind. He saw the dark lips of her vulva open and close, affording a brief glimpse of their pink inner depths.

"Aha. I get it. Why, you brazen little tart."

Kyle was still laughing about it when the bulk of Abraham loomed in the door to the barn.

"How's that nick looking?" he asked.

"Good enough. Don't plan to ride her, anyhow. Maybe lash a couple of bags to the saddle. Taking her on lead past all those tangles of brush to the north is smartest way to get through. Hey, need to ask you 'bout something."

Kyle dug into a pocket of his recently acquired buckskin jacket and hauled out a gold coin. It was one of Roy's ounce-size Kruger-rands. He held the round up pinched between thumb and forefinger so that it gleamed like a miniature sun.

"How about me giving you this in exchange for Buck?"

"You serious?"

"As death."

"Careful. That stud has proved he can dish out a dose of it."

"Right. So, we owe the big guy. Don't like the fate he's facing. You shouldn't just whack his balls off, then set him to work at skidding logs or whatever. Too much of a come-down."

Abraham wagged his head slowly from side to side.

"We can barely get a halter on that horse and lead him over to another corral. How on earth will you bring him all the way up to Arcata?"

"Got me a secret weapon."

Abraham looked skeptical. Kyle pointed to the mare's backside.

"Penny's going into heat."

Abe's broad face split into a grin. "And you think *that* will make him easier to control?"

"No, not exactly. But I know I can lead her, and I bet she can lead him. It'll give me a chance to look at Buck in a fresh setting. I mean, every horse is a person, right? No two are the same, and the personality of any one of 'em can evolve. We could bond in a new way, just the three of us, traveling together. Maybe being penned up all by himself has made Buck crankier than he needs to be. And I'm not real worried about him and Penny. That mare thinks she's at least half-human, so she's not about to take crap from any mere horse, even if he's a stallion.

"If it doesn't work? Heck, I'll let him run off. Put him out to stud with some of the bands of wild horses that roam California these days. That's a good, alternate retirement plan for the dude. Plus, it's one he earned, after he wiped the ground with Cooper for us. Even if he scoots away from me, I'll still get to Arcata with two horses."

"How—" Then Abe smiled. "All right, I get it, the one inside the other. Like those dolls. And I guess I like it. Deal." He reached out and plucked the coin from Kyle's hand. "But I know you've handed out some of these golden cuties as if they were cookies. Not about to run dry, are you?"

"Easy come, easy go. Just swapping 'em for gear and tools I want. Come right down to it, such things are just as valuable, if not more so. Don't worry, I'll be fine."

"Well, come on up to my loft. Got another item that might help you on your way."

———

Abraham handed Kyle the 1911 model of semiauto pistol Cooper had carried the night he died. The weapon was clean and gleaming, with a bit of extra shine in the places where its bluing had been worn off by use.

"Where'd you find it?"

"Up against a fencepost. Guess it skidded to a halt there, and kind of kicked up dust on itself. Borrowed some gun oil from the Tribe, and I wiped it down for you."

"Thanks. I mean, I love my .22, but nothing like a major hand-cannon for backup."

"Better to have it and not need it, than need it and not have it. How I'd figure it too. Never know exactly who or what you'll run into between the settled places."

"Which is why you stick around here, 'stead of hitting the road?"

"Well, this is a place I know, and one that knows me. Which makes for a more peaceful and predictable day, right?"

"'Specially now that Cooper and his gang have been sorted out. So, tell me. How do the final numbers look, with that bunch?"

"They lost nearly half of his outfit. Ten dead, seven wounded. Survivors are camped in quarantine outside the Portal. The ones who want, can enter to attend services and to do work. Then once they've been thoroughly vetted over the course of time, they can join up either with the Tribe or Elysian, according to their preference. Any who'd rather run off and take their chances on the Outside can do so. But once they choose that route, they can't return."

"I've heard the liberal approach was your idea."

Abraham shrugged modestly. "Oh, I gave folks some input on it, sure. Y'know, years of being around horses can give a guy some notion of how a herd should work, and how it might not."

"Elysian itself is at a fork in the trail," Kyle mused. "Now, it seems to be heading more down a democratic path. Makes sense. Authoritarian structures may work well to handle emergencies, but over the long haul they can leave people feeling unheard, resentful, and left out. I guess that's why the Elders decided they would elect the next Sayer."

"Michael? Yes. Great pick."

"Excuse me, did you say 'pick'?"

"Yes, I did." Abe chuckled. "What did you think I said?"

Kyle smiled. "And your Elders? How do they get seats on the council?"

"Oh, that deal was started five years ago. A year after Judith died. They're elected by the whole town."

"So, the change happened about a year after Ruth became Sayer."

Abraham cocked a look at him. "Think I can guess what you're driving at."

"It's a key to what's gone down. Her whole plot with Ephraim and Cooper was designed to restore power and authority to her. Her proper role. Hoped to reverse the course of local history. Of course, Cooper probably had his own notions. But that's only one thing I'm driving at. The other item I'd like to mention is, this might be the right time for you to run for Elder."

"Oh, please." Abraham rolled his eyes. "I'm happier up here. Horses are critters that I understand and can relate to. People, not so much."

"Yeah. For just that reason. Your heart is good, and your instincts are sound. Elysian might be able to truly use some of that. Look, the three main plotters of the grand authoritarian coup are dead as mackerels. Cooper, Ephraim and Ruth. And they croaked while managing to achieve the exact opposite of that they'd intended. The pendulum is now swinging hard the other way, here. I'd call that an excellent opening for major change. Think about it."

Abraham snorted. "Right. And now that you've poked that idea into my head, how can I *not* think about it? Thanks a lot."

"You're welcome."

"Hey, why don't you stay and run for Elder? Bring your wife on down. We'd find a place for you."

"Can't imagine anybody's got a mallet big enough to pound a square peg like me into such a round, round hole, pal."

"Well, I mean, as long as we're tossing around wacko ideas about what folks ought to do with themselves...."

"Best I can promise is, if our world settles down some more, I might drop by on some future day for a visit. As Aristotle said, a cure for fifty enemies is one friend. And Abe, I'd like to think of you that way."

"Guess I can let you do that. You've got yourself another deal, there. And I've got to say, until the next time we ever talk, I'll stay lit with curiosity 'bout how Penny and Buck work out for you."

Chapter 29

Penny stamped her hooves, swished her tail, and released a squirt of pee as Kyle tied her off to a hitching rail at Treetown One. Buck stomped around behind her and snorted, his eyes wide and his ears slanted forward. She commanded his undivided attention. Kyle considered mooring the stallion to the same rail but then saw that, if he did, the horses might literally tie themselves in knots. Anyhow, the mare already had Buck on short tether.

Instead, he unclipped the stallion's halter so Buck had full room to maneuver. The inevitable now looking to be well underway, he released his packs from the sides of the mare's saddle and loosened the girth and removed that too.

"Hey, be careful of my girl," he told the stallion. "No deep kissing on the first date, all right? And no kicking, gouging or biting either. Keep it fair."

He heard the door to the arboreal cabin open above his head. The big unit that Carlos had lived in was one of a lucky half-dozen structures that had been left unburnt. He looked up and scored a view of Red on the landing, stark naked except for bandages that wound around all his limbs and one that slanted across his chest like a bandolier.

"Hello, Red. What's up with your new look? Is wearing buckskins passé on the Pale now?"

"Nah," he said, waving a hand. "Clothes just kind of chafe all my sore spots. So, I'm having to go without 'em for a few days."

"Okay, that's a relief. I mean, I'm always a step behind fashion, but I'm not sure I'd ever be ready for a style like that."

"You want to come up, or what?"

"Yeah. Thought I'd drop by for a chat before I hit the trail."

"Sure. Do it. Jade's inside, I know she'd like to see you."

"'Cos she's seen more'n enough of you, most likely."

"Hah."

Kyle rooted through a pack, hauled out the box Roy had labeled "comfort"—one of the items he'd rescued from his wrecked kayak—and proceeded to tromp up the stairs. Upon reaching the landing, he gave a low whistle.

"Damn, Red. I heard you got tuned up a tad in the fight at Elysian. When you came to the Cuadra that same night, you looked all right. But then it was dark. By light of day, you're a wonder to behold! How do you feel?"

"'Bout like I got et by a wolf and shat off a cliff, is all. But I've been worse off."

"Have you? Makes me kind of surprised you're still around."

"Hell, that's one way I keep most folks amused. Me included."

Red pointed down at the horses. Buck was sidling up to Penny and nudging her. The top lip on his muzzle was curled up, exposing his teeth in a wide equine grin.

"Heard me a rumor you wanted to take that badass Buck on home with you. What happened? You get dropped on your head during the fight, or something?"

"Well, maybe I did back when I was a baby. Which would explain a lot. But it's more, I feel that me and Buck have a lot in common. Like we both do love Penny, and we both hoped to rush Colonel Cooper off to kingdom come."

"Your skulls could be similarly thick, too."

"Yep. And there's that."

"Way things go down there, you might end up with a pasture-bred foal into the bargain."

"In truth, that is my aim."

"Well, let's give 'em some privacy, while he gets her done. Come on in."

—

Red held the door open and beckoned Kyle to enter the cabin's dim and funky recesses. But now its smoky redolence seemed reassuringly familiar, even somewhat homey. Jade sat on a stump stool in front of a plank table that held a pair of quart jars full of a gray substance. She was hand-rolling a cigarette.

"Hi, Kyle!" she said brightly. "So, you've had about all you can take of the Elysian Valley, huh?"

"Oh, it's not like that. More, it's that there's no place like home."

"I remember that movie! Wish we had a way we could still see it."

"Well, there *is* a way. Got equipment up in Arcata, decent wind power and some archived discs. You could come visit."

"Could we?"

She shot a beseeching look at Red, who shrugged noncommittally. He pulled a cured deer hide off a peg, wrapped it about his waist like a kilt, came over and sat beside her.

"Aye, now you look like a proper laird of the manor," Kyle told him. He sat at the table, too. He pointed at the pair of grey jars. "What do you have there?"

"Carlos and Sally," she told him.

"Really?"

"We're just waiting for a good, strong West wind to come screaming over the ridge," Red said. "Then when the fog blows through the oaks, with all those big limbs thrashin' 'round, it's when we'll scatter the ashes and let 'em fly."

"Interesting send-off."

"Way we've always done it."

"Only bit I'd add, get somebody to play 'Ride of the Valkyries' on a kazoo."

Jade giggled. "They would *love* that," she said. Then she fell silent, heaved a sigh and looked sad.

Red appeared peeved. "Don't know what the hell you think you're kidding about, there," he said. "But I lost me my best pal, and I sure do miss him."

"Well, you can take a degree of comfort in knowing that you've done a decent job of filling his shoes. Moccasins, I mean."

"Not hardly." Red wiped the underside of his nose with a fore-finger. "Anyways, I've not been 'lected in yet by our whole crew. Not sure I plan to stand for chief, anyhow."

"Speaking of 'comfort,' how 'bout I pop this baby open," Kyle said. He thumbed the latches of Roy's box. "Then we can offer our toast to those dear departed. I mean, seeing as I'll be MIA for their ceremony."

"Hmmm." Red peered into the box. "What you got there? Damn my eyes, is that real tobaccy?"

"Yep. Sealed pouch. Might even still be good."

"Light it up, let's check and see."

Kyle slit the pouch open with the tip of Roy's blade. A tangy pungence—not unlike the aromas from a Virginia curing shed in midsummer—wafted from the opening. He wasted no time in plucking out a wad and stuffing a tuft of its fragrant shreds into the pipe. He tamped with a fingertip and then skritched a match. He worked his cheeks to get a red coal started, drew vapors into his mouth, sucked it into the top of his lungs, and then let the smoke drift lazily from his nostrils.

He nodded and smiled. "Uh-huh," he told Red. "You were right. It's real tobacco."

"Pass it here."

"There you go, skipper."

"Mmm. Umm-hmm," Red said, "a tasty reminder of my highly wasted youth. Jade, you want a hit?"

"Sure." She wrapped her plump lips around the pipe's stem, sipped smoke gingerly. "Ugh." She wiped her lips with the back of one hand, coughed. "That shit's nasty! How do you stand it?"

"Gets better, more times you try."

"No thank you, very much. I'll stick with this." She held up her hand-roll. "It's way more floral. And got better side effects too, I'll bet."

"Suit yourself," Kyle said, taking back the pipe.

"And what's that there?" Red poked at the flask.

"Oh, something that my teacher Roy used to call depth-charge medicine. Basically, it's five-star industrial drinking alcohol. Would you care to compare it against your 'shine?"

"Hey, thought you didn't indulge."

"Well, that was just before a battle. Now, it's the victory parade."

"Word, buddy." Red gave him a thumb's up and got to his feet. He tucked a fold of his leather kilt a bit tighter around his waist, walked to a shelf, grabbed three cups made from ends of cow horns and brought them back.

Kyle twisted open the cap of the flask and poured a hefty splash of clear liquor into each. Then he lifted his cup. "To Carlos. Brave guy. True leader," he said.

"Great friend," Red added.

"Sweet man," Jade said.

"If there's a Happy Hunting Ground, Carlos deserves to ride around on it," Kyle concluded.

"Hear, hear."

"And to Sally, she was a real den mother to the whole Tribe," Jade said.

"Didn't get to know her well," Kyle said. "But she seemed brave, too."

"She sure as heck was able to keep Carlos in check!" Red said. "I can think of no higher praise."

"Hear, hear."

They clunked their horns together, then drank. Jade lowered her cup, glanced down at it admiringly, and went for another swallow. Red sputtered for a moment, and his eyes watered.

"What is that, acid?" he said.

"Oh, in a manner of speaking. Old-school firewater. Kind you can't really find around much anymore. Usually mixed with other stuff. Fruit juice or what have you."

"Well, our corn 'shine is a ton smoother. You'll see." He snatched up a jug from under the table, yanked out its stopper with his teeth, and added a generous dose to each of their horns as they held them out, and finished by topping off the horn he held between his knees. "Made my drink fifty-fifty," he said, "So it can be somewhat tolerable. My mix, right there."

"Jade, what do you think?"

"I like the bite, all by itself." She smirked.

They just sat for a moment, all elbows bending occasionally as they savored their sips of firewater.

"So, what's your route out?" Red asked. "Central Valley, up and over, or you plan to bushwhack?"

"By bushwhack you mean north, then yeah, that's my choice. Valley way could show too many meanies. Like it did when I headed down, except now I'd be moving a lot, lot slower than I was then. Probably best for me to stay high. Like, take your brushy trail north off the Haul Road, go northeast from here until we hit the Jackass Ridge, then strike up toward the King Range. What do you think?"

Red nodded. "That's the way of it. You been to Petrolia? Well, the bridge there is still up over the Mattole."

"Good."

"Y'know, I might could give you a ranger escort off the Pale. As far as King Peak, maybe."

"Thanks, no. Inconspicuous is more my style."

Red snorted. "Coulda fooled me!"

"Hey. I'm humble as the dust."

"Well, you don't fool *me,*" Jade said. "And you never did."

Kyle smiled.

"I've got your bow quiver down there, lashed on my pack. Remind me to give it back to you before I go."

"Oh hell, just keep it."

"Really?"

"Sure. You earned it, and I've already got me another one goin', anyhow. Just backed it the other day."

"Grand. Thank you. Well, in that case, I'd just like to buy a few more arrows." Kyle dug in his pocket, then flipped a gold Krugerrand on the table. The coin wobbled and rang as it settled onto the wood. Red's eyes bugged out slightly.

"That what I think it is?"

"Probably."

"Don't think I got enough arrows to sell you!"

"Consider it a payment for as many shafts as you can spare. Plus, a down payment on any goods that come through you might want to forward on to me at HSU. That is, if you can figure out a way to do it. Add in a tallywhacker, right now. I'd sure like to have me one of those."

"Done," Red said. "Pick one out 'fore you go."

"And if you really like these things," Kyle said, as he tapped a finger on the gold coin, "I can think of a way you might be able to get more of them."

"Yeah?"

"While I've been here, I've been impressed with how the rangers do stuff. Not everything, but some things. Such as fighting. Strikes me that it might be useful if a squad of rangers could be sent for. I mean, if trouble breaks out again in Arcata, and I sent a message to you asking for you to ride north. As a kind of mutual aid thing. Would you do it?"

"Maybe." Red shot a glance at Jade, trying to read her reaction. "We'd think about it, certainly."

Jade looked at Kyle. "It's a whole new world," she said brightly. "He started doing that, just the other day."

"What, thinking?"

"Not only. Also, checking in with me to see what I think."

"Wow."

"'Nuff of that gibberish. Both you hush. This is 'portant. Now, you say, 'mutual aid.'" Red tugged on his beard. "It means your folks can come down to help us out, too?"

"Could."

"Then why offer to pay more of these?" Red tapped the coin himself. "If we're lookin' at a swap? Not that I'd mind, mind you."

"'Cos in special circumstances, incentives could apply. I just want to make my case in advance. Might be a move I'd need in a hurry, so I want you to get used to the idea. No tactic better than swatting an unsuspecting enemy with a rogue element. And what could be more rogue than a company of Tribe rangers? Be great to know that I've got you on tap."

Red threw back his dreadlocked head to laugh. "You really be a piece o' work, man." He slid the coin over to Jade. After she grabbed it, she dropped a hand to stuff it into one of her own pockets.

"That's what I'm told," Kyle said. "So. Far as getting a message down to you, how could that work for me? Right before Cooper kacked, he mentioned a system, 'Trystero.' Said that Ruth and Ephraim used it to kind of mail stuff to him."

"Yeah, that. Ask 'bout it on your back streets in Arcata. You might find it's been run 'round under your nose for a while. Traders carry and transfer messages for a fee. Like, if you gave one guy a handful of your .22 bullets, and he picked out ten for his share, and passed the rest on with your message to the next guy. Something like that. 'Course, a bag a' top bud can work the deal too, near equal well."

"How often do messages come to the Portal?"

"Just about every other time anybody ever comes by."

"Oh."

Jade waved her hand. "Hey. Kyle. Can I ask you something?"

"Shoot."

"That night you ran off. Just grabbed Penny off the picket line. So, how come you didn't keep on keepin' on? Ride north and home to your wife? Isn't that where you've always been wanting to get to?"

"Well. Thought about doing so that very day. Seriously! But then I realized there was no way I could puzzle out a path through all the brush and move fast enough to keep your rangers from catching up."

"Got that right." That was Red. And his sly grin.

Kyle poked up a forefinger. "Later, I realized that Sayer Ruth hoped I'd try to escape. She needed to deflect attention from the mystery of Rebecca's death. Reduce all speculation. Refocus people's attention on catching a culprit. When I show up? That's her big stroke of luck. A perfect decoy to lead everyone away from her and Ephraim. If I ran off from the Pale, then you captured me, my escape attempt alone would prove my guilt. And if I ran away and you *didn't* catch me, that would be even better for her. See, then I couldn't be dragged back to say anything contrary to her story. I'd stay the bad guy forever, your scapegoat, driven off into the desert with all the sins of a community piled on my back. Most especially, hers."

Jade slapped her palms together in applause. "Man, did you ever get Ruth," she said. "Always thought she was crooked as a skunk's back leg."

"Yeah, but there's more to it, darlin'," Red said. His index finger circled in a broad arc. "I'm sayin', the actual deal, okay? Dude right here purely does love all this shit. I mean, combat, mayhem and whatnot."

"What?" Kyle's forehead wrinkled.

"You. Don't try to bullshit a bullshitter. Been keeping my eye on you this whole time, pal. Tryin' to tell us, you both was scared of being caught, and you aimed to outfox Ruth?" Red narrowed his eyes and shook his head. "Those are the reasons you kept your butt 'round here? I cry horseshit."

"You do?" Jade.

Red went on. "Sure, you hope to get home to this Luz chick. Some. But there's a 'nother thing you want just as much, if not a whole bunch more."

"Yeah?" Kyle scoffed. "What?"

"To win!" Red chortled. "Now I see, just by lookin', I got you dead to rights. Bullseye." He turned to Jade, while jabbing his finger at Kyle. "See, this guy tries to come across as a lone wolf. Yeah, I admit he does play that act fair to middlin' good. But what he *really* hopes to do is end up top dog. He wants to lead a whole bunch of other guys into some kinda giant fight. Wants to puzzle out tactics and strategy and timing and all the rest o' that crap and figure a way to outsmart his opponent and beat him into the ground and so come out on top. Victory! That's what this man lusts for." He turned back toward Kyle. "Now, I couldn't see so well that night at the Cuadra. But I did see the way you stood over that bloody heap that used to be Cooper. You felt proud to win and pleased as punch. Am I right, or am I right?"

Amid this peroration, a flush slowly crept across Kyle's cheeks and then up his forehead to the roots of his hair. He sat silent for a moment, then said softly, "It is well that war is so terrible. Otherwise, we should grow too fond of it."

Red snorted. "Now, who the hell's that? 'Nother of your damn Greeks? You've annoyed folks all over the place with that guff." He looked at Jade. "Amongst his other charms, this guy's kind of a walking library."

"Not a Greek. But someone I bet you've heard of—General Robert E. Lee."

"Hah!" Red slapped the table. "Damn straight. Out in the hills I come from, folks still think he walks the earth."

"Well, if you appreciate Lee, at least his poise and dignity—apart from the cause he fought for, which was entirely odious—then you should take some time to get to know the Greeks. Don't take 'em lightly. Like us now, they had to put together a vision to help them cope with a truly harrowing set of days. They lost a lot of what made them great during a huge war. Then they became dominated by a foreign dictator and forced to engage in a much bigger war. One that took them all the way to India.

"Through all that tumult and turmoil, they tried to come to an understanding, a mindset, that would help them endure no matter what the times were like. And that's what a few of their brightest and best did indeed become able to do. It was the Stoics' holy grail. It's why I and my teacher Roy paid them so much heed. Their system is a map to sanity. You talk about my yen to win, which I must admit, is all too true. Yet there's another, better and deeper victory that must come first, one that enables any other kind. And it's a battle that all of us fight every day, in our own minds. And to win a triumph there, that's what I'm truly after."

"Whew." Red took a long pull from his drinking horn. "Testify, brother. Hey, can this guy yack, or what?"

A long, drawn-out whinny drifted up from ground level, followed by a few muffled thumps and snorts.

"Now, what could that mean?"

"I can't translate. We'd best go see."

Kyle went to the cabin door and out onto the landing, followed closely by Jade and Red. Below them, Penny stood contentedly, with a hip out to the side and a rear hoof slightly raised. Buck stood a few yards away, his head down and sides heaving. There was a bloody scrape along his ribs where it looked like he'd been kicked.

"Bet he tried for seconds," Red said. "And got turned down."

"Good. Since he looks kind of tuckered out just now," Kyle said.

"Are you two jokers talking about what I think you're talking about?"

"What do guys always and forever talk about?"

"Well, I know you always *think* about it. Just not out loud. Too often," she added.

"How old is Buck?" Kyle asked.

"Oh twelve, thirteen. Thereabouts."

"Closing in on middle age, then. Time to start pacing himself."

"Word to the wise," Jade said, glancing at Red.

"Hey," he responded. "When I go, I want to go with my boots on."

"No boots," she declared. "Those must stay on the floor."

Kyle squinted at the sun. "I probably should hit the trail," he said. "I'll need light to find us a flat spot by a watercourse in the next valley. Especially since it's a locale I know doodly-squat about."

"Right. Well, let's get you squared away."

They went back inside. Kyle picked out the 'whacker he wished to take, Red rummaged around, then came to him with a fistful of hawk-fletched arrows.

"Like those broadheads," Kyle said.

"Not hard to make. Cut 'em out of scrap, then shape and sharpen with a file."

"And I like that plan you guys concocted, to handle Cooper's men. One of the most Christian deeds I've seen here, you want to know the truth. Forgive all, then offer everyone a second chance."

Red shrugged. "Sure. But what else were we going to do? Slaughter 'em like hogs in a pen? That wouldn't be manful."

"No. And now you've got real guns, fuel and some vehicles. The bikes at least work. I predict a great leap forward. Get more stuff done, then ably defend all that you do."

Kyle gathered up his comfort box. Before he closed it though, he shook half of the tobacco out of the pouch and onto the table.

"You sure?" Red inquired.

"Why not? It'll run out soon enough. In a month, I won't know the difference."

"I take back every bad thing I ever said about you."

"Oh, sure. Likewise."

Kyle went to the door. Jade had remained on the landing. He gave her a hug and she gave him a peck on the cheek.

"Be fun to meet your wife, someday."

"That's what I always thought."

"Give her a hug for me."

"Hey. That woman's about to get plastered by way too much lovin' for a good, long while."

He descended to ground level and Red followed to help him tack up Penny and load his gear. Buck offered scant resistance beyond a token head toss when Kyle clipped his lead line to the halter and tied the other end to the rear rigging dee on Penny's saddle, using a trucker's quick-release hitch.

"Stay careful 'round the big guy," Red warned. "You might be handy, but he's a handful."

"If it doesn't work out, it just doesn't," Kyle said. "My bet's hedged, since Penny's carrying my gear." He put out a hand and moved toward Buck, who rolled his eyes and stepped backward, tightening the line. "Marriage has taught me that the best way to manage a herd is to throw in with the boss mare. Someday, I hope he'll get that, too."

He coiled Penny's lead in his hands.

"See you 'round, maybe," Red said. "Till then, happy trails."

"Oh, come on. Can't you sing it?"

"Don't want to scare your horses."

"Hey. Glad we ended up on the same side, Red. It's been a real barrel of monkeys."

Kyle gave him a salute, leaned back to wave to Jade, then marched up toward the Haul Road, leading his tiny parade.

"C'mon, Sweetheart," he said. "Let's get after it."

—

Afternoon sunlight angled through the oaks that lined the Haul Road, casting long bars of shadow across the dusty track. That crosshatch of natural camouflage prevented Kyle from seeing a man who sat on a boulder near the juncture where the road bent westward and the narrow path dropped off the hill to the north.

He kept so still that Kyle failed to notice him until he got close.

Samuel rose to his feet. At that moment, of course, it became obvious who had been awaiting Kyle's approach. A jute satchel with a shoulder strap lay at the base of the boulder, with his big staff leaning against it.

"How'd you know I'd come this way?"

"Figured a guy like you to take the smart route."

"You got some hankering to go north?" Kyle pointed at the bag. "Were you going to ask to come along?"

Sam emitted a basso profundo chuckle. "Being in Elysian, I'm halfway to Paradise now," he said. "Why would I ever want to move further off?"

"Okay."

"That bag doesn't hold baggage. Just put my lunch in it. Didn't know how long you'd be. Anyway, I hiked up here just to thank you, and to say Godspeed."

"Thank me?"

"You helped to put us back on the beam. Maybe nobody has said that to you yet. But we're grateful. All of us."

"I appreciate that, Samuel. And the place is lucky to have you, too. Everyone can breathe easier, knowing you're on top of the place and keeping watch."

They stood there for a second, just looking at each other, weighing something invisible, intangible. There was an unguarded warmth in Samuel's dark eyes now that Kyle didn't think he could match. He reached into his pocket, took out a coin.

"Here," he said, extending it in his palm.

"What's that for?"

"A present. Think of it as a souvenir. Something to remember me by."

"Don't need it for that. In fact, can't use it for nothin'. Keep it."

"All right, then." He let it drop back into his pocket. "Got to make tracks before I lose this light. Remember to take care of yourself as well as everyone else, Sam. Stay out of trouble."

"Always the plan."

Samuel stepped back and raised his broad hand.

"Adios," he said.

Kyle considered that. "Adios," he replied.

The End

About the Author

P aul McHugh is the award-winning author of six books and has also enjoyed an illustrious career in journalism. *The Blind Pool*—a political thriller— won first place in the Thriller & Suspense category at the 2019 Chanticleer International Book Awards. *Deadlines*—a

 journalism murder mystery—won a best mystery prize from the National Indie Excellence Awards and another from the Bay Area Independent Publishers Association. He held the post of outdoors features writer and editor for the *San Francisco Chronicle* for more than twenty years, and has also published his work in *The New York Times, The Washington Post, The Los Angeles Times,* and the *San Jose Mercury News.* McHugh is an accomplished outdoorsman who presently resides with his wife Dawn Garcia in Northern California.

CPSIA information can be obtained
at www.ICGtesting.com
Printed in the USA
FSHW010907081220